Queen of the Zoo

Black Migo

Lock Down Publications and Ca$h Presents

Queen of the Zoo

A Novel by *Black Migo*

Black Migo

Lock Down Publications
P.O. Box 944
Stockbridge, Ga 30281
www.lockdownpublications.com

Copyright 2021 by Black Migo
Queen of the Zoo

First Edition October 2021
Printed in the United States of America

Lock Down Publications
Like our page on Facebook: Lock Down Publications @
www.facebook.com/lockdownpublications.ldp

Book interior design by: **Shawn Walker**
Edited by: **Shamika Smith**

Stay Connected with Us!

Text **LOCKDOWN** to 22828 to stay up-to-date with new releases, sneak peaks, contests and more...

Thank you!

Submission Guideline.

Submit the first three chapters of your completed manuscript to ldpsubmissions@gmail.com, subject line: Your book's title. The manuscript must be in a .doc file and sent as an attachment. Document should be in Times New Roman, double spaced and in size 12 font. Also, provide your synopsis and full contact information. If sending multiple submissions, they must each be in a separate email.

Have a story but no way to send it electronically? You can still submit to LDP/Ca$h Presents. Send in the first three chapters, written or typed, of your completed manuscript to:

LDP: Submissions Dept
P.O. Box 944
Stockbridge, Ga 30281

DO NOT send original manuscript. Must be a duplicate.

Provide your synopsis and a cover letter containing your full contact information.

Thanks for considering LDP and Ca$h Presents.

Dedications

To Irma, a.k.a India, my first love, my mother, it's because of you that I want women to rule the world, to be empowered, to learn and know how to defend themselves, and to have a voice that men can't silence. Rest peacefully, Queen!

I have been a fuck up all my life—well, this should prove that I'm trying. Don't think for a second that because I changed up my hustle, I changed up on my goals and beliefs. Dude that's responsible for your untimely death; I had him down bad, blood on my hands and feet. God saved him. Next time—well, you know how I give it up.

To Jameia, my lil one, baby girl, the world is wicked and foul. It's up to me to protect you the best that I can from what I do in the streets and from what the fuckin' streets got in store for me. Papi loves you!

To my sister, Amber, I know what you've been through. I can't speak on it. Act on it. You're a tough lil mama. You are stronger than the men you fall in love with. I never changed up on you. If you have with anybody, and I do mean anybody, I'll still walk down and air them out. .

The little runaway—abused—misused—neglected—disrespected and violated girls. No mean: Hell The Fuck No! If a boy or man can't accept it and tries to take it from you, the first chance you get—kill his bitch ass! Your innocence is worth fighting for, even dying for!

~BMG~

Black Migo

Prologue

Hastily, Queenie moved throughout the room, snatching up her panties and bras tossing them into the duffle bag.

"I have to hurry. I have to hurry." Her hands shook tremendously. Every few seconds, her gaze shifted to her phone, waiting on Gary's call to come through.

"Lord save my sanity," she said in exasperation, sitting on the toilet to relieve her bladder. She swiped away tears praying Gary could hold true to his word. "God, don't let that animal catch up to us." She exhaled deeply.

Wiping herself dry, she flushed the toilet, washed her hands, and collected the rest of her belongings. After making sure she had every item, she hurriedly loaded the rental and slid behind the wheel. Her only line of defense was the trusted box cutter, so she pushed it into the front pocket of her pants, hoping that she wouldn't have to use it.

Easing into the Ashley Apartments, she cruised the parking lot slowly.

"Where is it? Where is it?" she whispered aloud.

Though she found the building, there was no sign of his truck, still. She searched for a place to park. Finding a post across the lot, she backed in so that she could be appointed in the direction of G-50's apartment and easily leave when ready. Cutting the engine, she leaned the seat back slightly to hide out of view while taking her cell phone out to check the time. It was a quarter past four in the morning.

Impatiently, she sent him a text.

//: *Babe, where r u? I'm here.*

A few minutes passed, still, no reply.

Her leg shook violently as her nerves took a beating. She needed one moment of peace to recollect herself and figure out the next best move but was unable to push the thought of such an insane animal hot on her trail out of mind. After too many seconds passed without her moving closer to her goal, she finally outgrew her patience and busted the move. First, she had to call Gary to be sure he was safe and sound.

He answered on the fourth ring, panting wildly. "What's up, baby? Are you already there?"

"Yes, I'm already here. I've been waiting for like twenty minutes."

"Where are you?" She took a peek over the dashboard.

"I'm at second post getting the rest of my money. I should—"

"Nigga, now you got the fucking nerve to be calling your bitch up while you're up in my house?"

"Tempest, get the fuck outta the way. I'm only here to get my shit and get the fuck on."

"You ain't getting shit! And tell that *bitch* to bring her ass the fuck over here to get you. So, I can fuck her ass up!" Tempest's angry voice blared.

"Bitch, chill out with yo' police ass."

Queenie was furious and hurt that she was even in his presence again since she was the one who called the police on them. He was making it hard to believe that he could just leave the chick alone.

"No, bitch, fuck you! Get your fucking money and get the fuck outta my house 'fore I call the police on your ass again."

"Queen, come get me from—"

She hung up in his face. She was not in a space for any more drama. Too much was going on. She needed to get her sister. Cranking the car, she reset the seat and checked the gas.

"Don't worry, Precious. I'm on the way to you now, baby," she spoke aloud, shifting the gear into drive.

Pulling into the Flying J on Fairfield Road, she parked at the gas pump jumping on Interstate 20 West to Augusta, Georgia.

"Fifty dollars on pump seven." She handed the cash over to the guy behind the counter, then went to the ladies' restroom to relieve her bladder before the trip. The nagging sound of her ringing phone was irritating. Suddenly frustrated, she answered her phone, "Hello?"

"So, that's how we doin' it?" Gary asked with attitude.

"What are you talking about?"

"Hanging up in my face. Matter of fact, fuck all dat! Where you at now? Come get me."

"I'm peeing at the gas station," she kept her voice low as she wiped dry.

"I'm pulling up to my brother's crib right now. Hurry the hell up, Bae."

"Okay, I'm on my may now." She hung up.

Flushing the toilet, she washed her hands again before rushing out to the pump. Her feet shuffled across the parking lot toward the dark blue Impala. Her heartbeat quickened when she noticed the familiar black truck across the lot.

"What da fuck?" she mumbled, struggling to keep her grip on the nozzle as the tank guzzled down fuel.

Her fears climbed to its peak when she realized there was no one occupying the vehicle.

"Fuck this shit." She snapped the tank shut and hopped into the driver's seat, trying to spot any familiar faces in the store. She cranked the car and shifted into drive, hoping to outrun the looming darkness when the fine hairs on the nape of her neck stood tall.

The cold steel kissed her perspiring skin as terror paralyzed her entire body, causing her racing heart to stop beating.

Click! Clack!

11

The perpetrator jacked the gun slide, chambering a heavy round.

"Bitch, you thought you could run forever?"

"Oh, my God." She became nauseous. "How'd you find me?'

"Pull outta the parking lot into the Hardy's across the street."

Queenie did as told.

"Park!"

When she parked the Impala, she cut the ignition, too afraid to make any sudden moves. "What do you want?'

"I should kill you right here."

"Don't!"

"I'll think about it."

Chapter One

Queenie swiped away tears, struggling to tame her frazzled nerves as she raced against borrowed time. With little to spare, she darted about her bedroom in a frenzy, collecting only basic essentials for the journey. Since the house she'd once allied home was eerily silent, the slightest sound made her body stiffen while panic threatened to cause her a stroke. Ears perked. She listened closely for any indication that immediate danger was coming.

Stuffing her book sack with all it could carry, she wiped away the stream of tears once again with the back of her shaking hand before pushing up the bedroom window. She tossed out the bag first, then pulled up her tight jean pants before climbing out onto the small roof section. Looking back at the window open last time, she swallowed her fears, took a deep breath, and jumped.

A loud thump sounded in the night when she landed on her ass.

A gust of wind escaped her lungs.

Her palm clamped tightly over her mouth to muffle the scream. To be sure she was in the clear, she waited a full minute to allow the pain to subside. When she got to her feet, a wave of adrenaline pumped through her, giving her the energy to sprint through each of the neighbor's backyards until she finally reached the edge of the neighborhood. The bag was strapped to her while she jogged as best she could, ignoring the aches of her fall.

It wasn't until four miles into her escape that a car pulled alongside her. The bright high beam lights were blinding in the night. Her heart threatened to explode with fear. Part of her wanted to break down and cry right there along the street as she sensed that her journey was over before it started.

She froze in place helplessly.

"Excuse me, is everything alright? Can I give you a ride?" The woman's voice almost made her cry tears of joy.

She turned to peer through the passenger window at the driver, and her voice cracked, "Yes, I need a ride."

"Come get in." The pretty face waved her over, hitting the unlock button.

Reluctantly, she nodded and got in, setting her bag on the floorboard between her legs with a sigh of relief as she strapped the seat belt across her chest.

"Thank you, I really appreciate it," Queenie said gratefully.

"No problem. Where are you coming from?" The woman pulled away.

"The summit."

"Damn, that's like three hours away on foot, right?" She cut her eyes over at her before focusing back on the road.

"Something like that," Queenie answered. "What's your name if you don't mind me asking, ma'am?"

"Krissy."

"Queenie."

"Okay, Queenie. Where are you going?" Krissy took a quick second to roam her attire then the bag with a knowing look.

"I don't know," she answered, honestly. "You can drop me off anywhere you want to as long as you can make it away from here and across town. That would be nice?"

Krissy nodded.

Queenie wiped away the tear before it fell. Her heart was extremely heavy, and her mind was going in a dozen different directions because the burden on her shoulders was almost too overbearing to carry. She was saddened by what she left behind. However, whatever it took, she'd be back.

Thirty minutes into the drive, she was nervous about what to do next. It had just dawned on her that she had no money or direction.

"You smoke?" Krissy broke the silence, pulling into the gas station. "Weed, of course."

"I've tried it before."

"I'm gonna run up here and get some cigars. I'll be back in a second." She parked at a pump, grabbing her purse and car keys along with her.

She left Queenie with silence as she watched Krissy hook up to the gas nozzle before strutting across the empty parking lot and her head high with confidence.

Minutes later, Krissy resurfaced. Since it was prepped, gas began pumping on its own. She opened the driver's door, sat, and cranked the ignition before taking a swisher sweet out and busted it down using her freshly manicured nails. It did not take long before she had the blunt rolled and lit.

"Take a few hits, lil' mama." Krissy passed the blunt, blowing a thick cloud out of the gaped open door.

She took the blunt from her fingers and took a strong hit allowing the smoothness of the Kush to relax her brain.

After closing the gas cap, Krissy pulled down her skirt before climbing behind the wheel. She took out the hand sanitizer and rubbed her palms.

"I'm going to try not to catch the damn Coronavirus." She smirked, taking the blunt and hitting it hard, blowing another thick fog out of the window. "So, did that make you feel a little bit better?"

"Yeah, it did, thanks."

"You seem pretty young. How old are you?'

"I turned seventeen today."

"Oh, really?' Krissy turned to get a good look at her face.

Queenie tried not to become uncomfortable. To survive, she knew she would have to put up a thick wall and sever all emotions from her sleeves.

"Happy Birthday."

She folded her arms over her breasts. "'Preciate it."

"I was thirteen when I ran away from home." Krissy took another pull as she pulled out into the streets. "I regret it sometimes because it was super hard, and I didn't know what the hell I was doing."

Queenie denied the blunt.

"I knew it in my heart when I rode past you the first time. You were running away from something. I wasn't gonna turn around, but I know that feeling. And now, from what I see in your eyes, I know you're running from something terrible."

Queenie cast her gaze out the side window, wiping tears away to keep from showing weakness. "Thank you again," she said softly. "For the ride."

"You don't have to keep thanking me." Krissy stuffed the burned-out blunt in the ashtray. "Do you have any money? A plan? At least somewhere to go for the night?" her tone was laced with concern.

She answered gravely, "I don't have nothing."

Just as she was about to express her thoughts, she answered the nagging vibration of her cell phone in the cup holder.

"Hey. What's up, baby?" she answered with glee. "No—I had to stop get gas and some cigars. I told you I got to head out early tomorrow." Krissy cut her vision to Queenie with a smile. "Baby, stop it. I'm on my way home now. So, what if it's two in the morning? I'm about to pull up." She giggled. "Okay, I'm almost home, love you. Yeah, you better. Boy, bye." She kissed the phone and smiled.

"You can let me out anywhere." Queenie set her bag in her lap.

Krissy sighed, biting her lip in thought. "How about this? Let me give you a place to stay for a few days until you can figure out what you're gonna do?"

"Seriously?"

"Why not?" Krissy shrugged. "I know what you're about to go through, boo. Trust me when I tell you, it's a hard life, hard times, and the struggle ain't no joke. Plus, I'm not much older than you. So, let me at least help."

Black Migo

Chapter Two

Krissy pulled into the driveway of a beautiful home, ducked off in the Forest Acres' area. Queenie couldn't help admiring the surroundings so far. She caught good vibes from the woman. So much had been going on in her life recently that she wasn't quite sure how she managed to keep her sanity.

"This is my casa." Krissy smiled. "Get your stuff, follow me." She got her purse and took half of the blunt out of the ashtray before climbing out.

Queenie trailed behind. Seeing someone like Krissy with her own place gave hope to her mission. As they entered the house, the smell of apple cinnamon attacked their nostrils.

"You can sit your things anywhere, Queenie."

Setting her bag beside the couch, she sat, taking in the modern decor that gave off a cozy effect.

"Bae!" Krissy called out.

Heavy footsteps could be heard vibrating the hardwood floors before he came into view. "What's good?" this deep, smooth voice echoed.

Queenie turned her eyes away quickly, caught off guard.

"Nigga, put some damn clothes on!" Krissy yelled play-fully.

"Shit, my bad." He covered his heavy package, back-peddling down the hallway, and bent the corner ass naked.

"Sorry, you had to see all that. I should've told him that I had company with me." Krissy removed the stilettos she was wearing, then connected her phone to the kitchen counter phone charger.

Queenie whispered, "It's okay."

"That's my man, Dirty. He's cool as fuck, so you ain't ever gotta worry about nobody bothering you while you're here. He doesn't play dat."

Dirty's heavy footsteps could be heard again. Soon, he came back into view wearing a tank top and sweatpants. He was every bit 6'6" and about 260 pounds of muscle. His skin was black as coffee. The curls on his head were even blacker. Queenie could easily understand why any woman could be so attracted to him. He was extremely handsome.

"Who is she?" he asked.

"A new friend of mine. She needs my help, so she'll be here with us for a few days. Now go back to the room so I can talk to her," Krissy explained.

Dirty looked as if he wanted to protest but backed away after looking Queenie over.

When he was gone, Krissy continued, "Do you have a job?"

"I did, but I lost it."

"Don't worry. I have my own business. I'll be able to employ you. In the meantime, these are my house rules. Clean up behind yourself, no company allowed, and no flirting with my man." She snickered.

"I wouldn't—"

"I'm just kidding." Krissy giggled. "My man is loyal, and I trust him," she expressed. "I'll get you some blankets and a pillow."

Queenie sighed deeply, appreciative, and hoped soon she'd be in a better position to help herself. When Krissy returned with the linens, she showed her where the second bathroom was and left her for the night. Tired and mentally exhausted, she laid back on the couch and fell into a needed rest.

***

Matthew entered his two-story brick home well after midnight. It had been another grueling workday for him, and after a long-exhausted day, all he wanted was to come home, shower, feed his belly and take advantage of the sleep he needed.

Dropping his keys on the kitchen counter, he listened to the silence of his home, thinking he'd heard something. He remained still, allowing a few seconds to pass. When nothing else seemed to catch his attention, he continued through the house to his bedroom, where he stripped down naked, then moved into the adjoined bathroom and started a steaming hot shower.

Standing before the mirror, he winced in pain as he removed the bandage from the foot-long gash across his chest. His menacing grey eyes glinted like burning stars as his fingers rubbed roughly across the healing stitches that held his fairly pale, white skin together. A silly grin spread across his sick face as he reminded himself how he inherited such a nasty scar days ago. He stared at it for another long minute.

"You're so pretty," his sinister voice gave him goosebumps.

He ran his fingers across the wound once more, tracing the slash from one end to another, allowing his index finger to linger a second longer. He was beginning to zone out, and before he'd allow that to happen again, he took the bottle of prescribed meds from the countertop, tossed back a variety of pills, and swallowed them down.

Grimacing from both agony and distaste, he climbed into the steaming hot shower welcoming the burn as the water hit his back. Life had spiraled out of control. His family had fallen to shambles, and the only person to blame was his wife, Destiny. It would always be her fault, at least that's what he told himself.

After twenty minutes, he climbed out, wrapping a towel around his waist, heading into his bedroom. The awful silence of his home was driving him crazy, although he hated noise. Battling with his conscience, he went out to check on his daughter.

As he descended the basement stairs, darkness swallowed him up. "Queenie, you sleep?" he spoke out. "Queenie?"

Silence!

Chills crawled up his spine, a cold sweat caused his skin to clam up, and his gut twisted with fear. Quickly he flicked on the light. What he saw sent panic through his chest.

"Queenie?"

Silence!

He checked the area in a frenzy. There was no sign of her. He bolted up the flight of stairs and through the house, flicking on each visible light switch as he searched high and low. He then dashed up the flight of stairs to his daughter's bedroom.

"No! No! No!" he yelled. "This can't be!"

There was no sign of his oldest, Queenie, and only one conclusion slammed into his mind when he noticed the bedroom window ajar. He raced over, sticking his head out to glance below. She had taken off.

"Ah, shit!" he growled at the new fear of chaos as he stormed to his room to get dressed in a rush. "Don't do this to me, Queenie. Not right now." He feared the worst.

Snatching up his pistol and keys, he left the house with heated haste. He wasn't sure how long she was gone, and there was no real clue as to how far she'd gotten. Her safety was his main priority.

In ten minutes flat, he reached every street of the Maywood Community. He knew she had a lot of friends. So, she could be anywhere.

"Where are you, Queenie, baby?" He tapped the steering wheel angrily to match the rapid drumming of his heart. "Where are you?" he spoke aloud.

Unable to think clearly, he went to her first option, he figured.

***

"Queenie! Queenie! Queenie!"

She scrambled to her feet instantly, both frightened and alert from Krissy shaking her awake from another nightmare. She stood in the living room with her fists balled in a fighting stance, ready for the fight of her life. Panting, she began to relax when she realized she wasn't in any danger.

Rattled, Queenie apologized, "My bad, I'm sorry."

"No, that's my fault. You were screaming in your sleep, and it scared me. Are you okay?"

"Thanks, I'm fine."

"I know we just met, but if you want to, we can stay up and talk about it if that'll help you feel better."

"It wouldn't," she said politely, noticing the sun had beat her out of her bed with its bright rays of light staining the hardwood floors. "Just another bad dream of mine."

Krissy watched her with sympathetic eyes as loud steps came around the corner.

"Baby, I'm gone. Call me when you get back in the city." Dirty kissed her lips while casting a quick glance at Queenie before heading out.

"I will, baby. Love you!" She smiled as she watched him leave and get in the G Wagon from the living room window.

"If you don't mind, can I take a shower before you drop me off?"

"How 'bout this? Take a shower and get dressed. You're with me today. But you gotta hurry. I like to be out of the crib at eight a.m., which only gives you about thirty-four minutes."

Black Migo

Chapter Three

The flaming, candy red paint beamed superbly under the bright sun. Drops of water and soap from a fresh wash fell on the 2020 Tahoe that was sitting pretty on 32-inch chrome rims as it sped up Broad River Road, leading the entourage. Inside, four of the five occupants that were preteens sat quietly, guns drawn, engulfed in silence, waiting for the word, *kill*. The driver, an eighteen-year-old dead set on the road, awaited further instructions from the walkie-talkie.

Tailing one vehicle back, the matte' black Suburban 2020 XLT sat high on Dooly tires, intimidating the streets with a monster truck attitude and heavily tinted windows to match the dark moods inside. The nineteen-year-old driver kept the race tight, gripping the wheel with one hand while keeping the other hand tight around the walkie-talkie.

The four preteens inside were zoned out and ready, gripping the handles of automatic weapons as the eerie silence drummed thick with tension in their ears.

Zoo sat comfortably in his black cherry-colored Wraith with his Dolce and Gabbana denim jeans and Tom Ford boxers down at the ankles.

"Turn the A.C. up a little bit," he told the driver, a twenty-year-old doll-faced beauty.

She glanced over her shoulder to assess his situation. "Is that good?"

"It's good enough, baby girl," he agreed, tilting his head back in ecstasy as the seventeen-year-old cutie he'd recently met at a gas station slurped and gagged on his thick manhood, hungrily.

"Am I doin' it right?" Cutie asked with the tip of his pole sitting in her cheek like a massive jawbreaker. He held the back of her head to keep the show going.

"Less talking, more swallowing."

Cutie went back to working desperately to please the stranger who had her awestruck at first glance, trapping her in thirsty-groupie mode. She sucked his sausage like she was auditioning on the mic, hoping to make the cut.

He could feel the pressure in his nuts build rapidly as the orgasm prepared to reach its peak. He made her head bob to encourage her performance.

"Don't nut in my mouth," she murmured. "I don't like it." She slurped.

"Keep suckin' dat dick," he raged, lifting his hips as the sweet meat swelled. "Suck it right, too."

Cutie hummed, grossed out as she received the milky load of seeds.

"Now swallow all the shit."

She grimaced with her head back, unable to swallow the cum; she shook her head.

"Aye, pull over."

"What-you-doin'?" she spoke with a mouthful in confusion.

"Get the hell out."

"Huh?"

He pushed the door open. "Hurry the fuck up. A nigga ain't got all day."

Cutie was going to buck back until she noticed the Desert Eagle .45 wedged between the seats. She climbed out on the curb spitting out the tarty goo. "That's so fucked up!"

"Shut the fuck up, stupid-ass thot! Take off," he told the driver.

Back-to-back, each of the vehicles came to a stop outside the fenced house on Apple Valley Lane. The back passenger doors opened, and the Suburban opened with three baby faces dropping out. Though clad in prep school uniforms and penny loafers, each of the kids' wore faces of stone-cold killers.

Upon further instructions, the back passenger door to the Tahoe opened, and four bodies dressed in school uniforms spilled onto the streets. Two of the four split, heading up the street on foot while the other two lingered back by the Wraith to prevent any sneak attacks as the first two entered the yard and approached the front door.

Zoo shoved the DE onto his waist, then grabbed his phone and walkie-talkie. "Baby Girl!"

"Yes, sir?"

"You know what to do if shit gets ugly."

She held up the Grenade from the cup holder. "I do."

He climbed out.

A short, curvaceous redbone dressed scantily in skin-cutting boy shirts and a tank top with her hair pinned up, giving her baby doll appeal, opened the door and stepped aside, allowing the trio to enter.

Zoo instantly recognized her nervousness since he was a master at reading body language.

"All good," the walkie-talkie chimed.

He entered the home with arrogance, ice grilling Zi-Zi on his way in. She followed him into the living room as one of the youngins sat on the front porch watching the street.

He finally spoke, "Where's everybody else?"

Zi-Zi swallowed. "They're here, smoking on the back porch."

"It smells like y'all been smokin' in here."

"We weren't, I promise." She cringed.

Zoo studied her face. At twenty-one, she had her body in check and beauty on the mark. He was used to seeing her feisty and ratchet, ready to fight anybody who offended her, her best friend or her older brother. However, the moment she spread her legs for him, he dickmatized her and later invited her to his mansion, where he took control of her completely. Having so much control made him superior, a trade he invested in well.

"Tell them to bring their asses in here."

Zi-Zi rushed away, returning with a timid Crash and Dae-Dae.

"What's good, big bruh? Everything straight?" Dae-Dae asked hesitantly.

"Little nigga, if my mufuckin' money ain't right in this bitch, hell nah, I ain't good," he retorted. "Now where the fuck is it?"

Cresha went to the attic door, pulled down the ladder, and ascended the stairs, retrieving the loaded duffle bag. She came back and handed it over.

Zoo unzipped and examined the bundles of cash.

"Hundred fifty stacks like you asked," Zi-Zi said.

"It's supposed to be one hundred and seventy-five k."

"But you said if I can have one-fifty by yesterday, you'd let us keep the twenty-five k and the slack on the package."

Whap!

"Bitch, shut it up." They all flinched when he smacked her. "That was yesterday, today is today." His huge hand sent her sailing onto the couch.

She got back on her feet slowly, holding her cheek as the red mark on her face instantly appeared. Her eyes watered with fear, yet she swallowed the blow and took up standing beside her brother, Dae-Dae who dared not intervene.

"I called you as soon as I made your money, Zoo," she replied. "If you want, I'll give you the twenty-five stacks outta my money."

"Good, 'cause I want that and the twenty-five k of the last bit of slack left."

"But—"

He removed the Desert Eagle. Zi-Zi sighed and downplayed her frustration. Any miscommunication at this point could get them all killed.

"It'll be twenty-five k and the slack, same as last time."

"No disrespect, big homie, but we're not goin' to be able to make that happen," Dae-Dae butted in.

"And why's that, huh?" He was seconds away from exploding.

"Them CBG Crip niggas up the street. They shot up the house twice this week trying to run us outta the hood. The police keeps comin' around, talkin' 'bout complaints. Whenever the traffic do pick up, them niggas jump out and jack all our damn customers at gun point to make sure they don't come back. It's almost impossible for us to eat right now."

"Oh, really?" He glared at Zi-Zi. "And you ain't bother to tell me nothing?"

"We knew you weren't tryna hear that," Cresha spoke up.

He whispered into the youngin's ear who took the money and returned with another bag, giving it to them.

Zoo spoke calmly, "Put it up quick. We're going for a walk."

"Which house is it?" he asked, nonchalantly.

"Both of them." She tilted her head to the two red brick houses neighboring the other.

Outside, a group of teenagers and an older man sat under an open car garage, smoking and listening to music.

Zoo was nothing shy of danger. He thrived on moments like these. Born and raised in the wicked streets of Kill'umbia, he was made to confront shit if he had any aspirations to make it further than his Pinehurst Projects. From the way things were looking, he was far beyond. The irresistible thirst for money, power, and clout kept him tangled in his own web.

The group of infamous Crips stood at the sight of their approach. They strolled down to the front yard's grass while the three vehicles crept along.

"Fuck y'all mafuckas want?" The Tookie Williams look-alike rose to the occasion with enough animosity in his voice to incite a riot.

Zoo smiled. "Who runs the show here?"

"Me. So, what's crackin'?" he spoke.

The group of Crips spread out across the yard in a stand-off. Their eyes rested on the whips and kids who wore blank expressions, seemingly harmless.

"Milli, holla at 'em." Zoo stepped back with a grin, finding no threat.

"Check it out, Big Swoll ass nigga," the young voice came to life almost humorously. "This is what's gonna happen, so listen up and listen up good because I don't repeat myself twice."

The Crips looked at him sideways before bursting into laughter.

"Little ass boy, how old are you?" Big Swoll cracked up. "Nigga, you still wearing diapers and got the nerve to be talking crazy to me."

"If you interfere with the spot up the street anymore from here on out, and I gotta come back, it's gonna get messy," Milli spoke loud and clear, meaning every word. "And that's word on all our mamas, nigga."

The goofy smirks fell away instantly.

"Y'all come down in Crip territory making threats?" Big Swoll gritted. "Like this shit sweet or sum'n, we gon' see—"

"You can either respect it or get disrespected out here on this pretty ass grass, nigga," Milli cut him off with confidence.

Zoo smiled broadly. Zi-Zi and her friend were watching in utter surprise while Dae-Dae was ready to run in fear of guns.

Big Swoll had heard enough. As he and his soldiers turned to retrieve their guns from hidden, yet easy to access spots in the yard, they were met with crooked juvenile smiles.

"Reaching for these?" a member of the sneaky duo asked, aiming the Mac 90 he found in the bush while his partner aimed the two Mac-10s steady at the group.

They had broken away from the group earlier to case the hood. When Zoo put them on point, they sprang into action as taught, sneaking up behind the guard Crips and relieving them of their hardware.

"You think we playing?" Milli asked.

Big Swoll turned his gaze once again to see the prep school preteens in his yard armed and ready for work.

"Hold the fuck up now." Big Swoll held up his hands in sudden disbelief. "Ain't no way y'all little bastards running down on us."

Flah!

Milli pulled the trigger. The thunderous explosion got their undivided attention. "Next time we gotta come up out here, you ol' head niggas getting dropped first, hear me?"

The Crips thought, heard, and went with the flow. "Y'all got that, homie."

Zoo whispered into Zi-Zi's ear, "You see that?"

"Yes."

"From here on out, every fuck up is on you. Now, take Cresha and start getting rid of my shit."

"What about my brother?"

"His soft ass is coming with me."

"Please don't hurt him."

"I'll think about it," was all he said before heading back to his Wraith.

He told Dae-Dae to get in as the girls fled the street. The Crips glared at the group as they shook down the area for guns,

31

leaving the drugs. Zoo knew it would be soon when he had another run-in with the Crips of Apple Valley. When they came, he'd always be ready."

Chapter Four

Queenie sat back in the soft plush leather seat after a hot shower, admiring the sleek interior of the 760 Li BMW once again as Krissy drove the highway on cruise control allowing the GPS to navigate. Strangely, she felt safe and protected in the stranger's company though they had only met hours ago. Even still, she slouched in the seat to avoid being seen behind the heavily tinted windows.

Krissy turned off the *Steve Harvey Morning Show*. "I can tell you're paranoid. I have a licensed Beretta .22 right here." She popped the glove compartment revealing the hot pink toolie, customized for a woman. "Ain't nobody gonna fuck with us, I promise you that." Her sassy attitude made Queenie smile. "I already shot a bitch once for runnin' up on me, so I dare another."

Queenie chuckled, delighted.

"So, not to pry, but who's Destiny?"

Her smile faded.

"Never mind dat," Krissy changed subjects, noticing a change in Queenie's mood. "When I ran away from home, shit was hard as hell, but I blamed most of it on myself. I was hard-headed, didn't wanna listen to no-fuckin-body, and that did nothing but forced me into a worst predicament."

"How?"

"Because when the bitches that were living in the streets was giving me game, I thought I knew it all and was too good to take heed. I felt that if that game they were tryna give me had any real value, the bitches wouldn't have been in the streets like me. Then when shit started happening to me that they had forewarned me about, I knew what they'd told me had to be worth something." Krissy switched lanes, picking up speed.

"And what was that they told you?"

"To listen and *pay-the-fuck-attention*. We all get one free fuck up to learn from. Make the same mistake twice, that's a wrap. Everything after that is another strike against you. And since we're bitches out here tryna get it off the land, we gotta be one-hundred times tighter, meaner, more cutthroat and more savage than these niggas we're running past."

"But you don't seem mean or savage." She took another good look at Krissy.

"And that's why I got all that I got now! These niggas think because I'm pretty with a phat ol' ass and a sexy walk, that there's nothing to be afraid of, and that's where I trick 'em." Krissy eased off the ramp. "*You* got that same look in your eyes that I had. With a little grooming, you'll be a boss bitch like me, maybe even better."

Queenie sat back in the seat. If she was going to survive the streets and complete her mission, she knew she would have to pay attention. As Krissy listened to the navigation system following its directions, she pulled into a shopping plaza, a bad feeling tightened her stomach.

She tensed up at the sight of the police cruiser parked at the entrance. Krissy noticed instantly that her skin turned red when her eyes got misty.

"We're in Florence, South Carolina, far away from Columbia. There's nothing to be afraid of," Krissy assured.

"I hate the police so much."

"Me too." Krissy parked." Fuck 'em. Now, are you ready for your first day on the job?"

"Uh—I guess. Where do I work?"

"Here, this is your purse, it's a tote. Stay close." Krissy got out after double-checking her makeup. "Money time. Let's go."

She followed closely as Krissy led the way through the city mall. Entering Macy's, they headed into the kid's department.

"Ooh, yes. This right here is cute." Krissy checked the size and cost of a toddler's outfit before draping it over her forearm. She then went through a few more racks. Though she appeared to be occupied with shopping, Queenie noticed her eyes behind the big shades roaming the floor. She looked at a few things wishing she had a few dollars in her pocket to buy something for her little sister, Precious.

As they continued to shop, Krissy removed a device from her own purse remaining discrete while removing plastic alarms from the expensive clothes with ease. It took a second for her to catch on to what Krissy was up to, and before she could ask any questions, Krissy was making her move.

"Don't make no scene. Stay still and act normal, okay."

She nodded her compliance.

"Look behind me," Krissy instructed.

Queenie did so, watching as she rolled up the bundle of clothes from her arm and in a swift motion, pushed the roll off her arm wand into the tote bag.

"Close it and act normal."

Her heart was beating fast, she struggled to keep her face calm and emotionless as butterflies fluttered in her stomach, making her feel the need to use the restroom. It suddenly felt as if someone was staring. So, playing it off, she took a quick survey of the room.

Krissy had another roll coming off her forearm, into her own purse. "Alright, let's dip." She smiled.

"Why are we going to the register?" she asked, timid, keeping her voice at a whisper.

"Cause, I'm gonna buy what I have in my hands. Gotta make it look like we were really doin' some shoppin', feel me?"

At the counter, Queenie ignored the cashier's gaze as Krissy spoke to the woman about perfume. She started to stress, she'd never done something so stupid in her life before, not even a thought.

"Okay, thank you. Bye!" Krissy waved.

Though she didn't appear worried as they neared the exit, strutting in a pair of heels, swaying her ample hips—she was.

Queenie stayed close, afraid the alarms would sound off.

"Don't panic, never panic. And if it does go off, just keep walking to the car like it can't be going off for you." Krissy read her nervousness.

As they made it through the exit, she breathed a sigh of relief. The cool day breeze was chilling against her perspiring skin.

"That's so crazy." She touched her beating chest.

Krissy giggled. "You did good."

"You could've at least told me something. A heads up would've been cool since I had no clue what was going on."

"I know, but if I would have told you, you might've been too nervous and probably backed out."

She said nothing.

"And since you carried out that bag, we split the sale."

"How much is that?"

Krissy started the car. "We'll see when we get back to the hood. In the meantime, the day is still early. So, let's make some money."

Chapter Five

"Now listen, put these shades on so nobody can see your eyes. I wear mine in every store I go into. Always peep the floor because whoever you think is just shopping could actually be undercover. Always keep your eyes open, pretty girl. I'ma need you to watch my back, a'ight?"

"I don't think I can do this, Krissy. I mean, I'm not a thief nor—"

"Nor are you going to be able to survive these streets if you don't take the necessary risks to get ahead. Would you rather sell some pussy or drugs? Because we can do that too if you really want."

"No, of course not."

"Then you can put in some applications and hope to get a job now while the economy is fucked up, or you can rock with me and run up a quick check. What is it? You comin' or what?"

Queenie nodded, emptying the tote bag on the back seat. She was considering backing out, but the way Krissy spoke without fear made her fold under peer pressure.

"We got to hurry up and hit this one."

She got out checking her five-foot-five curvy figure and silky-smooth, honey-caramel complexion in the tinted window before following Krissy into the shopping plaza. Soon, they were inside a men's clothing store looking around like shoppers.

"I cannot afford to get caught stealing," she whispered to herself. "I'm so scared."

Krissy stopped. "Huh?"

"Nothing."

"My bad, I thought I heard you say something." Krissy smiled, turned, and sashayed away.

The place was bare of customers with only a few making quick purchases and then leaving out.

"What are we looking for?" she asked, anxious.

"Hmm, I got a few orders. They should be right over here." Krissy lifted a pair of Levi jeans for inspection. "These are nice," she said.

Then right there in the center of the aisle, she used a device to remove the electronic labels.

Queenie looked around feeling exposed to the few dozen cameras. She was not trying to go to jail.

"Open your bag." Krissy rolled the dozen or so jeans into a bundle before sliding it off the arm and into the tote.

Queenie got scared when she realized her bag was over-stuffed.

"Go, meet me in the car. I'm behind you." The lump of fear got stuck in her throat. It felt like a setup. "Go, hurry up," she urged.

She was hesitant and frightened when she turned away. Adrenaline pumped, she swallowed hard, bee lining her way through clothing aisles, shaking like a dancer toward the exit.

"Don't panic. Don't panic. Don't panic," she whispered.

Her heart sank to the pits of her stomach when an old white man at the cash register glanced her way. Her neck got hot with color and her legs rubbery as she pushed the door open, expecting him to give chase. If the alarm sounded, she was ready to take flight. Where she was going, she wasn't sure.

But he hadn't and her heart pounded loudly in her ears as she hurried to the 760. The sound of the alarm disabling and doors unlocking was a sweet melody, as Krissy hit the button from the store.

She flopped in the passenger seat looking around. Shortly after spotting Krissy, the car's engine came alive remotely. She strutted across the lot with her heavy tote as if she was a model on a runway. Her long and silky weave blew with the breeze as her hips rocked, making her ass clap while giving her beauty a round of applause.

"Toss this in the back seat for me." Krissy eased into the driver's seat.

Queenie did as she was instructed while Krissy shifted the gear into drive.

"Is someone chasing you?" She feared the worst.

"Fuck no, I'm so dramatic sometimes." She grinned. "We are good for today."

Queenie sat back in the seat releasing a sigh of relief, and watching the road through the side-view mirror. Distrust for police kept her high alert and on defense.

"I can tell now you're gonna make it far in life and that's not me just talking. You're a quick learner and you listen. I may make you my partner."

"A partner like how?"

"Business partner, duh. We can get money together. All I gotta do is show you the ins and outs. Everything else will fall in line."

She asked, interested," How much will I make?"

"Depends."

"On?"

"How much work you put in."

Since Queenie had been sheltered most of her life with only a few friends in her circle that were either too bougie or wanted to be ghetto, she knew nothing about the hood except what she'd seen on the news, social media, or heard in music. Seeing the first item made her tingle with nervousness, dreading the unexpected.

"Have you ever been out here?" Krissy asked, pulling into a parking space. She shook her head no, taking in the struggle around them.

"These all my folks out here, family. Ain't nobody gonna fuck with you, nor me 'cause all these fools got big guns and they crazy." She killed the ignition, then opened the glove compartment, taking her pistol and pushing it into her purse. She began rolling up a blunt while waiting for her man to answer his phone. "I'm back in the city, baby. Yes, everything went well. Okay. I will. Yeah, she did good, too. Alright, love you, too. Yeah, see you when I get home."

"What now?"

Krissy lit the blunt taking a few hard pulls. "Pass me that bag." When she handed over the bag, Queenie retrieved the blunt from her fingers. Instead of taking a hit, she held it, watching Krissy closely.

"I'm not 'posed to be saying shit, but I really think me and you will make a good team if we stick together. You just have to promise me one thing."

"What's that?"

"To stay loyal to the ones you come up with."

"I can promise that."

"Good because I expect nothing less." She began removing clothes, folding the men's Levi jeans, and sitting them neatly in Queenie's lap until there was a large pile and an empty tote.

Queenie's eyes sparkled with admiration. So much trauma and destruction had rocked her days that one glimpse of sunlight shining down on her life seemed impossible, until now. Even still, she wasn't going to get her hopes up for anything promising. At least until she put old demons to rest.

Climbing out the car, merchandise in hand, there was a strong urge to vomit now that she was a runaway and a certain someone would be searching high and low for her whereabouts. As Krissy led the way across the street, she took in the area listening to the chick talk.

"This is Pinehurst Park. I know damn near everybody hustling out here. Ever heard of Black Migo? He writes books and movies about the 'hood."

"I think I've heard of him on Instagram."

"Oh, well everybody knows him. That's a real nigga and this is his 'hood. If I can, I'll try and hook you up with 'em since you'll need you a gangsta too and he won't give me the chance to suck that dick."

She repositioned the bag on her shoulder. "Why won't he?" Queenie grinned.

"Long ass story. I'll tell you about it later though," she spoke. "This here is Four Seasons Apartments. It ain't jumpin' like it used to, but it still and will forever be the hangout spot for a lot of drug dealers and bloods. See—"

As they rounded the building corner, small groups were scattered throughout the cul-de-sac of buildings, eating, listening to music, or hanging out of doorways watching the kids play.

Queenie instantly became uncomfortable with all eyes on them while Krissy paid it no mind, strutting her hips harder and enjoying the attention.

At the sight of their approach, a young guy no older than Queenie came their way with enough swagger to lend some.

"What's good wit' it, Krissy? Wit' yo' thick ass." He licked his lips.

"Boy! If you don't get the hell outta my face." She rolled her eyes playfully. "Where the hell yo' brother, G-50, at anyway?"

"Show me what that mouth does first, then I'll tell you." He cracked up.

Krissy burst out laughing while slipping a hand into her purse. With a swift motion, she jacked the slide on her Beretta. "I ain't gon' ask yo' ass again, boy."

The humor fell from his face.
"Speak up, I can't hear you."

Chapter Six

"Stop that goddamn running through here!" G-50 barked at the group of young kids chasing each other, weaving in-out of parked cars. "I ain't gon' tell y'all asses no goddamn mo'!"

Queenie had her sights on the group of men standing on the side of building C, smoking weed and drinking liquor while watching G-50's back.

"Aye, bruh. You gotta check Krissy 'bout pulling that lil' ugly ass .22 out every damn time she comes 'round here with that ratchet shit." Gary chuckled. "It's enough goin' on today around this bitch as is."

"Then tell your little ass brother to quit playing with me like I ain't official." She rolled her eyes. "He knows I'm with the shits."

"Yeah, what the fuck ever," Gary waved her off, leaving them standing outside of C-Building. "I'll be inside if you need me, bruh."

"G-50, you gon' buy all this stuff from me or what?" Krissy set the bag of merch on the Mustang. "I got baby clothes, too."

Queenie noticed other men approaching as Krissy began since they all were getting an eye full of her curves and beauty. The predatory look in their eyes made her feel like sheep amongst wolves.

"Who this is you got with you, Krissy?" one guy spoke, licking his lips while leaning against another parked car. His eyes undressed her.

"This is my friend, and she doesn't want to talk to any-body, Jroc."

"How do you know dat?"

"G-50, are you gonna buy all this stuff off us? I got things to handle." Krissy feigned irritation ignoring the guy's question. "We ain't got time for the thirstiness."

"Ooohhh, I like this one."

Queenie tensed up feeling his approach from behind. "Don't touch me." She removed her hand from his when he grabbed hold. No one saw him coming.

"Don't be touching on my girl, Zoo. She's too young for you," Krissy said, seriously. "Fuh real, gon' 'head somewhere."

"She doesn't look too young."

"Well, she is and she's off-limits, so back the hell up."

"You stay on some bullshit I see." Zoo grinned. "G-50, you buyin'?"

"Nah."

"You sell clothes too lil' mama?" he spoke to Queenie.

"Umm—yes."

"Whatever y'all got, lemme get it all." He retrieved a thick wad of cash.

Krissy nodded for her to turn over everything. "They're fifty dollars a pop." Krissy frowned at him. "Should tax yo' rich ass."

Zoo grinned, peeling away bills and tossing them on the hood of the car. Queenie collected the money before handing it over to Krissy, who continued to frown at Zoo with distaste.

She picked up the hundred-dollar bills off the car and handed them to Krissy who was mean mugging.

"Thanks, G-50. Call me when you need something else."

"Did I do something wrong?" she asked as Krissy drove.

"Of course, not. It's that nigga, Zoo. He irks my nerves every time I see him. I can't stand him. He thinks he runs everything and everybody around him. The attitude was strong. And if me and you gonna do business together, we need to get an understanding. Under no circumstances, should you ever fuck with him. Okay?"

"I got you," she answered wanting to know why, but decided now was not the time to be asking a lot of questions.

Parking in her driveway, Krissy removed the kilo from beneath the seat, stuffing it into the tote. "Always keep your mouth shut. Niggas fish for information. Don't give it to them. Whatever we do together, stays between us."

She nodded in agreement.

"This is your split of the money. I was stupid when I got my first taste of money. Don't be like me, tryna look fly and broke at the same time. Dress casually and stack your bread. Got it?"

She folded the money and stuffed it into her bra. "I'm listening."

"Good. Let's go shower up."

When they entered the house, Dirty was hanging up his phone call, coming around the kitchen island and into the living room. Though his face appeared calm, his body language was aggressive.

"Fuck is you still doin' over there in Pinehurst?" He glared at Krissy.

Krissy sucked her teeth. "Boy, don't be running down on me. I had to make a quick run. Why does it matter?"

Dirty gritted. "My nigga, don't show out in front of your company. You know why I'm tight. Where is my shit at? I ain't got time to be playin' these silly games with' yo goofy ass," his deep voice was loud even when hushed.

Krissy handed over the tote bag, keeping her mouth shut. When Dirty saw what he needed to see, he turned, headed down the hall, and slammed the bedroom door behind him.

"Don't pay him no mind. You can take your shower first. I'll take mine in the room." She left.

She sat on the couch trying to make sense of the day. So much had taken place over the course of a few hours. However, being overwhelmed kept her mind from drifting back to the days of pain and sadness. Days she so badly wanted to erase from her memory. Hanging around Krissy, she could tell would provide her with insight but not a place to call home.

Quickly she sifted through her bag for a change of clothes. Picking out something simple, she proceeded with taking a shower. As the water burned dirt away, tears cascaded as she thought about her mother and little sister.

"You good in there?" Krissy tapped on the door.

"Yeah, I'm coming out now," she called out.

Queenie rinsed her tears away before cutting off the water and getting out. She reminded herself to not show any weakness, she was officially on her own. Her means of survival were solemnly her responsibility.

***

Matthew stared back at himself in the rear view mirror, counting down from ten slowly to simmer down his burning anger that showed in his reddened eyes. His grip tightened around the steering wheel, the leather grips cracked under brute strength.

After releasing a small portion of steam to balance his attitude, he checked his appearance in the mirror before climbing out of his Black Tahoe. He knocked softly on the door waiting for an answer that came quickly.

"Hi, Mr. Wilks," a pretty, well-developed young lady answered the front door. "How can I help you? Is something wrong?" she asked, sweetly.

"Hey, Mariah," he glanced over at an inside view." Is Queenie here with you?" He tried not to sound the alarm. "She didn't come home last night."

"No sir. I hadn't seen her in months. She doesn't answer my calls, nor has she texted me back. Is everything alright?"

"Everything is fine. If you hear anything from her, let me know. Here's my number." He handed her a card.

"I will, Mr. Wilks. Have a good day." She smiled politely, closing the door. Clenched jaws, he headed back to his truck, tight chested, he rammed into a dead end. As he started his vehicle, he pulled away knowing that soon he had to find his daughter.

Black Migo

Chapter Seven

The body of cars eased past the concrete and steel fortress wall after being buzzed through the gate. As the Tahoe led the way, they traveled the smooth paved path around to the back of the mansion. He found himself parking the whip beside other luxury cars facing the wide-open range of beautiful green grass and tall pine trees that lined the theatre-styled property perfectly.

"This shit is dope," Dae-Dae said, impressed. "Nigga living like a king."

"Let's go." Zoo stepped out of the wraith. "Baby girl, have the youngins clean my car again."

The driver nodded.

"Is this where you live?" Dae-Dae asked.

"Sum'n like dat," he replied as the team of preteens stood around. Zoo whistled loudly. "Watch this."

Suddenly two icy white-coated wolves, male and female, came bolting from the tree line in a tense race toward him.

"What the fuck kinda dogs are those?" Dae-Dae was both intimidated and frightened hearing the rapid succession of thumping paws against the ground.

"Get 'em y'all, get 'em!" Zoo pointed, as Dae-Dae attempted to jump on the car but couldn't in time as one of the wolves caught hold of his pants leg while the other barked ferociously, displaying razor-sharp teeth.

"Oh, shit! Get 'em off me, bruh!"

"That's right, get 'em," Zoo instructed, amused. "Bite the bitch out of 'em."

The wolves ripped Dae-Dae's pants to shreds causing him to fall to the concrete.

"Arrgghh!" He tried to scare them away.

The wolves surrounded him barking and snarling viciously.

"I can't have bitch made niggas on my roster, feel me?"

"Don't let 'em bite me, bruh," he pleaded erratically. "This some fucked up shit you doin', dog."

Arrgff! Arrgff! Both wolves barked, circling and keeping him centered with nowhere to run. One command could have him chewed to bones.

Zoo burst out laughing with his youngins who showed no sympathy.

"Why the fuck you doin' this shit to me for, bruh?" Dae-Dae was on the verge of tears as fear of being eaten by an animal consumed him. "You wrong as fuck!"

"Nigga, with yo' scary ass." Zoo cracked up. "Sheba, Solomon. Sit!"

On command the wolves licked their snouts, sitting obediently, watching their Alpha while keeping eyes on a potential meal.

"Come gimme kisses." He patted his stomach. They came excitedly standing, licking his face. "Good girl, good boy. Now, run and go play."

Together, they rushed off through the yard getting lost in the woods.

"This some bullshit, big homie. Real talk." Dae-Dae stood, looking down at his destroyed clothes.

"You'll be alright. Bring yo' ass on," Zoo spoke.

The men followed up the flight of stairs to the second level of the mansion, which was adjoined to the back-patio deck and open kitchen area.

Large paintings of tigers, lion packs, hyenas, and wild animals decorated the milky, white walls gracefully. Small plants and corner trees gave off a tropical jungle theme vibe as sculpted glass, ivory, wooden, and clay statues of monkeys, elephants, giraffes, and other wildlife gave the room substance.

"Ti-Ti, Boo-Boo?" Zoo called as they entered the entertainment room. Exotic replies came back. The talking parrot and baby spider monkey came from the cartoons on television in an elated frenzy taking up both shoulders. "Did y'all miss me?"

The monkey smiled brightly, moving his head up and down. The bird did the same, shrieking, "Yeessh!"

He gave them both treats. "Finish watching TV, I'll be back."

When the pets scurried away, Zoo led the way into the far end of his three-story home with Pussy Boy keeping close. Unlocking the door, he entered one of the two master bedrooms, shutting the door behind them both, sensing the boy's uneasiness, he could almost feel his heart beating out of control. As he moved around the heavy desk, taking a seat, he noticed Dae-Dae's creeped-out demeanor as he stood still staring at the things around him.

"What's your worst fear?" he asked Pussy Boy.

"Shit, you, nigga." He gave a stupid look.

Zoo grinned, staring at him with dangerous browns that made him fidget. "What else, scary nigga?"

He answered, gravely, "Spiders."

"Like those?"

"Hell, yeah like those." He tried to keep his distance from the large wall of live spider tans ranging in dozens of poisonous species. The room was a spectacle of live creatures, exotic fish tanks, and insects. "Fuck is you doing with all this weird shit anyway?"

Zoo stood. "Fuck is you so pussy for?"

"Huh?"

"Come closer," he urged. "Since you can't hear."

"Nah, I can hear. I just—"

"I can't trust that all my hard-earned money and investments will get the proper protection it deserves if I got a pussy boy guarding it."

"I showed you that the Crip niggas been going hard on us in the valley."

"And you should've been goin' hard on 'em since that's my shit y'all pushin'. You can't risk losing it or it not getting sold in a timely manner, nigga. What, you think I got all this by being a pussy nigga?" he growled. "Fuck nah, boy! This shit took time, gangsta shit, and dedication."

Dae-Dae shivered, frightened beyond control. "I'm a hustla, bruh. I'on play 'round with guns. You know that, though. Zi-Zi told you."

"This Killumbia, South Carolina, bitch! Every kid and their grandma got fiya out this mufucka. You gon' get one, learn to use it and protect everything that belongs to me." He glared, viciously, then opened one of the spider trays. "This here is one of the most poisonous spiders in the world. Stick your hand in."

"I can't do it, bruh."

He pulled out his Desert Eagle .45. "Pussy, stick your hand in."

"Bruhhh!" he whined, dramatically. "Don't make me do it."

He shut the tank. "I'ma turn yo' faggot ass into a gangsta." He made for the door. "Come on, let's go."

Dae-Dae thought about bolting, but reconsidered. He remembered that there was at least a dozen shooters around the compound and he'd never make it out alive.

Zoo led him up a stairway to the third level.

"This shit feels haunted," Dae-Dae stated.

"It is." He tapped on the steel door.

A soft voice came, "Yes?"

"You ready?"

"How many with you?"

"Just one. He is a cold pussy."

"One second," the sexy voice said.

There was a brief pause, and then the locks unhinging could be heard. A breathtaking beauty opened the door dressed in a silky white gown that amplified her mouthwatering curves. She was far sexier than any woman they'd ever seen, with silky long hair flowing down over her shoulders and golden-brown, soft skin. Her lips were perfectly filled and she was heart-stopping.

She looked Dae-Dae up and down. "We'll make 'em tough. Let's get started."

****

One Hour Later

"Yeah, what's poppin', foo'?" Zoo answered the phone as he descended the stairs to the second level of the Mansion with Dae-Dae close behind.

"We're out back, bruh."

"Sayless." He hung up, and then grabbed the walkie-talkie. "Bring 'em up to my office." He entered the room poised and unrattled, the jittering and fidgety boy who stood there an hour ago was no more.

Moments later, a combination of knocks came on the other side of the door. Dae-Dae opened it.

"Damn, who the fuck is this new nigga all chewed up?" G-50 sized him up. "Looking like he tryna rec. He Blood?"

Dae-Dae sized the duo up. Zoo stood to greet them with a gang shake. "Ta'maine lookin' like he tryna put paws on the homie, Dae-Dae." He chuckled, instigating. "Nah, he ain't blood yet."

"Bruh, you know I'm with the shitz." Ta'maine ice grilled Dae-Dae. "Fuck you find this dark ass nigga?"

Flashing a wide grin, Zoo said, "Watch this shit. Dae-Dae, come over here."

They all watched him cross the room. Slowly and carefully, Zoo opened one of the glass trays that protected them from the spiders.

"Put your hand in."

The two guests stood back in suspense as the *stupid* nigga placed his bare hand inside. They all gathered around preparing to see the spider deliver a deadly dose. As he set his hand in the habitat unafraid, the spider lifted its front legs exposing its thick, long fangs in a territorial standoff at the far end of the footlong tank. A light hissing could be heard.

"That bitch big as his hand," G-50 said.

Zoo was entertained seeing his two men on edge, he went for it. "Argh!" He scared them both, causing them to jump in fear of the sneaky critters. He burst into comical laughter. Settling, he tapped Dae's shoulder. "Take your hand out, slowly."

He did so.

"Where you keep finding these weird niggas at?" G-50 asked.

After receiving further instructions, Zoo led them out of the room and down the stairs. Closing and locking the office, he spoke, "Since we ain't born gangstas and real niggas, the people raising us and the streets we're growing up in gotta show us how to be that way by example. Feel me? Niggas ain't birth Ta'maine into Blood gang, niggas introduced it to him, and then showed him how to be a Blood." He opened the entertainment room door. "Ti-Ti, Boo-Boo, let's go."

"You be doin' too much with all this wildlife shit, bruh," Ta'maine said.

"Nigga, don't like it, you can get the fuck out. You're lucky you're my cousin, I would've had your ass on some weird shit a long time ago."

G-50 laughed. "Don't do it to 'em."

Zoo took a seat on the back patio overlooking the entire backyard. Plucking seedless grapes from the bunch, he gave his pet monkey and parrot the fruit as he watched his youngins down below wash his vehicles.

"So, what's up?"

G-50 took a seat.

Ta'maine remained standing. "That's two hunnid racks on the back seat of my car, that's what I owe you."

"What good is my money doin' in the back seat and not in my grips off the rip?"

Ta'maine left to retrieve.

"We family, Zoo. Don't let the money and power you have change that."

"And what's that 'posed to mean?"

"Just what it means. You're me and Ta'maine's family. We all grew up together, even ran trains on thots together. The more money you seem to get, you start treating us niggas like soldiers."

Zoo chuckled. "We family. That's why we eat together, and I make sure of that. When it comes to this Blood shit, I got the high for the whole mid-state, which also means I got more status. That alone makes you and all the rest of the G-Shine homies, soldiers." His mood darkened. "Fuck is you sayin'?"

G-50 shook his head, knowing he had no wins in arguing.

"Say what's on your mind."

"Gimme Pinehurst, bump my status too low. Let me run my own line. We still do business as usual."

He glared at his cousin as if he could kill 'em and kill 'em again. "Fuck you drag some stupid shit like that your mouth fuh?"

"All the homies tryna turn up across the city. You got damn near everybody on low key status. Niggas smashing all our spots and the homies not with that sleeper mode shit no more, bruh."

"Them stupid niggas don't know nothing. If I hadn't done what I did, we all would've been tangled up in the last RICO with them Five-Nine brim niggas. All of them niggas got life sentences. Every one of them, fifty plus, homie," he snarled.

"We can turn up any moment and take over everything 'round this bitch."

"Then that's what we need to do, foo."

Ta'maine climbed the steps and set the bag tableside.

"It's too risky."

"A'ight, that's what's up," G-50 muffled his irritation. "So, what're we gonna do 'bout our dope getting into them Forty-eight boys' hands? They've been pushin' our shit all over Bluff Road and it ain't lookin' good."

"Hold up. Hold up. You mean to tell me that them niggas getting a hold of my weight after I told niggas specifically not to wholesale nothing to none of them mufuckas?" Zoo growled, then took a moment to regain control over his anger until he was able to hear anything else.

"We already know who's pumpin' hard down there. We just gotta learn who in our camp is getting wholesales. Won't take long though."

"Better not."

"But that ain't all. The dope is so good we can strong-arm anybody hood overnight. That shit turning Pinehurst into a

million-dollar spot. It also got all the other blocks goin' out of
business. For the last few nights, the wild niggas from Greene
Street been coming through, shooting up every little trap spot
and getting away. Three of the homes are done and getting
shot already and expecting you to give the green light. Hell, I
say we slide down on the turf and take the whole strip."

"Nah, this ain't the old age. Niggas ain't doing stupid shit
like dat."

"Then how else we gon' do it? 'Cause if the homies ain't
gon' get the chance to kill something—anything, them niggas
thinking 'bout flipping under somebody else. Niggas don't
wanna be affiliated with nothing weak or taking leadership
from a man that ain't on Blitz Mode," G-50 told him straight
up.

Ta'maine listened to the intense meeting unsure how it
would play out.

"That's because them pups can't think, and it's on me to
think for all of 'em. How we take them niggas block? You
gotta trust that a boss like me can move pawns and make *boss*
moves. A nigga with no vision can't picture shit, but a mufucka with an imagination can see it and make it happen. Y'all
keep doin' what y'all doin'. I'll make shit happen, a'ight."

G-50 sighed. "I hear you, foo."

Zoo sat back formulating a plan in seconds. He knew he
had to do what needed to be done in order to save face and
keep his bloodline stronger than ever. Though violence was
always an option in ruling, he was certain proper strategizing
won wars. And he needed to win without getting a federal in-
dictment.

"We gon' go 'head and get the hell up outta here." G-50
stood, giving him dap.

"How the hell you been getting these bad-ass kids to listen and do everything you say? I swear they worship you like you a God or sum'n." Ta'maine finally spoke.

"My damn kids don't listen to shit I tell 'em to do," Zoo broke out of his brief daze. "It's a secret."

Chapter Eight

"No. Baby, please!" echoed through the home.

The sounds of hands slapping flesh rang out, ricocheting off the walls. There was a fight, a struggle taking place.

The sounds of screams were being muffled, "Please! Please! No!"

A twelve-year-old Precious crept into her sister, Queenie's, room distraught face covered with tears. She no longer cared if her footsteps carried into her parents' bedroom as she came bedside.

"Queenie, wake up," her trembling voice, whispered. "Queenie. Queenie?"

Being rocked, she was startled from the slumber to see her younger sister's face inches away, masked with pain and ache. "What's wrong, Precious?"

"They're fighting again, make them stop it," she pleaded. "He's beating on mom again, Queenie." Those big, doe browns pleaded more.

The effect of someone crashing into a dresser and it into the wall sent vibrations through the house. Sharp cries of agony filled the darkness. Precious cried louder, fearing the worst. Helpless. Demands were made, the masculine voice so authoritative and threatening that both girls tensed with each word, frozen in terror.

"Queenie, do something," Precious begged.

She threw her covers back and jumped out of bed. Keeping her sister glued to her hip, they entered the hallway frightened. Her heart was beating so hard that she couldn't think as each step closer she took nearing their parents' bedroom made her chest tighten.

She attempted to turn the knob. Locked. Hearing their mother scream out for help and her endless pleas made tears fall from their eyes despite so many times she said they wouldn't see another.

"Open this door, daddy. Stop!" Precious pounded as Queenie began rattling the nob violently.

"Mommy!"

"Ma—"

The door snatched opened. The distant look in their father's chilling, grey eyes stopped their hearts with fear. The smile on his face was that of a crazed lunatic and too forced to be sincere.

He pointed up the hallway. "Go back to your room."

Destiny crawled from the fetal position over the door, her beautiful face battered and swollen. Even still, her smile shined brightly. "Go back to your rooms. Me and daddy are just playing, okay."

"Nooo, I wanna stay with you." Precious tried to push into the room, but her father prevailed.

"Go back to your gotdamn rooms!" his voice struck fear. "Now!"

"Queenie, take your sister and put her back in bed," "Destiny cried.

"Daddy, I hate you!" she shouted in tears, pulling her sister away.

The bedroom door slamming behind made them flinch.

"Why does daddy keep hitting mommy?" Precious sobbed.

She had no explanation and could only wrap her arms around Precious to console her. She couldn't say everything was going to be alright because it would be a lie, so she wiped her face dry again before laying her in bed.

"Put your headphones on and listen to your music."

"But I don't want to."

"Put them on." And she did so.

Pressing play on the iPad, the whimpering began to soften. After a while, she was off into an exhausted slumber.

Queenie could hear her parents in the other room still at it as she wiped stains from her own face. She kissed Precious on the forehead before heading to her own bedroom.

****

"Damn, girl. You alright?" the sound of Krissy's voice snatched Queenie out of the trance she had dozed off into.

Embarrassed, she wiped the stream of pain from her face. "My bad. I'm good, Krissy."

"You sure? 'Cause you zoned out for a hot second, then started crying. I need to know what's goin' on. Is everything alright with you mentally, emotionally? You can talk to me about anything."

The words were like sledgehammers pounding at the walls around her mind and heart. Walls she refused to let down or allow anyone behind. She was too ashamed to admit it; she'd only humiliate herself more than she currently felt.

"It's nothing. I'm okay. Started thinking about something."

"Queenie, baby, we're both grown. I'm only a couple of years older than you, but that doesn't mean anything. I'm concerned about your mental health. I don't want to be taking wild guesses about what's wrong, so I need to know. If we're going to be a team, I have to know what's going on with my partner at least."

"I miss my sister, that's all. Now can we—"

"Yeah, we'll get to the bottom of this another time, straight up. Now, how do I look?"

"Pretty."

"So, do you. I got competition. This is your bag for the night. I paid two stacks for this Chanel, so don't lose it. Come on and stay close." Krissy slapped the visor mirror shut before getting out.

Queenie found it difficult to wear high heels. Up until then, she'd never worn a pair. As she stood on concrete in a set of Red Bottoms suggested by Krissy, she felt saucy. The Seven jeans were a size too small, but hugged her curves like a drag racer, while the halter top clung to her firm breasts. A wave of Black Girl Magic made her confident as she followed Krissy to the club's entrance.

"Hey, big D-BO." She turned on the seduction. The big burly security guard glared over his clip board of guests.

"You're not on the list," he said sternly, giving his attention to the trio of men standing behind them. "Gentleman, this way, names please."

Queenie could feel the heat coming off her friend's glare. Once the group of men entered the security came back over.

"So that's how you handle me?"

"Last time you brought your ass up here on Dirty's behalf, you shot a bitch. I got my ass chewed out and nearly lost my job for letting you in. You of all fools should know this is a lowkey spot and that ratchet, ghetto shit you're used to isn't gonna cut it here."

"But that hoe ran up on me."

"Understood. That still don't give you the right to blast ol' girl in here. You cutthroat the chick on a sale, you knew she was gonna be tight."

"Fuck all that, I'm here to meet somebody for Dirty. Is you gon' let me in or not?" She gave him attitude.

His gaze roamed over to Queenie. "She's barely legal." Krissy noticed the predator in his eyes. "If she's with you, she's grown." He frowned.

She was uncomfortable, but Krissy had schooled her on how to use the beauty God gifted her with to get ahead.

"Are you letting us in? We ain't got all day," she asked.

He tousled his thoughts. He knew he shouldn't let them in, but couldn't resist the lust. Sliding the clipboard under his shoulder, he instructed them to turn around.

"Don't make me regret this," he spoke.

Queenie watched his hands, slow and deliberate. Secretly caressing her friends' figure, even squeezing her succulent back sided. Krissy never flinched when he searched her body, or as his massive hands roamed her breasts, the small of her back, and palmed her ass.

"Go 'head."

"What exactly are we doing here?" Queenie asked, looking around the crowded nightclub.

"This is a private party spot and my man couldn't come. I came on his behalf only because I hate to let that money go unmade." Krissy led them to the ladies' room. Checking beneath the stalls she made sure they were alone. "Open your purse."

It had not dawned on her until now that the Chanel bag weighted it. When she opened it, Krissy removed her Betsy Beretta .22. "Don't trip, I only did it because I knew he would've searched my bag more thoroughly." She set the gun on the counter. Krissy reached under her skirt and fingered out the package stuffed in her pussy. "Perfect place to hide stuff." She winked, rinsing her juices off in the sink.

Taken aback, Queenie watched and learned with amazement as Krissy arranged bags of drugs on the counter before stashing them on her person. Seconds later, she was being handed three bags.

"Do you have on panties?"

"Uh, yes."

"Stick two of these in your panties, but not in your pussy. This other one is kept in your purse. As soon as I get a sale, I'm gonna get them off you."

Nervous, she replied with a head nod. Shortly after, they were back on the dance floor pushing towards the bar. Men were everywhere gawking at the duo. She ignored the cat calls, whereas Krissy entertained them, twerking on random guys when a favorite song played. At the bar, a familiar face approached while Krissy had her back turned. She wasn't expecting to see him, but now that she had, her stomach was tightening.

"What's good, lil one?" he asked, eyes penetrable and staring into her soul!

She knew she was troubled the moment she laid eyes on him. She pulled her hand away from his. The weed smoke on him was strong.

"I saw you earlier, right?"

"Right. So, what's up with you and Krissy? Y'all still making money moves, huh?"

"That's none of your business."

He chuckled, unfazed by her sassy attitude. "What are you doin' later?"

"Why?" She cut her eyes to Krissy who was caught up in conversation.

"I like that slick mouth of yours. Maybe later you'll show me what else it does." He smiled lustfully while pinching her nipple through the thin fabric.

She held her breath, taken aback.

"I'll catch up with you 'round the 'hood." He kissed her cheek before she could avoid it.

She then watched Gary pass Krissy not bothering to palm her ass. She turned to pounce on him but before she could unleash a rain of blows, he was gone.

"What did that clown want?" Krissy with an attitude.

"Nothing."

"Nah, his ass wanted something," she said. "That lil' nigga cool, but he bad news and stays in some shit. Don't be fooled. Seeing him here lets me know the other Pinehurst boys here as well. Take this." She thrust the massive wad of money into a Chanel purse. "Gimme that dope, stay put. I'll be right back."

Queenie hurriedly handed over the drugs at the urgency in Krissy's voice. Suddenly, the room temperature began to rise with the thick tension that threatened to suffocate her as she clutched the purse tight in her arm. She kept eyes on Krissy as she made dope for money exchanges. In no time she rushed back, strutting with a purpose.

"I don't like this club's vibe tonight. Too many of the wrong niggas in here. Shit is throwing me off, so let's go, boo." She led the way.

The moment they crossed the dance floor, the over-crowded Mega VIP Section erupted with chaos, sending party goers shifting in different directions.

A riot broke loose.

Taking no chances, Krissy latched onto Queenie's arm dragging her through the club until they were outside, closing across the busy Gervais Street.

Flah! Flah! Flah!

Dudoom! Dudoom! Dudoom! Dudoom!

Lah! Lah! Lah!

A fossil of gunfire erupted close by, both girls ducked beside a parked Mercedes to avoid being struck by stray bullets. Neither noticed the masked man creeping up from behind.

"Bitch, give me that bag!" The perp growled, cocking the pistol slide, aiming at them both.

"Please!" Queenie fell to the ground. "Don't shoot us."

"Gimme the bag bitch!"

As he went to snatch the purse from her, more shots rang out in the distance stealing his attention. Another round of shots exploded nearby.

Pah! Pah! Pah!

The sound of the assailant smacking to the ground dead startled her.

Krissy jumped to her feet, pulling her. "C'mon, boo. Hurry, we gotta go!"

Chapter Nine

"Krissy, what just happened?" She trembled, double-checking over her shoulder for any police as they sped away.

"What do you mean what just happened?" Krissy grimaced. "We almost got robbed and possibly killed. The fuck?"

"But I think you killed 'em," Queenie said.

"No, the fuck I didn't. And if I ever hear you say some shit like that again, we got a major problem. If anything, I saved our asses. Bottom line, you ain't seen shit."

She took short breaths. "Okay. I didn't see shit." Her eyes watered. She quickly restrained herself from cracking.

That's right." Krissy dug the blunt out of her purse and added flame before taking a hard pull, then passing it.

She took a long drag filling her lungs with a strong haze. Slowly, her nerves began to settle.

"I know it was one of them clowns that I served in the club. We'll know in the morning." Krissy sent out a text. "I showed mufuckas once before that I'm nothing to play with and they still come for me." She sighed deeply in frustration.

"What's next?" Queenie hoped the police wouldn't come for her.

"Ain't nothing changed, we'll still get this money."

The rest of the drive they rode in silence. Entering Krissy's home, Queenie sat on the couch and kicked off her heels while Krissy went to the backroom to have a dirty conversation with her man, Dirty. She was in the process of getting her thoughts together when the friend returned.

"Hand me the cash out of your purse."

She handed over the purse. Krissy dug in the purse, dropping the empty bag onto the table. Quickly, she thumbed through the hundreds getting a count before subtracting bills and handing them to her.

Queenie took the money with hesitance. She didn't think she should be paid anything since she was living on her couch and wearing the woman's clothes. Having a place to seek refuge was enough. Coming from where she'd been, she would do anything free of charge, to stay.

"What is this for?"

"You were with me, so I gotta feed you. Ain't shit free." Krissy placed a rubber band around the money. "One thing I learned in the streets is you gotta take care of those with you while you can because one day the shoe may be on the other foot. Feel me?"

"Yeah, I feel you," she added the money to the other cash she earned.

"Go ahead and get some sleep. We got business to handle in the morning."

Having Krissy out of sight, she pushed the money into a small pouch she found in her bag for safe keeping. Exhausted, she laid on the couch with her mother and Precious heavy on her mind. Soon, if everything went as planned, she'd go back for them.

****

"You like when I do you dirty!
You like when I do you dirty!
I'll let you talk to the pillow. Promise I'ma make it last."

Tank's silky, bedroom voice spilled from the entertainment system as Krissy threw that ass back slowly and dramatically, making her man go crazy while she tightened the grip of her sugary sweet walls around his thick pipe like a suction cup.

She made the pussy pop and gush on him, drowning him with her thick, slushy, nectar aiming to make him cum hard and deep, she was done playing games with him. When they first met, he was getting his weight up in the streets. Adding her hustler's ambition to his team, he became a star. Every bitch in the streets was after him and his bag, but what they wouldn't know was that she was the one making sure he was good in every way that she could contribute. Now that she was half a million strong, she needed something more than a position on the team. She needed a major role in his life as the head bitch in charge.

"Oh. My. God!" she mouthed slowly so that he could read her lips over the music.

He pushed his wet thumb into her butt making her buckle and quiver as the orgasm escalated into an explosion.

"Shit!" she screamed into the pillow.

She looked back at him nearly cross-eyed and overwhelmed with lust. Satisfaction wrinkled her brow as sweat formed all over her back. The seriousness across his face always made her wet during sex.

When he gripped her love handles, he took complete control of her waist by holding her in place while he slid his black stretch of meat deep intending to break down every wall in his way. As his orgasm climbed to its peak, so did she. She lost control. As he came, the pressure from his pipe caused a chain reaction. Krissy nutted so forcefully, her bladder spilled over.

"Oh, shit, Dirty—Diiirrtyyy!" She quaked, long, and violently with a grin.

He flopped beside her. She shuddered and moaned, while slowly her senses came back to her.

"You gon' quit pissin' on me, girl!" Dirty jokes, loving the things his blessing could do.

"I'm sorry, baby. It's all your fault," she whined, fighting the sleep. "That dick is such a good boy." She found the strength to sit up.

"Yeah, I know." He stood naked. "Want something to drink?"

"Put some clothes on before you go out." She frowned.

"Mean to tell me, I can't walk through my own shit with my nuts out if I want to 'cause yo' ass taking in the homeless?"

"Baby, please, not right now, you finna blow my high."

"Blow your high hell. You need to go in there and tell that lil' chick to run her ass back home some damn where." He stepped into his boxers.

"I already told you she can't go back home. Something bad happened to her there. She didn't say much, but I felt it. I can't just put her out on the streets. You know how I feel about that, baby," her voice pleaded.

The look he gave meant he couldn't care less.

"Don't do that, Dirty. You know I'm not gonna go in there and wake that girl up just to tell her to get out," she kept her voice low.

"I'm not asking you. I'm telling you to go get this lil' bitch outta my shit. I got too much goin' on anyway to have some runaway chick here with the police or who knows looking for her. That's a problem we don't need 'round here right now, so go wake the broad up and put her ass out."

"No. Nigga, you got me fucked up." She stood her ground. "I'm bucking that shit you talking, straight up. Beat my ass, do whatever you gon' do. I can't fuck up shit and put that lil' girl out on the streets."

"That broad better be outta my shit when I wake up or both y'all asses getting the fuck out." He went to his side of the bed.

"And I'm telling you now, she is not going anywhere until I say, Dirty. That's my new friend. You can't keep running all my friends away because you're paranoid. She's cool, and I know she'll do what I need her to. So chill, I need her."

He laid in bed. "Let her ass be on my couch when I wake up."

Krissy climbed in bed beside him, giving him her back. "Bet not fuck with her, I know that."

Black Migo

Chapter Ten

He shook her forcefully. "Aye, home girl, wake yo' ass up."

Queenie snapped upright on the couch tired but alert.

"Get your stuff and let's go," his voice was hushed. She stood motivated by the urgency he spoke with.

"Huh? What's going' on?" She noticed her bag packed, ready to go.

"Get your shit, you gotta go, bruh."

Unable to protest, she got her bag, slung it over her shoulder, and glanced down the stretch of hallway to the shut door wondering why Krissy didn't have the heart to tell her to leave.

"But I don't have anywhere to go."

"That ain't my problem."

"Can I at least take a shower first?"

"Nah, you can't. The most I'm doin' is giving your young ass a ride," Dirty's tone was hard and cold.

"This some bullshit," she said inwardly.

She wanted so badly to confront her so-called friend allowing her to stay a few days, lying that it was cool when it wasn't. "Did Krissy tell you to put me out?" she had to ask while he drove.

"It doesn't matter, yo' ass gotta go. Simple as that. Matter of fact—" He pulled over onto a stop in the median. "Get outta my shit." He hit the unlock button.

She fought back tears fearing being exposed to the world. She took a deep breath. "Tell Krissy she's fucked up for this, fuh real."

She snatched her bag and slammed the door as hard as she could, before suddenly feeling overwhelmed with helplessness while watching him peel off into morning traffic. Sucking up her fears, she crossed the street and started walking up the busy Forest Drive sidewalk.

Ten minutes into her walk, she noticed the huge Wal-Mart sign up ahead. "That's what I'll do. I'll go inside and burn a few hours until I figure out what to do next," she spoke her mind.

The closer she got to the massive opening of a parking lot stretching hundreds of yards across with big stores on both sides of an invisible field like opposition in a competitive standoff, the more her nervousness climbed.

"Ain't this a bitch?" She sighed deeply, wiping away tears as the police cruiser slowed alongside her for a brief instant, then sped away.

Her heart was beating outrageously causing her to shiver. She watched closely as they turned into the parking lot, so fearing a run-in, she headed up a hill of grass into the wooded area surrounding the large chain of shopping centers.

"Eww. Oh, my God, yuck!" she whined, pushing past spider webs and bugs scurrying across the curb.

She saw how far she'd ventured when she noticed another police cruiser circling the premises, she pushed further and away from sight until she was hidden under cool shade. Sitting her bag on the ground, she removed a sweater from the bag and slid it on. It wasn't until she dug out the pouch of money when she realized nearly all her money was gone. Brokenhearted, she removed everything in a desperate attempt to find the cash. The pine twig ground was littered with her belongings.

"This shit can't be real!" she cried, stuffing clothes back into the bag. "She took my money, then put me out?" She sat on the bag with her face in her lap. "God, why am I being punished like this?" She needed answers.

For hours, she sobbed uncontrollably thinking of every explanation for her situation. When her tears ran dry, she wiped her face clear of anguish and counted what little remains of the stash.

"This bitch really left me with a hundred twenty-fucking dollars." She quivered, incredulously. "I really can't believe this shit." She pushed the cash into her sock.

Disgusted with how she was treated, she soaked up her pride and went to pee beside a tree. Having her bladder at ease, she returned to needing to figure out her next move. Time was draining out of the day, and she was afraid if she didn't do something quick, she'd be left for dead somewhere. So, walking to the edge of the woods, she surveyed the area. It all seemed perfectly fine until she spotted the police cruiser beginning another torpid round of security. Instantly, she fell back into hiding feeling trapped and cornered like a prisoner in a jungle.

The sun fell quickly from the sky, and as night came, so had her fears.

***

"Dirty, you did what?" Krissy yelled into the phone storming through the living room. "I told you not to do that shit! Now you gon' have that poor girl thinking I'm the reason you got her out the house. That is so fucked up for you to do, straight up!"

"You'll be alright. Now I can move 'round the crib with my nuts swangin' any which way I want." He chuckled.

"Nigga ain't shit funny. Ugh! You make me so fucking sick." She hung up in his face. "Corny ass nigga."

Seeing Queenie gone had her livid. Since she wasn't too big on having a whole lot of close friends, having a chick like

Queenie who she could groom into a protege would've been nice.

"Damn this nigga done fucked up my come up." She strutted to the shower. Now that she was solo again, she knew she needed to head out early to get a jump start on the day.

***

"This morning, 26-year-old, Ta'manie Evans was gunned down outside the private club *Top Floor*. Witnesses stated a fight broke out inside and ultimately spilled in the streets where several shots rang out, striking the male in the upper torso. Investigators are still unsure whether this act of violence was random or a calculated gang hit between two street rivals. WLTX will continue to keep you updated. More to come—"

"Stupid ass nigga." She cut the television off. "Shouldn't have tried me in the first place. Now, look at you. Dead as fuck for playing with me and my bag." She frowned, snatching up her purse and tote bag before heading out of the house.

Inside the BMW, she sparked up the blunt of Kush needing to mellow out the start of her day. The severity of the situation hadn't set in until her mind started drifting, causing her to sober up quickly.

After making the hour-long drive into Sumpter, South Carolina, she was anxious to get back to the city to find out what the streets were saying. Pulling into a small ice cream shop, she parked the car before sending out a text. Normally she'd go do a short round of boosting, but with new concerns, she had to be in and out.

Fifteen minutes later, a silver Porsche pulled alongside her hitting the horn to get her attention. The window rolled down. Instead of seeing Krock, her eyes settled on his wife, Venice, and sister, Shay. All good friends.

"Hey, girl. What's up?" Shay spoke from the passenger seat.

"Follow us." Krissy nodded her head, rolling the window up.

She followed the sports car further into the neighborhood until they were turning into a long stretch of paved road and trees, along both sides for miles.

"I swear I hate this country shit," she mumbled. Two miles into the drive, they pulled onto a dirt road riding it for half a mile before pulling out of the smoothness of a concrete driveway that looped around a cherry tree. "Okay, Krock, I see you got your bag up," she said aloud.

When Venice and Shay climbed out of the two-seater, they waved for her to come over.

She locked her car up and followed.

"What have you been up to, trick? Venice hugged her excitedly.

"Bitch, you already know, bag chasin'!"

"Dirty putting that dick on you good, too. Yo' ass thick as hell now," Shay chimed in, playfully.

This was something they'd done when getting together.

"Ain't it, girl? My ass is phat, huh?" She tooted her bottom up.

Shay slapped it. "And it's jiggling. Let me find out he's sticking that dick in the chocolate factory." She giggled.

Krissy laughed off her embarrassment. "That's none of your business."

"Cut it out, Shay. Like Zoo's crazy-ass ain't been diving in yo' ass fuh chocolate." Venice giggled. "Your ass ain't too big for nothing."

The mention of Zoo's name made Krissy tight.

Shay frowned her pretty face up. "That's so fucked up. I told you, I don't fuck with that nigga anymore."

"Ahh shit. Why, what happened?" Krissy asked, following Venice inside.

"Giiirrlll! Let me tell you," Shay drawled. "That nigga beat my ass the hell up because I caught him fucking another bitch at one of his damn apartments on some humbug shit, too. This silly ass nigga denied fuckin' that hoe even while his dick was fresh outta her pussy," Shay said, becoming agitated.

"Chile, these dog ass niggas a trip," was all Krissy could say, taking a quick glance around at her beautiful home decor.

"He lucky his ass crazy was with all them stupid young niggas or I would've been had somebody knock his pussy ass out."

"I'on think all that would've happened, but I feel you," Venice said.

"We all know he official and gon' do what he does."

"You act like you taking this nigga side when I'm your sister."

"I'm not taking his side shit, I'm just saying."

"Saying' what?"

"That if he hears bitches making threats, don't act like he won't send them fuckin' dumb ass Pinehurst niggas to kill our asses."

Shay sucked her teeth. "Fuck him and them Pinehurst niggas. All of 'em."

"Fuck all of who?" Krock interrupted. "I can hear y'all bitches way in the other room beefing. What's all this about?" He came in shirtless, in sweatpants, covered in sweat from an intense workout.

Neither bothered to check his language. He was rich, powerful, and unapologetically dangerous.

"Nothing, baby. We just talking." Venice went and kissed his lips.

Standing six foot six, two hundred and twenty-five pounds of chiseled muscle, she loved all of him.

"Yeah, a'ight. Leave the drama in the streets because I don't have the tolerance."

"It's all good, bruh!" Shay assured.

They all knew the severity of getting him worked up. With his power and resources, he could have any young killah in Sumpter murder any and everything.

"It better be," his voice held conviction. "Baby, you and Shay step out and let me have a word with Krissy."

Venice smiled, planting a kiss on his lips before leaving with Shay in tow.

Once they were gone, Krissy spoke, "Did Dirty tell you that the last batch was pure bullshit? He barely made his money back."

Krock frowned. "Why dat nigga ain't come tell me that shit himself?"

His grimace made her uncomfortable. "I'm just a messenger. You know I ain't got shit to do with what y'all niggas got goin' on. So, leave me out of it."

"Ain't that yo' man?"

"Dirty? Yeah, you know that."

"A'ight then. His bullshit is your bullshit and vice versa. You out, spending a nigga's money, looking sexy when shits all good, then you gotta wear the bad when it's bad, too," he said, dead serious. "Niggas respect the broads that be around when shit ugly because he can have any hoe he wants when he is sitting on a bag."

"You're right," she could only agree.

"I know. When you get back to Dirty, tell him I said pay me back half of what that last order was. I didn't know shit was barely decent until it was all gone. The bricks we holding now are one hundred percent better. I made sure to check and double-check. The Migos got it right this time."

"What's the ticket?"

"Twenty-Eight."

"And he owes you?"

"A thirty piece."

She did the math quickly in her head. "Your money is in the car. The other half, he wants down on another clip," she said referring to ten kilos.

Krock chuckled. "You came a long way, girl. That's what's up. With a bitch like you on his team that nigga can't fail. Tell Dirty that we gotta get up immediately. While you go find Venice, I'll get that ready for you."

Krissy hurried and found Venice who wasn't too far and clearly in ear shot range. She knew what that feeling was that always made her hot, while in his presence. If any opportunity ever presented itself, she was not sure if she could avoid giving him some pussy.

"You must've been reading my mind." Venice smiled.

"What?"

"If your ass ain't come out in another minute, I was coming in to pry your jaws off my man's dick," she joked.

Krissy chuckled. "Now, you know better. I ain't that triflin'."

"I'm just playing," Venice said. "Don't take it seriously."

"Bitch, I'ma fuck your man first chance I get, silly hoe," she wanted to say but kept it hidden behind a smile. "I know you're just playing," she said. *But I ain't,* she thought.

***

Kak!

Her eyes fluttered open.

Kak-Kak!

Queenie held her breath too afraid to move. Enveloped in darkness, she listened to the nerve-wracking sound of crickets, owls, and mother nature around her. She could feel herself being watched, by what, she was too terrified to find out. She lifted her head slowly from the bar her arms created to rest her head as she slept. She had no way of knowing exactly what item it was except that it was the wee hours of a chilly night.

Kak!

Her eyes shifted to the snap of a twig. She took short shallow breaths to avoid being heard, hoping she could not be seen in the night. The full moon high in the sky casted patches of ghostly shadows across the forest floor. As goosebumps prickled along her flesh, the eerily feeling of being watched grew stronger.

Kak! Kak!

The snaps became louder. Closer.

"I'm finna run, fuck this shit," she told herself, eyes dead set on eyeshadows ten feet away.

There was a soft movement. She was thinking of her escape, needing a straight shot to exclude danger. Queenie took in a deep breath, readying herself.

Kak!

Her senses tingled as she watched it come closer. She was preparing to dash at the sight of the full-grown possum taking careful steps across the twig floor. She gasped and quickly covered her mouth. She held her lips shut tight. The animal gazed her way. Its black, beady eyes frightening under the moonlight. Then in a swift, sudden motion, something fell from the sky. Its long, thick talons clamping on the rodent's back, slamming their weight down on the prey and tightening its grip. The owl cast its vision her way while using its claws to puncture the possum's heart.

The rodent struggled and eventually went stiff. Then as quickly as it swept from above, it took flight high into the trees and out of sight.

Queenie bolted through the trees, heart racing in her chest. In no time she reached the concrete, but instead of a Wal-Mart, she was standing in the larger lot of an Econo Lodge Inn and Suites. Out of breath, she stood in the parking lot panting wildly and sweating. She held her chest feeling disgusted by what she'd seen. She shook away the creepy vibe as she walked over to the stairs to sit.

"Lord, what am I gonna do now?" she sighed exhaustedly. Her mind was bogged with the constant situations flashing through her head. "This woman actually killed somebody in front of me." Her head shook. "Then got the nerve to take my money and put me out on the curb. Got me looking crazy," she whined, speaking aloud. "That chick better hope I don't run into her ass no again."

Queenie wanted revenge. Vindictively she spoke, "I should go back to that neighborhood and talk to Zoo. It'll crush her ass to see me with him, I bet."

As soon as she began putting her schemes together, the sun started rising as travelers started to leave.

She couldn't stay, so Queenie decided with the sun shining its light over the woods, she'd go retrieve her bag. Wiping away tears, she could only think of things she had to do in order to get ahead.

"I'll burn time in here," she said, entering Kim's Beauty Supply Store.

After two hours of gazing, she settled on a Remi wig along with big-framed dark shades that concealed a good portion of her face. Since she wasn't sure how she was going to make more cash, she had to budget what little she had. She was no longer a daddy's girl and would have to rely on the streets to provide her with day-to-day material.

Putting on her new look, she exited the store feeling safe. She thought about her stomach as it growled. Spotting the McDonalds across the street, she made her way over there. After ordering from the dollar menu, she took a seat at a corner booth.

"I need a phone," she said. "No, I need a place to live." She chewed on a French fry. "No, I need a miracle." She let out a frustrating sigh. "I really thought she was cool." Krissy came to mind.

She still couldn't believe how she'd been done. A part of her wanted to ignore the anger of being wronged, but she could only think of redemption. In just a few days she'd learned enough to survive in the streets on her own, and that's what she planned to do.

"That chick tried me." She shook her head. "I'ma steal that ho's hustle."

Black Migo

Chapter Eleven

Minutes turned into hours and eventually ended the day. She traveled store to store aimlessly, hoping to burn time and shoplift only to realize the sun had fallen from the sky. She had nothing to show off and still had nowhere to rest her head.

A repressed Queenie sighed hopelessly. "I am not sleeping in those woods."

She began her walk around the massive shopping area until she had the Econo Lodge in her sights.

"My stuff is in the woods, I got seventy dollars left to my name. I need a shower and I need a—"

"Hey, there?" the masculine voice called from behind.

She turned, caught off guard. "Hey"

"I see you chillin' by yourself."

"Something like that." She stood from the steps and out of the path of his handsome face. "Was I in your way?"

"Nah, nah, you good, shawdy." He came and stood next to her along the second-floor rail. "What are you doing out here all by yourself?" His hazel brown eyes traveled up and down her curves.

"Chillin', that's it."

"Are you here with them other chicks in room one-eighteen?" He sparked up the half of blunt, taking a hard pull and blowing the thick fog into the night.

Queenie enjoyed the exotic smell that made her senses tingle. "Uh, no. What girls?"

He chuckled. "That's real, shawty. I feel you can't trust mufuckas these days." He threw one of his thick dreads back out his face while pulling on the blunt.

"I don't know what you're talking about," she said, honestly.

He chuckled more. "I came all the way from Atlanta to fuck with y'all Carolina mamas and I can't even lie, y'all got some of the best pussy I ever had." He pulled hard. "I damn near don't wanna go back." He grinned.

"Can I hit your weed?"

"You can finish it. I'ma roll-up something else." He passed her the joint.

She took the weed, hitting the blunt a few hard times before flicking it over the rail. "I appreciate that."

"No pressure." He licked his lips with lust oozing off his gaze. "Me and my potnas been in Kill'umbia for two whole days fucking with your homegirls. They done made at least ten stacks off us alone. That shit ain't nothing." He rolled up. "Nigga tryna see what up wit' chu', though?"

"I don't get down like that."

"You ain't gotta keep up with the attitude. I ain't no police. I'ma real street nigga, Zone Six." He puffed on the blunt blowing a thick, grey cloud of pungent smoke into the night. "You wanna hit this, too?"

She took two strong pulls before passing it back. Unlike the last two pulls, it sent a euphoric sensation up her brain, down her back, and straight to her pulsating twat. The Kush sent tingles up her thighs making her box gush with sweet juices.

"That mufucka good as fuck, huh?"

Her head went up and down slowly as her soul seemed to separate from her body. *I'm high as fuck*, she wanted to say but was too stuck. Everything moved around in slow motion.

"You wanna hit this again before I put it out?" he asked, pressing up close on her.

She shook her head. Taking the last pull before stuffing it out, he blew the thick fog in her face.

I can't feel my face, she thought.

She watched the strangers move about, but was unable to hear or understand. There wasn't much she could not speak as the heart pace quickened.

He opened the door to the Suburban with heavily black tinted windows. Helping her into the passenger seat before going around climbing into the driver's seat. He set his seat back completely. Queenie watched him through slits. Her body was floating on clouds.

"What are you gonna charge me fuh dat kat, lil' hotty?" He pulled out a knot of big faces. "I gotta bill." He tossed the hundred into her lap.

Her eyes landed on the bill. Still, she was too high to reply. "I'm not 'bouta have sex with you." Her eyes said it all.

"Come on, get me right."

She shook her head in slow motion. He undid his designer belt and zipper, digging out the limp, fleshy muscle. He stroked it, wiggling the snake to life, her eyes locked in on his swelling member.

"I got condoms if you wanna suck it with one on."

She said nothing.

He chuckled, grabbing her wrist. She pulled away softly. He pulled her hand back to his shaft. "Grab hold of it."

She refused.

Removing the Revolver from beneath the seat on the dashboard. Instantly her palm opened, grabbing the hot meaty stick. He began to expand.

"That's right, jack my dick," he snarled, veracious. "I already paid you."

Bit by bit, her senses returned. Soon she was able to speak though, her mind was a fuzzy cloud. She serviced him with a hand job for over half an hour as his muscle swelled more, she was able to comprehend the situation. He threw his head back in ecstasy on the verge of a climax.

Suddenly, Queenie jumped out of the seat, swinging the door open and quickly leaving him nutting all over himself. She ran back up the sidewalk toward the stairs clutching the hundred-dollar bill. Her mind was in every direction, she was panting in a rush to safety.

"Oh, my goodness," she whined, still high as hell.

She went up the flight of stairs looking for him. When she couldn't spot him, she sat on the steps fidgeting with her hands.

"Bitch you thought you could run forever?" He bolted up the flight of stairs, gun extended before him, his glassy, red eyes were soul-piercing.

"Gimme my shit back!"

"Here, I'm sorry."

The bill landed at his feet. Terror had her legs frozen afraid to be shot. He bent down and picked up the money, throwing it back in her face.

"Nah, shawty, I paid for you to get me right, so get me the hell right." He pulled out his cum soiled penis while keeping the pistol aimed. He stood directly in front of her blocking the review of the streets and keeping her trembling body trapped. "I ain't got all day, shawty."

Her voice cracked, "You're scaring me."

He checked for cameras. "Bitch, eat that dick up!"

"Nooo!"

"I said eat—"

"And I said no!" She kicked him in the pelvic area as hard as she could, sending him tumbling backward on the concrete.

She stood surprised at her reactions, but couldn't sit and make sure he was down for good, so she ran past him down the stairs.

"You stupid bitch!"

Bloom!

The gun blast was deafening.

Queenie tripped over her feet and crashed into the line of bushes.

The sounds of his heavy footsteps coming down the flight of stairs sent her into a panicked mood. She scrambled to her feet running as fast she could, landing on the hotel premises toward the Wal-Mart and shopping centers. Her sprint slowed along the dark street. The black forest to her left, the highway to her right. Ahead was a long stretch of road. She willed herself to run, but there was another long stretch of road she would have to turn in order to reach safety. She was too exhausted and her mind was discombobulated. Tears chased one another down her face, as she took a glance back behind her. She wasn't out of danger yet.

The black Suburban backed out of the parking spot and shifted into gear, the engine could be heard revving as it accelerated. She dashed across the street and jumped the ditch afraid for her life, scuttering into the dark ghostly woods. Spider webs covered her face as she zig-zagged through tangles of vines and brush with the SUV coming to a screeching halt.

"Fuck you too, bitch!" he roared.

Bloom! Bloom! Bloom!

The pistol flashed and a hot, red spew of fire sent cannon balls crushing through the trees. A petrified Queenie fell to the ground to avoid being hit. She hugged the ground whimpering, listening to the burning tires speed away and watching its tail lights disappear toward the highway.

Trees groaning, cracking from being struck, echoed through the forest. Branches were crashing to the ground causing her to cringe. She refused to move, resting her head on her forearms in tears while watching the backstreet. Police came and left. Still, she laid in hiding, crying with no way of knowing how her future would play out, until the sun-kissed the day.

Getting to her feet, she said, "Fuck this, I'd rather go back home."

Chapter Twelve

The entire morning, she searched the woods for her bag until she finally located it untouched. It was the only thing she could feel good about all morning. After smacking away dirt and bugs nesting on the bottom, she threw it over her shoulder while debating with her conscience, whether living at home is a lot easier than living on the streets.

"That's a lie!" she spoke aloud.

Under no circumstances was she willing to return home unless it was to retrieve Precious and no one could convince her to live under their father's roof ever again.

Then she had an idea, reaching down she snatched her socks only to learn every dollar she had left to her name was gone.

"No. No. No. No!" She searched her things in a frenzy. Tears welled in her lids all over again. "This shit cannot be happening."

Desperate, she set out retracing her steps until she jumped the ditch, walked up to the motel, and spotted the money. Her heart fluttered with a moment of happiness as she dug the bundle of money out of the bushes, she tripped and crashed into. After wiping her face dry, she brushed away dirt from her clothes and weave, then strutted across the lot with confidence just as Krissy had shown her, approaching the elderly woman going room to room house cleaning.

"Excuse me, Ma'am. My name is Queenie. I'm seventeen and homeless."

"Oh—my," The short black woman held her chest.

"Sorry for startling you, but I wanted to know if you could help me get a room for the night. I have some money, I just need a place to rest for the night," her voice cracked. She wiped away tears.

"Lord." The woman cast her sights on the sky. Tussling with her thoughts. She gazed at Queenie up and down with sympathetic browns, setting the vacuum aside. "Are you okay, child? Are you alone?"

"Yes, ma'am I'm alone," she smiled shyly.

The woman bit the inside of her lip. "I can get in trouble for this, and may even lose my job if my supervisor finds out. Old Hag is looking for any reason to have me fired, anyway."

"I understand. I only need somewhere to sleep and wash for the night. I'll be out in the morning."

"Don't worry, child. The Lord will bless me for this." She closed the room door. "What's your name again?"

"Queenie Wilks."

"Alright, Queenie what a beautiful name to have. I'm Patricia, but you can call me Ms. Pat. Now, the rooms are sixty dollars a night, with my discount it'll be around twenty-five a night for a single bed."

"Are you gonna charge me for getting the room in your name?"

"Sweet pea, no. How about this? You seem like a good young lady searching for your purpose right now. I'm sure you'll find something close to your heart and become great at it. I won't charge you anything."

"Thank you, I really appreciate it." She unrolled the seven ten-dollar bills, took the money and headed to the front office.

Queenie took a seat on the edge of the walkway between two parked cars. She feared the man with his gun would appear any moment, but she was too tired to even care. However, finding someone to help her out, she knew there was only one place those gifts could fall from.

The woman paid for two nights in order to get them for $25 a night and figured that would be best. She walked back over to Queenie. "Here's your room key. There are two cards so don't lose them. You're in room three-twenty-eight on the opposite end. Come, I'll show you." She gave her the keys.

Queenie followed the woman who reminded her so much of her own grandmother, Nancy. Climbing the flight of steps to the third floor, she was relieved to find her room facing the steps to the third floor, sitting in the corner of the walkway with the ice and snack machine nearby.

"Be responsible, Sweet pea. God will bless you on your journey and trust the plans he has for you." She touched her hand before walking away.

"I really appreciate it," Queenie whispered, as the woman hurried away.

Breathing a sigh of relief, she threw off her bag, kicked off her shoes, and flopped onto the bed mentally exhausted. She still couldn't believe Krissy had done her so dirty. As her body began to relax, she found herself struggling to stay awake, until she dozed off.

Hours later she fought the sleep away. "Uh-uh, I got two days to figure things out and I can't do it sleeping," she said, getting up with a burst of energy.

Making sure the door was secured again, she stripped down and took a must-have shower. Having only $20 to her name, there was no way she planned on ending up back in the woods. She'd rather run home than experience one more night in the dark and to be sure it wouldn't happen, she dressed and headed out.

Entering Wal-Mart, she grabbed a cart and began shopping for household products. Since she didn't have any clientele, she aimed to get what may be needed. After hitting the cosmetic and hygiene aisles, she then hit the clothing department stuffing her cart. Two hours later, she pushed the cart through the crowded store trying to figure out the next move.

"How am I going to get this stuff out the door?" she whispered. "Regardless, it's leaving with me no matter what."

Queenie paused at the fresh fruits. Thankfully she'd worn her shades concealing her wandering eyes. Survival made her desperate. She wasn't quite brave enough to go with her first plan of rushing out the sliding doors full speed pushing the cart, so with a second daring plan, she went to the self-checkout lines.

A pregnant woman with a full cart of groceries rang up her items. In the seat of the buggy, a toddler smiled happily at Queenie. The adorable little girl gave her a contagious giggle while she waved her hand.

"She is gorgeous," Queenie said, once the mother rang up the end of her groceries.

"Oh, yes she is. A handful at that, too." The woman turned, it was evident where the little girl had inherited her looks. "Terrible twos."

"What's her name if you don't mind me asking?"

"I don't mind." She turned to add the change to the machine. "Her name is Dynasty, her daddy named her."

"That's crazy, that's my sister's name, too," she lied, feigning astonishment.

"For real?"

"Yes. My mom named my sister, though."

When the woman turned to remove the receipt, Queenie handed the toddler a toy from the rack.

"Great minds think alike," the woman said, pushing the buggy towards the exit.

Queenie pushed her cart right alongside the woman. "Yes, they do. How far along are you in the pregnancy?"

"Chile, any day now. I can't wait either, this boy is killing me." She rubbed her belly keeping the cart right alongside Queenie's.

Queen of the Zoo

She glanced ahead at the exit, a young woman who looked as if today was her first day on the job stood marking receipts. The detectors went off on a couple up ahead. Queenie got nervous as they neared, she wanted so badly to chicken out, but she didn't have time to waste. She was not willing to leave empty-handed. The woman peeked into the couple's bag then looked to their receipt allowing them through without hassle. The pounding of her heart made her deaf to the pregnant chick.

"What's his name gonna be?" she finally asked.

The exit was coming up quickly.

"We've decided on a few so far, I'm still picking."

"Why not a junior?" She shot her last question to make it appear as if they both shared a deep conversation.

Queenie strolled on the woman's left side putting the Wal-Mart employee on the right side of the woman. The little girl, Dynasty, continued to play with the toy.

"Juniors are so cliche if you ask me, I think—"

Beep! Beep! Beep!

The pregnant woman stopped, blocking the employee's view of Queenie who used the distraction to continue through the exit. Behind her, she could hear the girl snapping at the baby.

Queenie rushed out with her cart. She didn't expect to get away with so much so there wasn't a plan. However, excitedly she pushed the cart across the lot as fast as she could.

"Oh, please let me not get caught."

She reached the McDonalds shortly after glancing back over her shoulder to be sure no one was chasing. Panting out of breath, she spotted a blue-ribbon cab parking. Giving the male driver no chance to get out, she rushed to his window.

"Sir, will you give me a ride to my place? I'll pay extra."

He looked from the cart back to her. "Get in."

Her smile beamed brightly. "Thank you."

Black Migo

Chapter Thirteen

Queenie picked over the things she planned to sell, double-checking her decision before creating a load she intended to take to the streets. There was already a guess of what she wanted to make as well, as long as things went according to plan. Never had she thought she'd be stealing to take care of herself, she hoped to make the best of it.

"Okay, sell this. Keep all this and sell another time." She organized the piles of merchandise.

Once everything was stored in its proper trash bag, she took another quick shower and changed her clothes, dressed and ready to go, she called the cabbie and headed out in the afternoon.

"Where to, miss?" he asked politely once she scooted in beside the bag of merch.

"Uh, do you know where Pinehurst is?"

"You sure that's where you wanna go?" He watched her in the rearview mirror.

She ignored the warning in his tone and nodded her head.

He stared at the meter shrugging his shoulders. "Pinehurst it is."

Expecting a long drive across town, she was surprised to see that Forest Drive was a straight shot to the neighborhood she sought after, making it easy to remember directions. She decided where to be let out, handed over the $9 fare, and climbed out at the Pinehurst Park Gym.

"Be safe out here, young lady."

There wasn't much activity in the streets since the pandemic had some people in fear of leaving their homes. However, that wouldn't stop her or the others looking to make a come-up. Recognizing the Four Seasons Apartments, she headed that way ignoring the nervousness in her gut.

From the doorways, eyes watched her like prey. Chicks holding their babies studied her. She wasn't sure what she was doing, but she was determined to learn on her own. Noticing the parked Mustang, she hauled her bag toward the group of men hanging around hidden from the streets.

"Aye, lil' mama. What you are doin' 'round here all alone?" A fat, sweaty man asked, the predatory look in his eyes gave her chills.

"Umm, I—I'm—"

"Who you know around here?" another asked, gazing with suspicion. "You ain't twelve, are you?"

"No, I'm not the police. I hate the police," she grimaced.

Fat Sweaty cracked a smile. "She got tight 'bout dat."

"I thought she was finna pull the strap or sumin." Another laughed.

She felt uncomfortable being stared at by five grown men who looked as if they wouldn't hesitate to take advantage of her young tenderness.

"So, who do you know 'round here?" Fat sweaty asked.

"Nobody."

"So, what the fuck you want?"

"I'm tryna make some money."

Fat Sweaty's smile brightened as he flashed two rows of gold teeth. "Whatever that ass gon' cost me, I'm paying."

"Uh. No, I'm—"

Another cut her off." What does that mouth cost?"

"Nigga, you always be first on all the new bitches comin' through here. Sit yo' washed-up ass down somewhere," one said, his diamond five-point star necklace glistened under the sun.

"I'm not a fucking prostitute!" she barked. "Quit trying me like that, fuh real."

The group of men bristled at the sharpness in her tone. She was not going to be disrespected again. Outnumbered and all, she was ready to put her new box cutter to productive use.

"I came all the way out here to sell y'all some stuff. If y'all not gonna support my hustle, okay, thank you anyway. Bye."

"Damn, I like her." Fat Sweaty grinned. "What're you selling?"

She set her bag on the hood of the Mustang. Her eyes scanned the area hoping to spot the handsome face guy that Krissy made her promise to avoid.

"I got toothpaste, toothbrushes, floss, different kinds of deodorants, soaps, body washes, shampoos. I also got socks, boxers, tank tops, and under shirts too." She began setting items out.

Slowly, the men touched the merchandise. When they started pulling out thick wads of money her heart fluttered with excitement.

"You right on time," one said. "I was finna be on my savage shit."

"Yeah, me too," another added. "What is all this going for right here?"

Queenie looked it over. "Thirty dollars."

"That's love." He handed over the money.

When she pulled out a Wal-Mart grocery bag for him to store his items, she knew they'd enjoy her business.

In less than ten minutes, every item was gone. She contained her urge to smile and almost choked on excitement. She had nearly two hundred dollars in her hand and was anxious to make more.

"We all got kids. So, if you hit up any clothes bring all that through. Let this be your first stop," Star Chain said.

"I got y'all. Appreciate it, too." She waved, turning, and walking away.

"She got a phat monkey and a phat ass, too."

She didn't have a cell phone, so she was standing in the park looking crazy. "I should've asked one of them to let me use their phone." She took a glance back at the apartments as she started walking through the park to Pinehurst Road. Remembering the route in which the cabbie arrived, she utilized it to find her way out of the hood.

"Yes, thank you! Thank you, thank you." She smiled and thumbed through the $200 she made.

She figured that from this point, the only way for her was up. Queenie pushed the money into her back pocket as a black Sedan sped past. Reaching the corner of Pinehurst Road and Forest Drive, she glanced at the CVS than to the corner store across the street. Joyful, she entered the store in high hopes of calling a cab. As the Arab handed her the phone to make the call, the black Sedan parked outside.

In the blink of an eye, four masked, black, hoodie-wearing hoodlums rushed inside, guns drawn, aimed, and barking commands with life-threatening tones.

"Oh shi—" She belly-flopped to the ground in tears, hating her luck. *Please don't let them shoot me,* she pleaded inwardly.

"Everybody on the fucking ground!"

"Give over the motherfucking money!"

"Open the register!"

Two of the goons jumped the counter at lightning speeds and unleashed a brutal attack by pistol-whipping the Arab before he could reach his handgun.

"Get. The. Fuck On. The. *Ground*!" one barked with the butt of his rifle crashing into the man's skull.

The second assailant applied feet to his face, knocking him out cold. Before ravishing the cash register and counter for money and valuables. The other two secured the customers sprawled across the cool tile floor praying this was not the day they died. Queenie trembled violently, blinking away tears of fear. The last time she almost got robbed someone got killed. This time, she hoped she was spared. Everything was happening so fast that she held her breath when one of the gunmen aimed his weapon at her face as she crossed the store.

"Did you call the boys!" he growled, snatching the phone out of her grip, smashing it on the floor beside her face.

"No. I—"

"Ho shut the fuck up!" He patted her down, barrel resting on her temple.

"Please, Nooo—I—"

The gun kissed the nap of the neck. "I said shut the fuck up!"

Her heart sank to rock bottom. Tears stained the dirty floor. She lay motionless, too afraid to move. Traumatized. As she began to grieve the fact that every dime, she'd just made, all that she had to her name was swiped away in a hot flash. She would've preferred for him to kill her than to leave her to wallow in misery.

Her heart crumbled to dust as she watched the four robbers run backward out of the store, waving their weapons until they were inside the black Sedan, speeding up the block.

Queenie's bones shook like dice. Emotionally she stood to her feet in defeat, looking at the frightened people around her. "I can't believe this shit! Why do you keep doing this to me? Damn!" she screamed, outraged.

Nothing was going right, so much of her wanted to give up and call it quits. One fall after another, never did she think it would be this hard, nor did she think getting to her sister could be so grueling.

There was a voice in the back of her head telling her to run out into oncoming traffic, headfirst and end the misery. She started to entertain the idea, but after speed walking for nearly an hour to blow off steam and simmer down her anger, she noticed the massive Wal-Mart sign high above the trees. A breath of fresh air filled her lungs.

When she reached the room, she kicked her shoes off, locked the door, and fell onto the bed in anguish and exhaustion. The only cure to her pain was the slumber that she found herself crashing into.

Chapter Fourteen

Well-rested, Queenie woke from the night's rest sore with aching bones. She prayed that the day before had been a nightmare, but the moment she rubbed her hands over her pants pockets, bra, crouch, then socks, the harsh reality of her situation landed on her forehead like a bag of cement.

"Fuck! I'm broke!" She sat up right.

The other half of the merch she had left from yesterday's heist was set on the table. So, there was hope.

Sighing deeply, she stared at the box cutter for some time. The weight of the world was far more than she figured she could handle. For a moment, she wondered if running back to a place she went through so much hell to run away from, wasn't such a bad idea. The streets were unforgiving, there was no love or sympathy. No win and a future in taking loss after loss.

Tears welled in her eyes. She was cursed with bad fortune and the razor could take away all the pain, all the torment, and all the demons chasing her soul. The razor slid out of the handle slowly, its sharp point peeked from hiding. She played with ideas. Her will to die was winning until Precious's face came into view, she withdrew the blade and set the box cutter down, shaking away all thoughts.

"I'm going back out there," she said while stripping down for a shower. "Yeah, I'm going back," she repeated as she turned on the water, then it hit her again." Fuck mannn, I ain't got no money!" she whined.

***

The walk to Pinehurst Park with a bag of stolen merchandise hoisted over her shoulder wasn't easy. Her feet hurt, and her eyes stung with tears. She crossed the green grass and soft ball field into The Four Seasons Apartments. She was suddenly exuberant to see the crowd of men sitting around the same as the day before. She was hoping to run into Zoo, but when she didn't see him, she went back to hustler mode.

"Yo' ass back?" Fat Sweaty asked, blowing out a cloud of weed smoke. "I see you came back with all dat ass, too." He chuckled.

She rolled her eyes and twisted her face at him.

"Damn, lil' Momma. You out here on the grind like we are, ain't you? J-Roc asked, sizing her up.

"I gotta get mine like you gotta get yours."

"Good word. Who's your man? All that beauty needs some security," J-Roc continued. "Where is your girl at?"

"I don't need a man. I came alone, I got some more stuff if y'all don't mind buying."

"If I keep buying, you gon' have to start bussin' it for a real nigga."

"Mannn shut the fuck up," Star Chain told Fat Sweaty. "Show us what you got."

Queenie stepped over to the Mustang, skin-crawling under the lustful gazes. Soon, everything was sold, it was clear she was selling out because guys wanted to flex. But as long as they were spending, she didn't care. As the day began to wind down, she realized she had to hurry and get back to her room safely with cash.

She took a seat at a park bench, quickly organizing the knot of money, and out of the corner of her eye, a police cruiser eased down the road a little too slowly. She tensed instantly, chest tight with fear. As she went to stuff the money in her crotch in case she had to run, someone jumped over the back of the bench sitting beside her.

She jumped, startled. "What the—"

"Bitch. Don't move." He glared. The chrome pistol shined under the sun.

She froze in horror. "What did I do?"

"Where is that money at?" he gritted.

Queenie looked from the pistol to the police car in disbelief, as she was getting robbed again in broad daylight. She shoved the money into her panties.

"Give it to me!" He grabbed the back of her neck.

"I'm gonna scream."

"Scream and I'll blow your top off," he growled in a hushed tone. "Think I give a fuck 'bout the police?" he spat. "Now gimme the fucking money."

"No!" she challenged.

"Oh, yeah?"

"I'm not giving you shit!" She tried to shake out of his grip.

She feared the worse as the police cruiser turned off the block. There were no adults in the park, so survival was up to her.

He cocked the gun, his menacing eyes paralyzing her with terror. "Dig in that pussy and give me that money. I ain't gon' tell yo' ass again."

"Just shoot me, I don't even care anymore!"

A smile spread across his face as he started to chuckle. "Yo' ass is a crazy, girl. I like that. Might have to make you my lil' bitch." He pushed the pistol into his pants and his entire demeanor changed instantly.

She stared at him confused.

"Why you are lookin' at a nigga like dat?" He sat back coolly.

"What do you mean? You just tried to rob me."

"No, I didn't. If I was gonna rob you, I would have shot yo' pretty ass first, then took everything, but I didn't because I was just playing."

"That's not how you play." Her emotions were high.

"You act like you don't remember me." He turned on the charm.

She looked at him closely. "I do. From the club? Before people started fighting and shooting." She remembered. "I don't remember your name, though."

"Gary." He took out a cigar, bustin' it down. "You?"

She sighed. "Queenie."

He smirked. "My Queen."

"Never."

"And what was you doing, was it necessary? Is that how you make friends?"

He licked his lips. "Had to see what you're made of."

Chapter Fifteen

Queenie kissed her sister, Precious, on the forehead before exiting her bedroom. She wished her parents would go back to the happy and loving family they once were, but so much had happened that normalcy would never return. There wasn't any amount of counseling in the world that could repair their home. So, for the time being, they all dealt with it.

Closing her bedroom door, she eased under the covers and balled up into the fetal position with her hand cupped over her ears to muffle the heated argument. The hostility in her father's tone always made her tremble. His once loving, caring personality was no longer, as darkness filled the back of his eyes and gloom hovered wherever he moved.

"Please, Father God, help them work it out," she whimpered, with tears rolling from the corners of her eyes. "Make them stop fighting and make daddy stop beating on my mommy." She sniffled.

As she started her conversation with God, her eyes grew heavy with sleep. She would fight the slumber until the heat coming from down the hallway simmered to nothing. Finally, she heard her father grumbling under his voice, stomping on his way out of the house, and slamming the front door shut behind him. Most of her hoped he'd never return for her mother's sake, but she knew that was unlikely.

"God, help mommy be strong. Don't let this mess Precious' head up. Protect our family, keep daddy safe and help him change," she continued her prayer. "And look after us, every day. Amen!" she finished, feeling a weight being lifted from her heart which also led to her drifting off to sleep.

As quickly as she dozed off, the front door could be heard slamming shut. His heavy stomping rattled through the house.

She rolled over, pushing her head beneath the pillow to drown out sounds, and returned to her needed rest.

Suddenly, there was another presence inside the bedroom. Her spirit sensed danger, she stirred awake to investigate, only to find herself staring down the barrel of a .357 Blue Steel Magnum. Terror paralyzed her to the bone.

"Make a sound, I'll kill your mother and Precious, understand?" his voice was low, yet brittle as the winter's cold.

She nodded her head. Every drop of her knew he was telling the truth. His hand touched her smooth, youthful face as tears welled, threatening fall. Confused and scared, her innocent browns stared into his icy grey's searching for answers. Gently he ran the knuckle down her cheek to erase the spilled tear. Mentally he was fighting a war, she could see it in his eyes.

Slowly his touch traveled down the cradle of her neck, collar bone, lingering. She held her breath too afraid to move.

"So, you love your family?"

"Yes, sir. With all my heart." She trembled.

A faint smile graced his lips. "Will you sacrifice for your sister?"

She swallowed hard, nodding while holding her breath as his touch continued its descent down and over her well-developed chest. More tears dripped.

"Answer me!" His eyes flared with anger.

"Daddy. Please. Don't hurt me," she managed, but her words fell on deaf ears as he groped her breasts, keeping his gun trained at her temple.

"You're sacrificing for your sister, okay," his voice was low and sinister. "Say anything and you'll watch them both die." He lifted her shirt up over her head, exposing her chest. Keeping her blind with the shirt, he pushed her back onto the bed as she began to whimper.

She shuddered, struggling to keep quiet, then she tried to resist," Please Da-Daddy—don't!"

The barrel of the revolver was pressed to her head. She was unable to see him. The metal was tempted to blow her thoughts.

"Don't. Fucking. Move," he growled.

She cried harder. He ripped the boy shorts away. As she struggled against his assault, her efforts were fruitless. With a strong grip over her mouth, he silenced her cries while snatching away her innocence like a thief in the night.

There was no remorse, no guilt, nothing in his eyes when he pulled his bloodied penis away and straightened his clothes before leaving the room and returning to another heated assault on his wife,

Queenie laid in a pool of her blood, sobbing uncontrollably, wishing she was dead.

***

"Damn, bruh you good?" Gary waved the lit blunt of weed in her face. "You tuned a nigga all the way out."

She quickly turned her gaze away, swiping the lone tear sliding down her sun-kissed skin, "My bad, I zone out."

"Where'd your mind go? I was asking questions and you straight up ignored a nigga."

Now that she had run away from home, all she could think about was the past and everything she endured. But she wasn't going to humiliate herself more by putting her business in a stranger's lap.

"First of all, you just pulled a gun out on me acting all crazy. What do you think this is? We're not cool." She stood.

"So, it's like that? You gonna walk?"

"What does it look like?"

Gary followed with a smile. "I'ma walk with you on the strength you're in my 'hood and that I'm laying claims on you first before these other niggas try." He blew a cloud of smoke in the breeze. She had to admit. Gary wasn't as cute as the guys she was used to from her neck of the woods, but the hood appeal and rugged edges made her feel safe. In her heart, she was running from demons, and protection was needed. But she couldn't fight the urge to be childish and had to make it hard for him. "You ain't gotta walk with me. I'm grown and ain't *nobody* claiming me."

"That's what you say now. What are you mixed with?"

"I'm white and black. My momma's black. Why you ask?"

"Cause you look good and I'm tryna fuck." He smiled. "Look like you might need your cherry popped or sum'n, too."

Immediately she felt uncomfortable,

"I'm just fuckin' with you, dawg. Stop getting all serious." He laughed. "You got an anger problem."

"Whatever. Do you have a phone I can use?"

"What kinda question is that? Everybody got a phone except you." He handed her his phone.

She called her cabbie. Handing it back once she was finished, she leaned up against the gym building to wait patiently for her ride.

"So, you're bout slide, huh?" He put out the blunt.

"Duh. Apparently."

He chuckled. "I see Krissy got you trained well."

Hearing that name made her disgusted. "I'm my own woman."

"Yeah, nigga, I see that. But we all need somebody around to have our backs nowadays."

"And who you got?" She cut her eyes to him." I don't see nobody."

"Because you can't see 'em don't mean he ain't there though." He lifted his shirt to expose the butt of his pistol. "And he grown as fuck, too."

"Well, I don't need yo' ass to have my back because I got my own. You're my age. You can't do nothing for me except put me into some damn drama. And right now, I'm good on that."

"You gon' put yourself into some drama next time you pull up out here without me on your hip."

She kicked off the wall as the cab turned into the parking lot. "You're going to get the drama next time you pull that broke-ass gun on me again, nigga," she snickered playfully.

"Oh, so you wanna talk shit now that your little cab ride done fuck' round and pulled up, huh?" He cracked up with laughter as she headed away. "And my shit works perfectly."

Before climbing into the back seat, she flicked him a birdie, hoping he could read her lips as she said, "Fuck you!"

Black Migo

Chapter Sixteen

"Brick, we gotta do something about this shit, fuh real. We ain't made not one serve in damn near two weeks straight. You keep saying shit is going to pick up and go back to normal, but I don't see that happening. Here it is, we've had these same two kilos of dope in this mufuckas house, taking penitentiary chances fuh no fuckin' reason!" Rucci fussed at her husband,

"How the hell do we go from a million-dollar Trap Street to nothing?"

Brick sat back on the couch staring at the two blocks in a daze. Though he was listening to his wife and feeling every word, the truth was, he had no real explanation why shit was the way it was. "The coronavirus bullshit got everybody scared to come through, baby. But trust me when they get the vaccine, shit is gonna pick back up. That's all I can figure the problem is."

Rucci craned her neck. "Nigga, you're talking to your wife. None of them little thots you run around getting your rocks off on, so don't fucking play with me like I'm not in these streets with yo ass," she spat.

"Then what the fuck is it, tell me? Cause if you got any idea what it is, you can tell me and I'll solve it, bruh."

"So, you are playin' stupid?" She placed a hand on her voluptuous hip. "Because if we gon' be doin' that I'ma take my ass home. I've been in this bitch every day waiting on some money to come through so we can get rid of this shit and keep going as usual but if you wanna act up, so be it."

"Chill out, bruh." He sighed in frustration. "You doin' the most right now."

"No, the hell I'm not. You're not doing enough."

"And how is that?" he sneered. "Tell me?"

"Bitch, you already know. You know that shit you're tryna push is some fuckin' trash ass dope. Zoo done took all our fucking clientele with that powerful dope, and you're trying to ignore it," she didn't care to speak her mind.

He held a line of fire inside. She knew too well that he'd lay hands on her if she continued the loudmouth shit he hated so much. However, she needed to strike a nerve.

"Ain't shit 'bout this work trash. That Pinehurst shit is just better. But it ain't gonna stop our show."

"Brick, baby—it already did. We ain't made not one penny in two whole weeks. What we've been spending has come outta our stash. What you need to do before that nigga try and come take over Green Street is go take what they're pushing and bring it back over here. Mix it, change the stamp, whatever, do something fast."

"I hear you. Come over here and slide on this dick." He needed to release some pressure.

"Boy! I am not fucking you in no stinking ass trap spot. We got a whole house where we can do all that."

"This is the same spot we came up off too, so gimme some." He unzipped his pants. "Let's get it!"

"Nooo—" she complained, avoiding glancing at his muscle. "We'll do it when we get home. Now put it back up.

He grinned mischievously. "Go on home then, I'll be there later."

"And what are you finna do?"

He stood pushing the P89 Ruger onto his waist. "You'll see, later. Now get the fuck on before I take that pussy."

Rucci rolled her eyes playfully. "Better come home with some fuckin' money, I know that."

***

Queenie was dressed bright and early the next morning with her wig and shades on, baggy jeans, and sweater, along with her tote bag. Her heart was pounding hard in her chest when she set her mind on a challenge, she had always dared to do things even with fear standing in the way. Today would be no different.

Pulling the door shut exiting the room, a smile formed across her face when she spotted Ms. Pat heading her way.

"Hey, child. I see you're up early as well." Ms. Pat spoke softly.

"Yes, ma'am. Good morning. I have to try to find a job."

"That's a good start," the woman dug into her shirt breast pocket. "Here's a number you can reach me at any time. I had a dream, God put you in my thoughts, so I put you in my prayers. It's not every day you run into a young lady as beautiful as you are, living in the streets."

She took the number, reminding herself she needed to get two phones. "Thanks, Ms. Pat, that's sweet and I really appreciate it."

Ms. Pat smiled, gazing at her lovingly. "You remind me so much of my granddaughter, Stacy. She was really brave like you."

"Something happened to her?"

"Unfortunately, yes. She was gunned down by police last year outside a bank."

"Huh? Are you serious?"

She nodded, her mind drifting back to that horrible day. "She had a mission to make it out the hood with her friends, and nobody, not even me, God, or the law could reach her, to change her heart. She did what she felt she had to do. To change her situation no one but death could stop her."

The woman's words had touched Queenie. She swallowed her emotions and kept her heart solid as stone. "I'm sorry for your loss, Ms. Pat. I really am. But I have to go. I don't wanna miss the bus."

"Sure. Don't hesitate to call. I'm here for you."

She turned feeling the strength in her words. The only thing she felt she would need Ms. Pat for was a few more nights at the motel. Nothing else. She didn't need anyone trying to change her mind or mission. Whatever Stacy did was on her, because whatever she decided to do, was on Queenie. Shaking off Ms. Pat's words she made the short walk to the shopping place beside Wal-Mart.

Since she wasn't trying to hit the same place twice. She decided to hit the Men's Rugged Warehouse across the parking lot. Seeing all the stores made her excited knowing she would be able to steal and sell.

But as she walked through the men's department store, she realized that everything she picked up had bulky devices bound by metal that could only be removed by cashiers after being paid for, if not, the alarm would sound.

"How the fuck I'ma get this?" she mumbled, thinking aloud she remembered Krissy using a device to remove the same piece with ease. When she couldn't figure out an idea, she continued to another store hoping to think of something.

Ripping open the flip phone by Verizon, she purchased for twenty dollars, she activated the prepaid service. Once activated, she saved numbers she could remember then called one of her best friends.

"Hello?" Miranda answered,

"Hey, girl. What's up?"

"And who is this?"

"It's me, Queenie."

"Oh my God, Queenie! Where in the hell have you been? You haven't been to any of our online classes or web chats."

"The virus had us all home, right?"

"Still, I've been calling you. We all have. You've missed so much schoolwork. Are you even gonna be able to catch up? Lord." she sighed. "Seems like forever."

"Miranda, I'm fine. I'm not worried about any of that right now. So much has been going on that it's the last thing on my mind."

"I know, I heard, and I'm sooo sorry about your mother. That was so sad. My mother still cries for her, you, and your family."

"Don't remind me." She fought back tears. "Well, I was just calling to check up on you."

"Wait. Don't hang up, Queen. I miss you. You're my best friend and I know something is going on with you, but you're too tough to let anyone in. I don't know why you won't speak to me about it, or any of us. We've all been wanting to let you know that we're all here for you. Nothing has changed." Her words were heavy and sincere. "You know how to fight but if anybody messes with you, I'll fight for you. Any day, even if it means getting my ass whooped during the process. You know how I am."

She cracked a smile, all her childhood friends were military brats from loving families the same as she. And though none of them are as tough as her, they were diehard loyal friends she could always turn to. But there was always that part of her she kept from them, too ashamed and embarrassed.

"You still there, Queenie?"

"I'm here." She shook away thoughts.

"You should've come over so that we can catch up."

"Someday. Right now, I have too much going on." She sighed.

"Okay—" There was a short pause." "How's Precious?"

Her heart ached. "She's okay."

"How is your dad holding up? He has to be feeling crushed behind this."

She swallowed hard, anger heavy in her chest. "He's doing okay, too. Listen, I have to go alright. If anyone asks if you spoke to me, tell them no. Not even your parents, hear me?"

"Uh...Sure. Why not though?"

"No reason, just respect my wishes."

"You know I will."

"Thanks. And I'll call you later."

"Love you, G—"

Queenie hung up on her. Setting the phone down, she debated whether or not to call her aunt and speak to Precious. She wanted to hear her sister's voice, but she felt there was no need to alarm her aunt. She figured she'd leave Precious in Augusta, Georgia without stressing behind her. She took what she managed to steal from multiple sites in a trash bag and she headed to Pinehurst.

***

"Where are you at?" Krissy placed the phone on speaker once Dirty answered on the second ring.

"What's good, baby?"

"I'm back in the city. Where you?" she asked.

"My grandma's house."

"I'll be there in fifteen minutes." She hung up, keeping her attitude discrete.

Regardless of how good business was, she was still feeling a type of way about how he handled things the day before.

Pulling into the driveway of his grandmother's Ridgewood home, she continued past the fence and into the backyard cut off from the community.

Spotting Dirty across the yard in a conversation amongst young boys. The moment the boys saw her, they quickly got Dirty's attention. He wasted no time dismissing them before coming over.

"You thought that shit was cool to stay in Sumpter overnight with my shit, huh?" He grinned, eyes flowing up her ankles to the camel toe, then up her slim waist and braless chest. The one-piece, baby blue leather bodysuit did nothing to contain her womanhood.

"Dirty, I'm grown. I already told you that I do what the hell I want."

To keep from spazzing, he laughed. She could tell he was tempted to lash out. "You gon' make a nigga break that glass jaw of yours, baby. Where my shit at?" he asked in a nasty-nice tone.

"Where is it supposed to be?"

He popped the trunk, removed the duffle, unzipped the bag, and took a quick inventory. "It's only eight bricks, I thought you said, ten. So, where the rest of my shit?" He glared.

She screwed her face up. "Nigga, your shit? First of all, I negotiated that deal so that you could get eight things instead of five. You were paying him thirty a piece for what you owed on ten bricks of garbage. I talked him down to letting you own half of that and put that one-five on a new batch at twenty-eight stacks a pop. So, now you owe him a hundred and thirty racks instead of two hundred and eighty, nigga."

"Fuck all dat, bruh. Where the fuck my other two at?"

"Those are for me."

He looked at her like she'd lost her mind. "Fuck you mean for you?"

"Nigga, you would've been paying two-eighty k for that load. Instead, you're paying one hundred and thirty grand for eight. You ain't losing nothing. Besides, a brick is my price for taking all the risks and the other brick is compensation for what you thought was so funny yesterday morning when you put my friend, Queenie, out on the streets. You ain't know what we had going on and only thought about yourself." She crossed her arms, standing on the decision. "You got some good dick and you're super crazy, but without me, there is no you."

"So that's how we do it?"

"That should teach you to stay outta my pockets and I'll stay out yours."

He nodded, frowning. "You're lucky we at my people's house, I swear yo' ass better be glad."

"I'ma ignore them weak ass threats. You got your shit, that's that. Next time, you drive to Sumpter to meet with Krock, nigga." She flopped back into the driver's seat. "I'ma start charging you for everything."

His grin made her uneasy. The silence made her uncomfortable. When he turned shouldering the duffle, she sat watching him head inside, unsure of what to do next.

"I ain't finna wait on his ass. I got my own shit to do, the fuck," she mumbled, pulling out the driveway.

As she navigated through Ridgewood, the realization hit her. She'd been so caught up with focusing on the money that a possibility of her getting identified for murder had slipped her mind completely.

"I gotta get rid of this dope," she whispered, taking her phone out, scrolling through contacts for someone who'd cop from her. "And I gotta find my little friend, Queenie."

As she headed home, she got someone on the phone.

"What's up?" he answered.

"You, me, us, never them."

He chuckled. "Still being childish. What do you want?"

"You."

"Stop it, for real. What's up?"

She set her feelings aside. "I need to see you and I got something you might want."

"If it's some pussy, I'm good. You are too messy for me, bruh."

She rolled her eyes. "Bitch, fuck you." She giggled. "It's my hoe, though. She was tryna get fucked really good and only you can fuck her right," she spoke in code.

"Pull up then. And bring some rubbers witcha."

Black Migo

Chapter Seventeen

The moment she pulled around Zoo's mansion out of sight from the streets, deep in the country parts of Heyward Brockington Road, her stomach tightened into knots. As much as she tried to hate him, her mind and heart wouldn't allow it. She made sure to stash one of the bricks of coke at home before coming down to meet with him. Past experiences with him kept her on edge and today was no different.

Swatting away mosquitoes and gnats, she walked up to the back door knowing at some point when she turned on his street there were eyes and rifles trained on her that she could see. Before she could tap on the door, it swung open with a preteen glaring up at her with an assault rifle draped over his shoulder. It looks fake, but she wouldn't bother to ask.

"Where Zoo?" She looked around.

The youngin locked the door down with a steel bar. "Put your phone into a basket. You'll get it back when you leave out. Your gun too."

"I ain't leaving my gun, hell no, that's not happening." She looked down on him like he was crazy for making the suggestion. "Your boss, Zoo, should know me better than that."

He jacked the slide on the mini-AK 47. "Aye homegirl, Zoo don't run this door, I do. And I say you leave your phone and your gun. Don't make me add all your clothes to the list." His eyes were big as he started undressing her in his mind.

She sucked her teeth. "Whatever. Y'all some stupid ass niggas." She placed the items in the basket.

Once done he got on a walkie-talkie, from thin air another youngin appeared to escort her upstairs.

"The fuck kinda shit you got going on up in here?" she complained, entering the massive bedroom made into an office, along the wall was a built-in six-by-six-foot fish tank filled with exotic fish. In one corner spiders secured behind glass tanks.

"Y'all step out. Go feed Sheba for me," he told two more of his young killahs who watched her with deadly stares when the door closed behind them.

He leaned back in an imported Haitian leather chair behind the desk, kicking his feet up. "Told you, you would need me before I need you." He smirked, gazing up at her figure.

Her nipples stiffened as she imagined what he was thinking. "I don't need you or no nigga." She looked around. "I just wanted to get rid of some good product."

"For a bitch like you, that shouldn't be hard being that you're fucking damn near every nigga in the city."

"No, the fuck I don't fuck with every nigga. I fuck with one, and he's my man, so don't try me like a thot," she replied, bitterly.

He chuckled, leaning up to rest his forearms on the desk.

"Still hatin' ass nigga, huh? Tell me why you don't like me, Krissy? It's been so long I forgot."

"Nigga, you know why I'on fuck with you. You fucked me and my homegirl Ebony and got us both pregnant. Then you beat both our asses when we were going to have your kids, making us have miscarriages." Her emotions stirred. There was still a lot of love buried deep for him that she tried to stuff away but couldn't suffocate.

"Even after all that, you found out I was fucking Shay and came back begging me to leave her alone, talking 'bout you miss a nigga shit. That's your homegirl, but you still let me fuck the shit outta you." He smirked. "So, why are you mad at me? I'm just a good fuck, with plenty of dick and deep pockets."

A knot formed in her throat. She wanted to cry. To be his woman even after it all is said and done was something she

124

yearned for. He was Zoo, there was no other. Her heart was emotionally bonded to him despite each effort to detach all ties.

"Don't make this all about sex. You beat my ass, too."

"And you still ran back."

She rolled her eyes. "Nigga, fuck you," she gritted. "I fuckin' hate you. You're lucky I'on got my gun, I'll—"

"Say it, it'll be your last," he challenged her with fire in his stare.

She bit her tongue.

"That's right Watch your mouth when you 'round me. Yo' nigga a wanna-be, I'm a gangsta. You know the difference. Now, where's that coke? I'on got all day, my nigga."

"I want a thirty-five stack for it." Her face was mean.

"Keep that shit, I got my own shit going thirty a pop."

"Twenty-nine."

"I'll give yo' thot ass twenty and let you suck my sausage."

"Fuck you."

"I'm fucking with you." He smiled, revealing a mouth filled with diamonds shining with clarity. "I'm serious about that twenty stacks, though."

"Nah, twenty-five and I'll give you my ass to kiss on the way out." She set the block on the desk.

Zoo picked it up, examining the stamp and its scent. "This that Sumpter work. Krock is networking in my city? He knows better. That's yo' folks, ain't it?"

"Yep."

"I'ma give you twenty-five k just because. Bend over and let me kiss that ass," he joked.

"Fuck you, pay me. Now," she relayed with the attitude. "I got shit to do."

Zoo pulled a neat stack of hundreds out of a drawer. "Where is your little homegirl? The pretty one with all the curves."

"Don't worry about her, she's too young. You're a grown-ass man."

He licked his lips. "When I want something, I get it, you know that."

"Queenie doesn't like you. She doesn't do creeps." She counted the cash.

"So that's my future wife's name, Queenie? I like that."

"You better not think 'bout it." She stuffed her money into her purse. "She already has enough problems as is, she doesn't need yours."

He nodded, her words were going in one ear out the other. He pressed a button on the desk, then summoned one of his youngins who escorted her out.

It wasn't until she reached the interior of her car when she sighed a breath of relief. Zoo had her so deep in her feelings that her body was coated with sweat. As she drove home, she was unsure what to feel and unable to think clearly.,

"If he thinks he gon' fuck with her, he got me fucked up."

***

Matthew was growing frustrated and irate with each passing minute. With his job demanding the majority of his time, the search for his daughter was wearing him thin with stress. There hadn't been much sleep since she ran away, and as far as he was concerned, she hadn't contacted any authorities or he would've known by now. He was hoping that maybe she knew not to. However, her absence was destroying his consciousness and ability to make rational decisions.

After speaking with his supervisor earlier, he wasted not a second hitting the streets in order to find out where Queenie was holed up. Figuring she was big on her friendships, he decided to give each of her friends a crack. Since Mariah had been his first option, he placed her at the bottom of the list.

Pulling his black Tahoe outside the house he suspected to be Miranda's parents, he parked, taking a moment to get his mind in order. Figuring since there are no vehicles in the driveway that either of the parents were home. Recently the Governor approved citizens to return to work immediately, with students looking forward to starting the next school year.

As he climbed out, the side door of the neighboring house opened with a mature young woman emerging, trash bag in hand. From afar she was familiar and as she neared, hauling the bag to the edge of the road, he recognized her instantly.

Miranda was stunning, and he'd parked outside the wrong house. But that complicated nothing. Stepping onto the sidewalk he walked over calling out her name.

"Hey, Miranda, mind if I have a word?" His smile was warm and unalarming.

"Hi, Mr. Wilks." She returned the smile, tossing the bag into the curbside dumpster. "I'm sorry for your loss, it was so sad." She pulled the spandex shorts out of her crotch area.

"I appreciate it. Say, your parents wouldn't happen to be home will they?"

"No, Mr. Wilks, both are back on base," she replied, "Hopefully I'll be able to go back to school next year."

He nodded. "When was the last time you spoke to my girl?" She gazed up at the sky. "Hmm—I'd say. Maybe six months ago. She's not the same, it's like she changed. On everyone."

"Yeah, she's been very different and difficult lately. We're all concerned for her mental health. I'm trying to get her all

127

the help I can, but she just won't let me." He rubbed the back of his neck.

"We've all noticed that about her."

"So, she hasn't been over either?"

She glanced back at the house. "Nope."

His gaze followed hers, wondering if someone was watching them from the blinds. "You do know you can get into trouble if I find out you're lying to me, right? I'd hate for it to come to that."

"Mr. Wilks, I wouldn't. That's my best friend, but you're her father, I'd never lie to you."

"So, you haven't spoken to her lately?" he pressed.

"Uh, no."

"And she's not inside?"

"No, sir."

"And if she was, you'd tell me?" He studied her.

"I have to get back inside," she said politely, though his gaze was making her uneasy.

He waved with a friendly smile, watching her every young, tender curve as she turned and strutted away. He watched until she was safely inside, waving him goodbye before closing the door. Sighing deeply, he slid into his truck undoing a top few buttons to his shirt. He turned the A.C. up to cool his rising temperature, then took another glance at the house, before shifting into drive. He could only replay Miranda's answers back in his mind, something wasn't right. She had told him a bald-faced lie.

Matthew laughed at his reflection in the mirror. He hated to be lied to and misled. "The audacity to lie to me of all people. Stupid kids these days."

The longer he thought about it, the angrier he became. Using brute strength, he gripped the steering wheel as tightly as he could. The leather cracked in his hand. He exhaled deeply to relax the beating heart-racing away from him. When he pulled in front of his home, he collected the mail, then headed inside. Locking himself in, he proceeded into his bedroom where he stripped down for a steaming hot shower and eventually into the comfort of his bed.

That was—until the sunset.

Black Migo

Chapter Eighteen

As the cabbie moved at a steady pace with evening traffic, Queenie did a quick inventory of the merch she had available to sell once she reached Pinehurst. After a grueling long day, she knew this was not an occupation she would consider a long-term career in. Too much risk, not enough reward. Once she tied the bag up, she made sure the box cutter was clipped to her waist before making a call.

"Answer the phone," she murmured.

"Hi, this is Miranda. Sorry I can't pick up the phone right now, but if you leave your name and number, I'll get back with you. Bye."

Sucking her teeth, she hung up, redialing the number only to see the same results. As the cabbie turned into a community, cruising up Pinehurst Road, she tried the number once more. The things she was certain her friends would be able to assist her with it would have to wait another time. Momentarily, she put her game face on as the cab came to a stop at the park. Paying the cab, she sent a quick prayer to God for protection and made sure to put the money in her crotch area, before climbing out and shouldering the bag of stolen goods.

Nearing the Four Seasons Apartments, her stomach tightened into knots, Aware of her surroundings, she felt the dangers lurking, yet today, the streets were more active as the community had a festive vibe that drew her in. However, she wouldn't drop her guard.

"Okay, that's what I'm talking 'bout. Look who's back with us." Fat-Sweaty rubbed his nasty belly.

"What's good, cutie?" Star Chain smiled. "See you back at it."

"Up early, up late," she countered with a blush. "Gotta get it, right?"

"You already know," One said. "I wish my baby momma's pussy-ass had a hustle bone in her lazy ass. All she wanna do is get pregnant by niggas, put their asses on child support, beg for money, complain, beg, complain and beg some more."

"Yo' ass funny as hell." Jroc laughed. "How much are you paying on child support?"

"Nigga, I ain't paying that shit. The fuck I look like?"

"A daddy."

"Fuck y'all niggas." One walked away.

"You still ain't got no ass for sale yet?" Fat Sweaty asked, lustfully.

She pulled the box cutter from her waist real slowly so that he would follow her every move. As she pushed the nob up the sharp razor point came into view. The funny smirk on his face turned into a nervous grin.

"I'll shoot the shit out your pretty ass if you swing that blade at me."

"You think I care?" Her eyes were darting while her heart pounded in her chest wildly with fear and adrenaline. "I told you once, I ain't gon' keep telling you. I'm not a prostitute."

"Man, Fat-Ass, leave lil' mama alone. She out here tryna make her money and you wanna be on some stupid shit." Star Chain said,

Fat sweaty scowled. "Nigga, mind your damn business. I do what the fuck I wanna do. Your own damn kids don't listen to you and they are both only four. You think I'ma listen? Hell no!"

"Aye lil' mama, don't pay this stank nigga no mind. What have you got for us today? You got any lotions?"

She mean-mugged Fat Sweaty, but turned her attention to the group of guys checking the merch and her body. It was no secret they wanted to get their hands on her tenderness. "It was a bad day for me, but I got a little bit of everything."

Noticing Queenie had all the drug dealer's attention, a few neighborhood chicks came over to get a good look at her. She instantly felt the jealousy beaming from their gazes as they pretended to check out the remaining items.

"Like girl, where are you from?" the prettiest of the trio of chicks asked boldly while holding a bottle of shampoo and ice grilling her.

"Does it matter?"

"Bitch, I was just asking your ass a simple question. But since you wanna have a smart-ass mouth, I'ma keep this shampoo and this soap."

"You ain't taking shit from me!" She wasn't going out like no punk.

"Aw, shit nah. A hoe-fight. I got twenty dollars on the booster, boo," Fat Sweat joked, pulling out a wad of cash to instigate the situation.

"And hoe what the fuck you're gonna do about it?" The second prettiest of the gang of chicks poked her chest out ready to jump in.

"Get your ass beat the fuck up out here!" the third chimed in.

Queenie shoved the first filled hand into her pocket to keep from losing money while the second hand popped the box cutter hidden behind her back.

"Bitch, what's up?"

Star Chain stepped in between them. "Strawberry, y'all bitches back the fuck up with that silly shit, dawg. Y'all always making the hood hot. You and your funky ass homegirls, back the fuck up."

"Boy, fuck you." Strawberry hurled the bar of soap at his face. "And bitch, you better be glad these thirsty niggas in the way. We would've mopped yo' ass up out here."

"Leave my stuff!" she spat, but the trick had already begun walking away with her merch making a joke out of her.

"What does that shit cost?"

"Don't worry about it," she told one of the men who wanted to pay.

"Damn, I was hoping to see some ass and titties swinging. I'm telling you, ole Booster boo here looked like she was ready to rec," Fat Sweaty clowned.

As she was getting ready to walk away and head to the park bench to wait for her cab, she got startled.

"Uh-huh. Caught yo' ass slipping." He slid the trick bike to an abrupt halt in front of Queenie. "Where that bird at you flicked to me?" He hit the kickstand.

She blushed, but quickly erased it from her face. "I don't have time for your shit today. I'm not in the mood."

"Damn, my nigga. What I do already?" Gary held his hands up in mock surrender. "You are always on defense."

"And you're always in my way, so move."

"Why do you have an attitude with me?"

She frowned. "This is your neighborhood, right?"

He took a look behind her at the group of men. "Point out the mufucka that got my boo mad right now and I'll blow his fucking face-off," he said seriously. "Come on, show me. Who it was?"

Queenie checked over her shoulder. When her eyes landed on Fat Sweaty his nervousness became clear. Gary's threat had traveled. Instead of starting any trouble knowing at some point, she would have to return, she decided to spare him.

"'Preciate it, Gary, but I can fight my own battles."

"Next time I'ma air this shit out. Now, can I get a hug?"

134

She looked at him crazily. "Nigga, no."

"You mean as fuck, girl."

"So."

"If I put this dick on you, it'll soften yo' ass up," he joked.

"I ain't no prostitute, so don't play me." She glared. "And I'm not eye candy, so stop looking at me like that, creep."

As he reached the corner, a Tahoe sitting on 32-inch rims bent the corner into the apartments. His voice went hush. The sparkling candy apple red glistened in the sun. Behind it, the burgundy Wraith rounded the corner as well. The entire complex went silent watching both vehicles nervously.

"Shit!" Gary exclaimed just above a whisper.

"Who is that?"

"Somebody done fucked up," that was all Gary said before the Wraith came to a stop behind the Tahoe, a few feet away from them.

The passenger doors swung open on the truck with three violent adolescents. Each appears to be spaced out mentally, in a trance like state. They opened the back door to the Wraith standing guard.

Her heart fluttered the moment she laid eyes on him. With his wrist in freeze control and neck below zero, the jewels glistened flawlessly the moment the sun touched him. He was sexier than she credited his last run in, and with the boss status radiating off him, authority was his gift. When he opened his mouth, diamonds shone like stars, however his demeanor was aggressive. She held her breath watching him as he moved towards the group of men with murder gleaming in his eyes. He stopped in the center of the parking lot. "Yo' Fat-Fuck, bring your ass over here, nigga."

"Huh, me?" the man Queenie named Fat Sweaty asked. "The hell did I do, Zoo? W-what's going on big homie?" he asked timidly, stepping over cautiously.

"I'ma ask you this once. Lie, and you know what's goin' happen," Zoo growled. Behind him, one of his young killahs lifted the FN-57 as a chick pulled out her phone to record.

"Drop it or I'll splash your ass!"

The chick dropped it instantly, frozen with fear.

"Big Ray, who the fuck told you it was cool to sell my shit to them country ass niggas?" Zoo glared.

"Bruh I-I'on even know what you're talking about. That's my—"

Wham!

"Bitch, shut the fuck up!" Zoo smacked him in the mouth, sending his fat massive frame crashing to the concrete." You think this shit is a game? I told y'all stupid niggas watch who the fuck y'all selling my shit to."

Big Ray touched his mouth coming back with blood. "Bruh, that's my word, I ain't sell them niggas shit." He spat red on the pavement.

"And you stand on that lie?" Zoo ran his hand over his chin. He turned and laid eyes on Queenie, flashing her a smile that made her weak.

"Damn right nigga. Fuck I'ma go behind your back and do some stupid shit like that for, bruh?"

"I was wondering the same thing. When you figure it out, let me know? Right now, though, sleep on it." He turned easing into the back seat of the Wraith as one of the trios of young killahs walked up and stood over Big Ray snickering.

Clah! Clah! Clah! Clah!

The deafening explosions echoed off the apartment buildings sending everyone ducking for cover. Big Ray's body went limp and lifeless. The shooter dove into the Tahoe as the drive took off out the lot with Zoo's Wraith close behind.

The violent wails of women and children pierced the air adding more chaos to the hostile situation.

"We gotta get the fuck outta here before twelve pull up on us." Gary hopped onto his trick bike.

"Where are we going?" She was traumatized and shaken. She'd witnessed two murders in a week and was having a hard time shaking images away.

"Get on these pegs. We gotta go. I got a strap on me!" he snapped. The urgency in his voice sent her into action, clinging on as he peddled away. She feared and hated the police as much as everyone else, so hearing the sirens in the distance made her panic.

"Hurry up, I hear them coming." She grabbed onto his shoulders.

Gary peddled hard turning onto Mercer Street, then up Magnolia, and back up towards Twonotch Road. Queenie recognized the black sleek sedan instantly. Stopping in their path, the driver's door swung open. Her heart dropped and her face contorted with distaste.

"Queenie, get off the bike. Let's go."

"Fuck you!" she spat.

"Don't go with him, they're gonna have you in some shit!" Krissy yelled, desperate. "We need to talk anyway, come holla at me."

"I'm good." She waved Krissy away. "Hurry up and get me outta here, Gary," she said.

He shot them across the busy road and through a shortcut.

Queenie glanced back over her shoulder to see Krissy glaring her way.

Black Migo

Chapter Nineteen

"And where are we?" Queenie hopped off the pegs, anxious to get somewhere safe from police.

"Waverly Street Apartments. My grandma's house, it's where I live too." He hit the kickstand, wiping his face dry of sweat.

She looked around the set of horseshoe-style apartments. There was a calm vibe about the place that made you feel at home. The moment Gary pushed open the apartment door leading her inside, she knew they had to be in the Ghetto Still. A thick haze lingered in the room from a scented incense. The couches were old and worn, the off-white carpet was now a khaki color, littered with patches, stains, and cigarette burns. Though there was a dull appeal, everything was neat and tidy.

"This is my room. You can have a seat on the bed." He closed and locked the bedroom door behind them before removing the gun from his waist, setting it in the dresser.

She tried to hide her disgust.

Gary chuckled. "You scared of roaches?"

"Uh—duh. They bite, right?" She looked around afraid to move.

"None of them bitches bit me yet. I'on think they bite though." He lifted a back window to get a breeze.

She took a seat at the end of the bed, resting her elbows on her knees enjoying the cool air. She was overwhelmed.

Tap! Tap! Tap!

"Open this door, Gary," the feminine voice demanded.

"Go away Grandma. Damn!"

Tap! Tap! Tap!

"Boy! Don't make me break this damn door down!"

"Go 'head. You gon' pay for it, too."

"No, the *hell* I ain't either," she fussed.

"Yes, the hell you are, too."

Tap! Tap! Tap!

"I ain't gon' tell your ass no more. Make me call G-50," she threatened.

"So, you act like I give a fuck. Get off my damn door!" he yelled, turning to face Queenie. "She just wanna come in my shit to be nosy."

"Let her come in so she can go," she replied.

Gary kicked off his shoes. "Nah, she wanna beg."

Tap! Tap! Tap!

"Open this damn door. You black, ugly, sorry ass nigga!"

"I'm gonna let her in here, fuck." She brushed past.

He shot daggers her way, turning and glaring at his grandmother. "Why are you running down on us?"

The grandmother looked around the room, then to Queenie who stood ready to go. "What's your name, baby?"

"Queenie."

"I'on know what you see in this little dirty motherfucker, but he ain't shit. And a pretty girl like yourself can always do much better."

"I'm 'bout ready to knock yo' old ass out, granny, get the hell outta my shit."

"This my damn house. I'm not goin' nowhere until you give me something to smoke. My check finna hit in a couple of days and you know I got you," her voice softened. "Come on now, I'm your grandma."

"You already owe me two hundred. I want my shit, too."

"Boy, I'm just tryna get high right now. Gimme something for fifty dollars and I'll owe you two-sixty."

"Maannn—" he drawled.

She could tell she was contemplating his decision, but like a seasoned vet, she pressed him out. "Hurry up so I can get out y'all way. I know you tryna get you some butt, so I won't bother y'all no more today."

Queenie wanted to check the woman, but couldn't. Gary reached into his shorts pocket. "I'm going to the bank with you, too," he said, digging into the sandwich bag. When he dropped the stones in her palm, she twisted her face with disapproval.

"Hell nah, I want something bigger than these, You're not about to give me the smallest dimes in the bag, let me pick my own shit!"

He tied the bag up. "Better get the fuck out my face, grandma. You ain't 'bouta be in here tryna D-Bo me in front of my girl."

"Give me something else to go with this, Gary. A crumb, that's it."

"No! Now get out." He pressed her toward the door. "Bye." He locked her out.

Queenie watched the exchange in confusion. She sat in the spot she deemed clean enough. "Why do you talk to your grandmother like that?"

Gary set the bag on the dresser. "She don't respect that soft boy shit. That's how we talk to each other. I gotta talk shit and buck on her every time she comes with that thirsty nonsense."

"You sold her weed?"

He chuckled. "Hell, nah. Granny smokes crack. That straight drop too. Gon' have her ass in there clutching, stuck all night."

"How can you sell her that stuff? She's old and that's almost like killing her, right?"

"It ain't gon' kill her. She gonna be high as fuck though." He laughed. "Besides I'd rather serve my granny than to have her walking the streets tryna find some shit then a nigga robs or hurts her. She got a habit, she gon' spend her money regardless. So, I might as well get it."

Taken aback, she was at a loss for words, rubbing her temples needing to give her mind a break. "I need to go. I gotta get some rest, it's been a very long day." She sighed deeply.

"Shit, take you a nap then." He pulled out a small assault rifle, placing it bedside for quick access. "Ain't nobody gon' fuck wit' you."

"What are you doing?"

"I slang dope out my window when the sun set. Which is soon, so I gotta set my lil' shop up. Why, you paranoid?"

"No, I'm just asking. You're moving around too fast."

"Whateva, this is how I do. So, you ain't gonna tell me nothing about yourself so we can get to know each other a little better?"

"No."

"Why not?"

"Because I'm not tryna be cool with you." She grinned. "You move like you have too much going on."

"Yeah, tryna get some money," he countered. "Ain't that what you doing? We can get it together. I'll show you the ins and outs. Get the ball in motion asap."

"Why can't you just boost your clothes? It's easy."

He shook his head. "That shit is a waste of time. I'd rather make five hundred to a thousand per day than to settle for two or three hundred. And that's only if you have a good day," he spoke. "Too much risk, not enough reward."

She gave it some thought. She wanted as much money as she could immediately in order to be able to get Precious and move far away from Columbia to start fresh.

"I don't know 'bout that right now. That's kinda out my league."

"Ain't no pressure. It's good to know you don't fuck with ole' girl, Krissy. That may have saved you from the bullshit coming in the future."

"Why do you say that?"

"Cause, that night I saw y'all outside *Top Floor* we got into a situation. One of the homies got shot. He thinks Krissy slumped Ta'Maine, he is not one-hundred percent sure, though. They got her on the suspect list in the hood."

Her heart pounded. "Do the police know?"

"Nah, not about that. The streets are gonna keep it to the streets."

She became nauseous.

"But fuck her. You good, you're with me now and you don't fuck with her at all, so you're clean. You don't need to get caught up in that bitch's drama."

"I feel you," she said. "But aye, I gotta go. I got to wash and change my clothes. We'll talk later." She got up to leave. "Call me."

***

Sometime After Midnight

Brick watched from a distance as the last of the police left the Four Seasons Apartments with no leads and only a dead body who told no tales. Sitting comfortably in the black-on-black F-Type Jaguar hidden behind heavily tinted windows. He cracked the driver-side glass allowing the thick pungent smoke to spill into the light as he pulled away at the potent blunt of Brick, a combination of Kush, molly, and coke. His eyes were wide as saucers. It was as if he was talking a glimpse into the future. Snuffing the blunt out in the ashtray, he sat back allowing his mind to do it thang. In just a few minutes the animalistic mentality that kept him alive and at the top of his game, kicked in full swing. It was time to eat.

Jacking the slide of the P89 Ruger, he trusted the .30 round extended clip would be enough to help him fight his way out in case shit popped. Licking his chapped lips, he took a sip of the warm pint of Hennessy resting in the side door panel, wincing as it burned on the way down. Putting the bottle back, Brick pulled the skull cap down low before climbing out, pushing the door closed gently and concealing his pistol.

Police circled the block every few minutes on high alert. Since Pinehurst wasn't a place wanted to be caught red-handed by enemies, nor identified in any matter of violence in light of the hood's deadly act in retaliation he made sure to move unseen. Blending in with the darkness he stood against the apartment building. Across the street was the Four Seasons. Since he didn't have the manor firepower to go in alone, he schemed on another spot.

Enveloped in the pitch-black darkness, like a bandit he peered into the bedroom of the one-level apartment. A dancing light illuminating the room from a flat-screen television gave him visuals. The woman laid sprawled across the sheets completely naked. His dick grew stiff. Pistol out, he removed the window screening quietly, glad the room was behind the apartment and out of sight. Setting it aside he looked around cautiously. Using great ease, the window slid up. She didn't budge, instead, she continued to snore lightly.

Brick wasn't sure how he wanted to enter the crib, so he went with his best option. Moving the blinds aside he swung his leg over the sill onto the bed. The moment he stepped his weight in she turned startled and jumped from the slumber to face him.

"What are you doing?" She cringed. "Get out!"

"Shut the fuck up!" he growled menacingly before slapping her with the pistol. "Where is the bag?"

"Nigga, fuck you!" She spat blood and teeth. "I ain't giving you shit."

In a violent manner, he snatched her up by the hair, slung and jerked her forcefully to the floor before pistol-whipping her twice more. "Your ass is gonna die here if you don't give me what I've come for, I know you got it. I watched you for two hours," he spat barely above a whisper.

"Bitch, nigga you got to kill me."

He rocked her jaw with a mean left hook, nearly sending her to sleep. She groaned in pain fighting to regain sense. "Get outta—my—shit!"

"This shit ain't a game." He knocked her out.

Standing up he began his search beneath the bed. When he found nothing, he ravaged the closet top to bottom along with a small closet. Figuring what he'd come for wasn't inside the room, he used his shirt to open the door.

"Where the fuck this shit at?" He rushed into the living room past the second bedroom and began tearing the couches up then the entertainment system.

"Who the fuck is you, nigga?" The childlike voice ambushed.

"Yeah, bitch, who the fuck is you and what the fuck you doin' in our mama's house? You tryna jack us?" the second kid added, unannounced. The two teenagers glared from the hallway, ready to pounce. Brick aimed the strap. "Where the fuck the money and dope?" he snarled.

Neither budged. "The big homie Zoo gon' kill you, fool."

He had the black pools of murder glaring back at him. Something about their demeanor and aura made him feel as if violence was the only option.

"Don't let 'em take our shit!" The bloodied and toothless woman staggered down the hallway using the wall to steady her balance.

Without more, the shortest of the boys raised the .25, pulling the trigger. The blunt force tore into the top right shoulder, but he was too high and numb to feel it. He ignored the blast and let this gun retort.

Klum! Klum! Klum! Klum!

Each of the residents crumbled to the carpet like dead weight. In a desperate frenzy he crossed the room in two strides, gun extended.

Klum! Klum! Klum! Klum! Klum! Klum!

The bright flashes of each discharge were the result of homemade facelifts. "Motherfuckers. Fuck Pinehurst!" He winced at the tingling sensation. With rapid speed, he finished checking the living room and then the boys' room where he found the black duffle. Unzipping it quickly, his heart fluttered with excitement. "Bingo, bitch!"

Zipping it closed, he shouldered the bag before setting his goods aside and rushing out into the hall. Seeing the pile of bodies, he stepped on them as he made for the front door. He peeked out the blinds. No one was coming, at least that's what he thought. Taking no chances, he took out the cigarette lighter, lit the cloth on the table until it was aflame, and tossed it onto the couch, which turned into a blaze.

Climbing out the window in which he entered, he crept back toward his car with haste. A police cruiser turned off the block unalarmed, as he opened the car door white flashes of blinding light erupted from the park tree across the street. The thunderous explosions filled the night. Bullets whizzed overhead missing by inches and buried themselves in the car interior.

"What the fuck?" He was caught off guard.

Krraatt! Krraatt! Kraatt!

The three-round bursts from an assault rifle were aimed at his face.

Klum! Klum! Klum! Klum!

He returned, tossing the bag into the passenger seat and then shifting his car into reverse burning rubber in an attempt to flee. Bullets ricocheted, glass shattered, the passenger side airbags deployed upon being riddled.

"Fuck this shit!" He glanced over his shoulder, steadying get wheel as he fled the 'hood in reverse. Police sirens were close. He vanished.

Brick climbed out with a wicked grin as he inspected the bullet-riddled car as the garage door closed. Snatching up the bag, he snuffed the rest of the blunt out before entering the side door of his home.

"You are busting up in here like you the police and shit." Rucci twisted her face and awoke.

"Bitch, get up." He smacked on the light switch. "Get this shit in order." He dumped the duffle bag full of contraband.

She checked the wound with a knowing look. "What the hell did you do, baby?"

His wide eyes were crazed. "You said don't come back without money."

"Baby, your ass is crazy. I know it's gonna be bullshit behind this, huh?"

"Fuck that!" He stepped out of his jeans, his joint sprung from hiding. "Give me this mufuckin' pussy!" He snatched her thong off, bent her over, and sent his meat plunging deeply.

Before she could protest, her sweet tone echoed throughout the house. "God Daaammmnnn!"

Chapter Twenty

Tap! Tap! Tap!

"Ughhh—what?"

Tap! Tap! Tap!

"What?" she whined, stirring from a peaceful slumber.

Tap! Tap! Tap!

"Who is it?" She lifted her head from the pillow only to flop back into its plushness too tired to get up. "Go away."

The motel room door opened letting in a gust of morning air. "Housekeeping," the woman said.

Her head shot up now fully awoke.

"I'm sorry. I was knocking for a while. I didn't hear anyone."

"My bad. It's check-out time already?" She sat up covering her nudeness.

"Yes, ma'am. I'll give you a few more minutes to get yourself together," the housekeeper spoke shyly, backing out of the room and closing the door.

Queenie hurried and dressed, skipping the shower while trying to reach Ms. Pat on the phone. She rushed to pack her stuff but hoped to get in touch with the woman. "Pick up. Pick up, Ms. Pat."

Getting the voicemail for the dozenth time, she shut the flip phone in frustration.

"Hello. Front desk, Amanda speaking."

"Hi, good morning. I'm in room three-twenty-eight. I wanted to know if I can come down now to pay for another night?"

"Sure. Is the room in your name?"

"It's in my grandmother's name," she thought quickly. "I can't reach her on the phone right now."

"I'm afraid I can't do that. The motel has been cracking down on us lately. Any little thing could cost us our jobs. Sorry, I can't help," the woman's voice was genuine.

"It's okay. Thank you." She sighed, setting the phone back into its cradle.

Tap! Tap! Tap!

"Housekeeping. Sorry ma'am, but I have to start cleaning this room."

Queenie swallowed the attitude. She quickly stuffed her valuables into her bag and then the extra into a trash bag. As she descended the flight of stairs, she kept an eye out for the black SUV and Georgia boy while trying to figure out her next move. She searched the massive motel for Ms. Pat to no avail.

"Hey, excuse me," she got the attention of another housekeeper. "You wouldn't happen to know Ms. Pat, would you?"

"I would. Ms. Pat called in sick today. I'm actually filling in for her."

Damn! she thought. "Okay, I appreciate it."

Sitting on the curb beside her luggage she voted by no chance was she going back to the woods. Having only two options, she dialed Miranda's cell.

"Please, friend, I need you to pick up," she mumbled, listening to the ring.

Her heart broke when she got no answer. She sent texts, even redialed. After a while, she gave up having no choice but to explore the last option. Swallowing her pride, she called the cabbie who answered on the first ring.

"Can you come get me?"

"Be there in ten minutes." He hung up.

Exhaling, frustrated, she stared at the number for a long minute before making the call.

Answering the first ring, "Yooo."

"Is this Gary?"

"This who number you called right?"

"Can I come over?"

"Gary, who is that?" the female asked in the background.

"Mind your fucking business, bruh," he snapped.

"Nigga, it is my business!"

"You can come through," he told her. "How long before you pull up?"

"Twenty minutes maybe. Text me the address."

"I asked you a fucking question!" the female yelled.

"Bitch, you—"

Queenie hung up, she had no idea what that was about and didn't care.

A wave of nervousness filled her as the cab came to a stop outside the Waverly Street Apartments. She handed him the cash. "Thanks, J.D."

"Anytime, Queen. Hit me if you need me." He pulled away.

She dialed his number nearing Gary's apartment. There was screaming in the background from the female raising hell. He opened the door for her.

"Come in. What's all this shit you got with you?" He looked her up and down with confusion.

"My stuff, I couldn't just leave it."

"You should've told me you were bringing luggage."

"Should I have left it?"

"Bring yo' ass in the house." He grabbed the trash bag. "I'ma put it in my room. My granny will fuck 'round sell all yo' shit so she can get high."

"Who was that yelling when I called? I'm not tryna have any drama, Gary."

"I'll introduce you to this bitch then." He pushed the bedroom door open. The female sat on the edge of the bed sniffling, hair in disarray, and wearing a pained expression.

Queenie felt sorry the moment their eyes met.

"So, this is the bitch you're kicking me to the curb for?" She stood wiping away tears. She was gorgeous and shapely, with hazel brown eyes that had now been replaced with burning ruby reds that glared at him. "You think you're just gonna fuck me and put me out like I'm a fucking jump off, nigga? You got me fucked all the way up. And who the fuck is she?"

"Tempest, I told you. She's my home girl. Yo' ass trippin', my nigga. Take your stupid ass home before I turn up."

"I'm sorry, I shouldn't have come."

"Nah you good," Gary said, "Tempest get the hell out before I get mad, straight up."

"I can't believe I let this young nigga fuck me." Tempest gritted stepping into her flats. As she bumped Queenie with the shoulder expecting a reaction she wouldn't get. "Matter of fact, I'm not going nowhere. Nigga put me out," She smacked him.

Queenie stepped back out of the way. The scowl on Gary's face said it all. Tempest quickly changed her mind.

"Bitch, you—"

"Fuck you, Gary. I'm leaving." She snatched the door open and stormed out before he could lay hands. Just when she thought Tempest was gone, she was at the back window. "You pussy-ass-nigga! Fuck you and that raggedy-ass bitch you with."

Gary snatched up the assault rifle. "You think I'm sum'n to play with?" He stuck the barrel out the window.

"Okay, I'm sorry." Tempest hauled ass.

Gary turned, cracking up.

"All this because of me?"

"She better be glad you're here. That bitch knows I'on play around." He set the gun down. "So, what's up with you? You stole some new shit? I'll go with you so you can sell."

"I don't have anything to sell, that's my clothes and stuff. I lost my motel room. Since I'm not old enough, I can't get one and need somebody else's I.D.," she told him. "And don't act like nobody ain't just got killed."

"Yeah, so? That shit ain't nothing new."

"Do you think your friends will be good?"

"Who, Zoo and them? Man, that nigga rich ass fuck with a million lawyers probably. He is good. Ain't nobody see shit and neither have you."

"Duh, I'm not stupid."

Gary answered his phone and said a few words then hung up. Shortly, three people were outside the back window with money in hand. She watched him as he checked the screen connecting to the hidden camera to give him a wide view of the back so that no one could sneak attack him.

"What's good, Auntie? What y'all want?" He opened the bag of dope.

"I got $80.00. Is it the same stuff from last night?"

He dropped the stones in her palm. Seeing how big they were, she hurried and thrust the cash into his hand. In under five minutes he made almost two hundred dollars and she wanted to learn.

"And that's all you gotta do?"

"Easy money. Way safer than stealing clothes."

"I see. Why'd you put your girlfriend out?"

"It doesn't matter, she gone and you're here."

Knocking on the bedroom door got their attention. "Gary, are you ready?"

"Nigga, is you ready?" He yelled back.

"I am. Let's hurry...I'm tryna play bingo later."

He looked at her. "You're riding with me. I'll show you how to hustle later when we get back down?"

She answered with a head nod.

"Boy, who got the damn car you have me riding in?" Grandma Esther strapped herself in with a seat belt, eyes darting everywhere while she rode shotgun. "This motherfucker looks like it's stolen."

"What if it is?"

"We gon' sell it."

They all cracked up.

"Chill out, granny. It's legit."

"Legit how?"

"A crack rental. Damn, why do you always gotta know shit?"

"Cause I wanna know mufucka." She twisted up her face.

Queenie tried to restrain from laughing ,but watching the two go back and forth was comical and entertaining,

"Yo' old ass needs to mind your business."

"I ain't old, I'm sixty." She scowled, "And slow your ass down. Why the hell you gotta speed?"

"Because the bank might be closed or something and I want my money today. I ain't got time for them crackhead games you be playing."

"I don't give a damn. I can't get high and you ain't gon' get paid if we both die. Now slow this damn car down."

He grinned while running a red light. Queenie gripped the door handle frightened as he sped through the streets.

"We gon' get there. Just sit your ass back."

"Gary, it's Thursday. You don't see all these damn police out here?"

"Since when have you ever given a damn 'bout the police?" He chuckled.

"You're gonna give me a damn heart attack!" she shouted.

He laughed harder. "How much is your insurance policy?"

She punched him in the shoulder." Yo' ass ain't getting shit."

"That's a lie. All the shit I gotta put up with," he instigated.

She turned to face him, jaw dropped. "Nigga, no you didn't. Okay, remember that when yo' ass get sick. I'ma leave your ass high and dry."

"No, you ain't either."

Skeet!

The car came to a screeching halt in the bank's parking lot when he purposely stomped the brakes, jerking forward and scarring granny. Gary burst into laughter at her frightened facial expression. Queenie found nothing funny since the woman spat up her dentures.

"Hurry up and go get my money, girl," he said humorously.

She hurried and snatched the seat belt loose. "Fuck you!" She got out, slammed the door, and stormed into the bank.

"That's fucked up you scared her like that." Queenie giggled.

Gary sparked up a cigarette and turned the music on. "That's my boo, I gotta fuck with her ass every day."

She shook her head. "Y'all two is crazy."

Black Migo

Chapter Twenty-One

It was intriguing to Queenie to watch Gary hustle like it was second nature to him. She'd always been attentive in school so picking up things in the streets she knew would help her means of survival. Was easy.

"Do you always talk shit to your customers?" After he cursed a fiend out for begging.

"Nah, but sometimes you have to go, or they'll run all over you."

"I can feel you on that. Are you gonna help me make some money?" she asked. "And do you have someone who'll get me a room for the night? It's getting really late."

"Of course, I'll help you get some coins, ain't no pressure, and as far as a motel? You're gonna have to wait until tomorrow."

"What you thought I was doing earlier when we got back? Changing my sheets." He smiled.

She found it amusing. "So, you were already planning to have me over," His smile told it all, "You trippin'. I ain't on nothin'. You staying or what? I brought some roach spray too so you can spray around the bed."

"Yeah, you were really scheming."

"You do that, and I'll call my brother to re-up. What're you tryna invest?" He took out his cell.

"One-hundred."

"Two-twenty-five will get you a quarter ounce."

"How much can I make off that?"

"At least four-fifty."

"Okay, I want it." She removed the money from her bra." And you're gonna make sure I see all my money, right? I don't have that much money and I honestly can't afford to take another loss."

"That's my word, I got you."

She handed over the money." I'm gonna spray around your bed then take a nap. It's gonna be a long night I can tell."

"Sure is."

***

That morning she woke from excruciating pain stabbing between her thighs. Agony sucked the breath out of her with every movement. She wished it was all a terrible nightmare, but waking to trembling legs, a tender vagina, and dried blood brought her back to a harsh reality. As the tears began to fall from their faces, she managed to stand and go check on her sister.

Yet, as she touched the doorknob, she found herself holding her breath at the sudden announcement of the front door opening and shutting. Heavy boots could be heard stepping up the stairs. They traveled down the hall where Destiny could be heard groaning in pain.

"Get. Off. Me!"

"Get the fuck up you whore!"

"No—stop!"

"Get off me!"

Queenie prayed it was the same nightmare and that she had not yet awoken, but everything was too real. Heart pounding, she backed away from the door. Hearing her mother's plea compelled her to intervene, but fear of repercussion froze her in place. She was lost in the middle of her room.

Fear was in her mother's voice. "Matthew, let me go!"

Wham!

The struggle was over, Queenie held her hand over her mouth while cracking the room door open to see her mother being dragged down the stairs unconscious. She hurried and shut the door back looking around for something to be used as a weapon. Opening the dresser drawer, she eased her legs into jean shorts while taking the box cutter and stuffing it into her back pocket. She had made up her mind that nothing would happen to her sister.

The sound of his boots stomping their way up the stairs filled her with anxiety. She looked around the room where there was no place to hide. Thinking quickly, she slid back beneath the covers and pretended to be asleep as she listened for any indication of him entering Precious' room.

Morning sun spilled in the front hallway window and under the door. The moment he headed her way, his shadow was seen, He opened the door, then with a quickness snatched her by the hair and out of bed.

"Daddy, no!" she wailed.

"Shut the hell up, Queenie, before I shoot your ass." He forcefully dragged her out the room, down the stairs by the hair.

"No, Daddy. Please!" she cried, attempting to pry his strong grip away. "You are hurting me."

"I'm not gonna tell your ass again." He glared down at her, pulling his pistol from his waist.

She went silent as he pulled her through the house and down into the basement. The overhead light shined brightly illuminating the entire space. Her heart nearly stopped beating when she laid eyes on her mother.

"Stand your ass up," he growled, jerking her to stand.

"Dad! Let us go!" she yelled to her mother who was cuffed to steel overhead pipes, struggling to stand.

"Matthew, why are you doing this to us? We're your family," Destiny cried. "You have to let us go. You have to take your medicine."

"You know why I'm doing this."

Whop!

He smacked her.

"Daddy, please, stop!" She tried to slip off the cuff, but they were clamped tight, almost cutting off her circulation.

"Quiet! Not another word or I swear to God." His eyes were daggers. "Your mother is the reason for all this. She's the one to blame for everything."

"What're you going to do with Precious?" she whimpered.

"Don't worry about my baby girl. She's at her aunt's. And since school is out, you don't have to worry about anyone coming to look for you." He duct-taped her mouth shut. "And neither will you."

Together they tried to yell through the tape. "Keep it down dammit!" he shouted. "I'll see you two whores when I get off work," was all he said before everything went dark.

***

Matthew placed the pistol into the holster of his work belt before slamming his glove box shut. Fully dressed and geared up, he spoke to one of his good friends, who was ready as well to beat the streets.

"I'll be glad when this Covid-19 bullshit is over with. I tell ya' having my family around all damn day is driving me and my wife nuts," Officer Jacobs complained. "The lockdowns are messing up my groove."

He snickered. "Tell me about it."

"So—how's your kids? I can't wait 'til we can enjoy thanksgiving together again. I have to get some of the famous sweet potato pie Queenie makes. Hers is absolutely better than my wife's."

"That's because my wife was black. Yours is white." He smiled.

"Yeah, that I know. It's still hard to believe your white ass even had a woman that loved you, even cooked for you." Jacobs buttoned up his uniform shirt as they headed out of the building towards their separate vehicles. "Does she know how much of an ass you really are?"

"Of course, not because I'm a saint."

Jacob cracked up. "Saint my ass. Us white boys are dirty as your boxers."

"Don't let anybody else hear you say that they'll have our asses under investigation."

Jacob opened the driver's door. "Nobody would even care."

"Still, that's nothing to joke about. They'll be all up in our business and right now I'm not up for it." He opened the door to his own squad car.

"Understood, Pal. Say—how about I come over later for a beer?"

"Hmm, I'm not sure that'll be a good idea. Me and my family are practicing social distancing at home. I can't risk exposing my family. Maybe another time?"

"That's fine with me, say—"

Officer Matthew held up a finger listening to dispatch." I gotta go, Pal. It's my zone. Chat later."

Working with the Richland County Sheriff's Department for 10 years came with its perks. There had been new promotions offered, all of which he refused since he knew it would only come with more duty and paperwork, he would rather be driving his cruiser.

As a retired Sergeant from the Marines, he suffered many mental illnesses obtained over years. It was only his immediate family who knew what conditions existed and would always strive to keep his business at home. Yet, slowly with each passing day, the medication was getting weak and useless, allowing his wicked mind to control his actions.

Cruising Hard Scrabble Road, he noticed three African American teenaged males exiting a local gas station. Although dispatch had cleared the last call, he would still pursue any group of Blacks in the predominantly white community. Without notifying dispatch, he hit the sirens to get the boys' attention, hoping one would run. Turning off the blaring noise, he parked and jumped out. He made sure not to activate the dashcam and body cam.

"Got me some fucking niggers, " he said inwardly enjoying his day already. "Fucking, fellas, where you are coming from?"

The chubby one spoke up for the group, "The store. Buying drinks and snacks. What did we do?"

"You're in violation."

"Of what?"

"Being fat and ugly, your black ass," he retorted. "You all up against the wall. Any weapons, drugs, crack pipes on your personal I should know about?"

"No, sir. We're too young to smoke crack," someone blurted.

"Fat Nasty boy, you twitch one more time, I'm gonna bust a cap in your ass and say you threatened my life. Hear me?"

"But I don't have a weapon. You already searched me."

"You're black and aggressive looking. Now stand up against the wall and don't fucking move. I'm warning you."

"We're not moving," they defended.

"Shut the fuck up or I'll shoot you all right here." He patted them down.

"Next time I catch any of you around here, I'm going to lock your asses up for trespassing."

"But we stay around here."

"Well, tell your black, skank mother to relocate."

"You're a racist cracker."

"What did you say?"

"We're gonna have you sued. Watch. My mom is a federal judge. She'll have you locked away forever."

He wanted to unleash a hail five of gunshots on the teens, but he had to refrain and suck up his ego. He sent them home after confiscating a few dollar bills that he'd slipped from their pockets.

As he pulled away from the curb, he couldn't help but speak out loud, "Hate these fuckers. Black bitches are like roaches. Kill 'em, they'll keep on coming back."

Black Migo

Chapter Twenty-Two

She jumped from the nightmare in a cold seat panting frantically while clutching her chest to calm her heart. Shivering violently, she hadn't realized until now she had been crying in her sleep. Sniffling, she wiped away tears gazing around the room until her sights landed on a set watching her closely.

"My bad, was I yelling?" She wiped the sweat from her brow.

Gary finished his money count. "Yelling? How about fighting. You see I'm way over this mufucka, right? You've already kicked me twice."

She smiled. "Don't make me feel bad."

"Just saying. You got my back fucked up. I think I need a massage."

"I'm not doing that now."

He chuckled. "I'm just fuckin' wit' chu. What the hell was you dreaming about? It was too real, huh?"

Face flushed with embarrassment she replied. "It's a lot going on in my head that I try not to think about. Every time I go to sleep it comes back to me in my dreams.

"Tell me what's going on?"

"A lot."

"Like what?"

"Too much to talk about. Stuff I don't feel comfortable talking about to anyone. At least not right now."

"You're just like my sister, Meesha. Always holding stuff in."

"Or maybe I don't wanna let any of it out right now."

"Could be that too." He handed her some cash.

"What's this for?"

"I'm serving both our dope together. That's some bread towards your package."

***

"I don't give a fuck 'bout you having an attitude." She twisted her face up into something nasty. "You fucked up my money, I fucked up yours. Now you have to respect it, Dirty," Krissy told him.

"I ain't gotta respect shit!" he spat.

'You're right, you don't have to do it but you're going to. I respect yo' hustle, it's only right you respect mine." she cut the shower off. "I ain't never came between your bag so don't come between me and mine."

"I'on know who the fuck you think you're talking to like you're running shit but that gotta stop. Put it on chill."

Krissy rolled her eyes, snatching the shower curtain back fully, exposing her dripping wet nakedness. "You put your shit on chill, nigga," she sassed.

"You think 'cause I'm a bitch, I'm 'pose to let you run all over me like I'm nothing. Hell no! I'm a boss bitch. And you need me just as much as I need you, so don't act like you don't."

"Bitch, whatever close the damn curtain. I don't wanna see you putting on no damn maxi pad, tampon."

"Nigga, you the one in here taking a shit while I'm show-ering, how 'bout you get the hell out," she ranted, in no mood to be fucked with. Seeing Queenie the day before with Gary had her scared for her own wellbeing.

"You're always tryna run me."

He burst into laughter. "I was here first."

"Don't try and start with me, you know I was here first." She put on the pad then panties. "Ughh, you make me so sick. And you fucking stink!"

"You'll be alright."

She stormed out holding her breasts into the bedroom to apply deodorant and lotion. Dirty was beginning to get on her last nerve intentionally picking with her. She had too much to worry about and wouldn't be at ease until her little friend was back under her wing.

Fully dressed, she touched up her makeup quickly hoping to make it out of the house before he finished on the toilet. However, that wouldn't happen, He came out with a mischievous grin.

"Where are you rushing to?"

"I got things to handle."

"No, you don't. Sit still until I get out of the shower." He took her car keys off the dresser before heading back into the bathroom and beneath the steaming hot water.

"Dirty. Gimme my keys! I gotta go." She followed. "You're always on some bullshit. This is exactly what I am talking about." She glared as he showered.

"You got something you wanna tell me?"

Her stomach tightened. She hated this side of him, the mind games and mental warfare. He knew how to pressure the truth from her. "No, you got something you wanna tell me." She folded her arms and crossed her legs.

He chuckled. "So, you are doing shit and the streets talk more than my Grandma, so I'ma give you the benefit of the doubt to let me hear it from your mouth then to assume what's being said is true." He washed his nuts then ass, with her watching.

"She sucked her teeth. "You're always trying to play games."

"What you wanna tell me?" he pressed, eyes penetrating hers. "We ain't got all day, bruh."

"I ain't got nothing I wanna say except give me my damn keys."

"So, you ain't had nothing to do with that top floor situation?" He cut the water off, wringing the cloth dry.

"Why would I have something to do with it?"

"'Cause, I know you were there on my behalf. And while you were there, somebody got rocked to sleep. Last time you checked some broad for running up on you, right?"

She answered, proudly." Yep. And that's what she gets."

"You had a beretta twenty-two when you did that, huh?"

She remained silent feeling uneasy. Dirty chuckled. "That nigga Ta'Maine got killed with a twenty-two. Whoever shot 'em left shells. And I'm willing to bet them three bullet holes in that nigga came from your gun. You probably ain't even thought to replace the bullets missing from the clip." He wrapped the towel around his waist.

She licked her dry lips. "I didn't do anything."

"If he's dead, that's because he made you feel threatened. I'm yo' nigga, we a team. So, if you wacked a nigga, that means we whacked a nigga, boots. If niggas gonna come for you, of course, they gonna come for *me*. And before I let a nigga catch me slipping, you needa put me on point."

"Baby, I don't have nothing to do with any of that, I promise."

"I don't believe that, bruh."

"Well, I'm telling you the truth. What's so hard to believe?"

He studied her face. "You know your ass better than me. If you can't trust you, then you know I can't trust what you're saying."

"Make me slap the shit out you, Dirty. I'm telling you the God's honest truth. I didn't have shit to do with that nigga getting killed and anybody lying on me, telling I did something can suck my dick!" She spat. "Now give me my key."

"So yo just gon' leave me in the dark? Like fuck me, huh?"

"No. But I ain't got no light to shine on yo' black ass. So, what the hell."

"You do know that was Zoo's people?"

She watched him closely, though fearing the truth may come out, she had no intention of crying over spilled milk, so she kept her game face on. "Fuck you tellin' me fuh' like I give a damn? I already told you I had nothing to do with that, baby. So, stop trying to press me."

He extended the keys out to her. When she went to receive them, he pulled back quickly. "You ain't getting these 'til I get me."

"You want some head, daddy?" her voice softened, she set the purse aside, He didn't have to reply. She knew what he needed and gave it to him to kill the questions. Falling to her knees she gave him some sloppy conversion that left him lost in the sauce.

Krissy pulled to the driveway quickly, wiping away traces of cum from the corners of her mouth. Digging into her purse she opened the small bottle of mouth and took a swig to refresh her breath, zipping through traffic.

"This little bitch cursed me out like I'm the one who put her out. I know that's why she's in her body," she mumbled aloud thinking back.

"Where the hell does she hang out? I don't even know," she answered her own question. "She can't be too far though." She drove through Pinehurst, she made sure to have the Pink Beretta .22 cocked and on standby resting in the Chanel bag for easy access. Despite what the streets were saying, she wasn't moving like a suspect.

Turning off Pinehurst Road onto Schoolhouse, she crept up the block slowly, scoping her surroundings. With the sun out and sky a cloudless blue, a beautiful day bought out the community. Several people still wore face masks in fear of catching the deadly virus, while others moved about carelessly. Police cars frequented the streets high alert. It Was evident something new had transpired across the street.

Pulling into the Four Seasons apartments she suddenly had a change of mind, the one way in and out, she continued around back. In the far right corner, two police cars sat ducked off watching the entire lot. Tensions were extremely high. Police were at a standoff with the neighborhood, everyone refused to offer any details. Confidential informants were hushed.

Feeling safe behind tinted windows she turned in the lot with the intention to leave peacefully. Stepping into the street, G-50 blocked her path. His hands gestured for her to pull over and park.

"Fuck is this crazy, fool doing?" She whispered, rolling down the window. From the side of eight buildings, a little girl no other than twelve pointed the 9mm, its red beam marking the side of Krissy's head.

"Park or she'll dog your ass right here."

"But?" She turned frantically to the police cars still behind them, barely visible and nearly out of sight.

"Fuck twelve. Park this mufucka and holla at me or Lil' Mama gonna redo your makeup. Hurry up and park," his tone was bitter and cold.

Krissy glanced over at her purse. She wasn't ready to die but was ready to defend herself. "What's up, G-50? You act like you ready to hurt me or something." She stepped out of the car, purse tucked and clutching the pistol. His smirk was golden. "If you play stupid, it'll happen. Now, I'ma need you to keep shit a stack."

"What's up?"

"My homie, Ta'maine tried to rob you at the *Top Floor*?"

"No, not that I know of. Why?"

He chuckled. "You're a funny ass bitch. Was somebody else with you that night?"

"My homegirl, yeah. She was there. She'll tell you the same thing I'm telling you," she replied with confidence. "We ain't see them niggas."

"Where she at? I'ma question her ass, too."

"Why?"

"Because if her story doesn't match yours, you know what's up." His eyes were burning red. "Homie left seven kids, we gotta raise 'em now."

"So! That's what his ass gets for trying me." She wanted to say but held their tongue. "Well, it's gon' match, I'm innocent. Now, if you're finished, I'ma go about my business," she sassed.

He grinned deviously. "You can go. When you get some baby clothes, stop through."

"Don't worry, you know I am." She flopped behind the wheel. Putting out the apartment she sighed deeply. Cutting up the A.C. she needed to find Queenie—and fast.

Chapter Twenty-Three

"So, we're laying down and letting them mufuckas take over your hood?" C-Lo questioned the big homie Crip who was built like Tookie Williams.

"Of course not, cuz," Cloud said above the music. He stood under the open car garage late into the night with a cigarette pressed to his lips." We're gonna smash the gas on them niggas. They gotta know shit ain't sweet."

"Hell, nah, it ain't," another Loc chimed in. Since Zoo and his youngins ran down on 'em over a week ago, tensions were high. "Them niggas took some of our straps and got the audacity to suck up and the money coming through this, but then expect us not to get it out the mud."

"Big Homie, I say we run-up in that crib, drop 'em all and take everything. Fuck 'em," C-Lo spat, agitated. "This Crip land, cuz."

Cloud watched the steady flow of drug clientele come and go from the house several yards down. Listening to his little homies was amping him up. However, survival wasn't all violence. He had to think things through and through. But he had to admit he was feeling exactly what they all were feeling. Since most of the city's businesses hadn't reopened, a majority of their families were still unemployed and going broke waiting for financial relief from legislation, leaving the burden of responsibility on each of them.

"I agree too, Big Homie," Luke added. "We took the hood from the Blood niggas, to begin with. The Feds came down on them and finished it off. It'll make no sense to let that Zoo nigga pump his shit out here. He thinks we are soft. He thinks he got all the sense to. Watch, before you know it, them G-Shine niggas gon' be popping up through here tryna evict the Locs. We gotta quit them niggas before they act up."

Cloud nodded, listening but still in deep thought.

"I don't think them niggas built like that anymore, anyway. Since the Feds snatched up all of them Five-Nine Brim niggas every blood in the city been low-key. They ain't tryna stand no heat right now. So I say we crush that spot, run they ass up outta here and go back on defense," C-Lo said.

"Call some of the homies in line to put in work." Cloud liked the sound of that. "Tell 'em bring the chirps through. Y'all mount up. We gon' run down on them niggas."

The crew grew hyped with excitement. "'Bout fucking time, cuz."

***

"Cresha, don't forget to wash your fuckin' hands after you got money from them people. Bitch, ain't tryna die from no virus before we can spend the bag and add two five-K Bundles."

"Giiirrll!" Cresha was amplified with attitude. "You're finna drive me the hell crazy with this bullshit you keep saying like I'm not already doing this shit in the first place. You act like I'm tryna catch this shit. Damn!"

She rolled her eyes. "I'm just saying like I'm not already doing this shit in the first place," Zi-Zi mocked.

"What the hell ever," Cresha softened. "What is up with your brother? Ever since he took that trip with Zoo, he's been on some different type shit. Like. It's kinda cute on him."

"The hell if I know. One thing I do know is that he's serious. He doesn't joke anymore, doesn't smoke or drink with us. He is super defensive every time somebody comes through. When I looked into his eyes the other day, it was like he wasn't there anymore."

174

"Girl, I was saying the same thang," Cresha hushed her tone so that Dae-Dae couldn't hear them in the other room. "He is a killah now, girl. I'm telling you. Whatever Zoo did got your brother on a whole 'notha level, and I've been thinking about throwing him some of this pussy. I ain't had no dick this year."

Zi-Zi laughed at her best friend's comment but took everything else to heart. Something strangely different was going on with Dae-Dae, who had always been afraid of guns since a child when they both witnessed their father gun down his own brother for sleeping with his wife, their mother. Now, after hanging with Zoo, Dae-Dae had the .40 in his grips all day and night, watching the door and windows as if he were expecting something. It was almost scary but necessary in their line of work.

"If you give 'em some ass, you better not break his heart."

Cresha chuckled. "I hear you, bitch. How much more before we have that psych nigga's money? I swear I'm sooo scared of his sexy ass. If he wasn't so dangerous and powerful, I'd be a little open to say that to him when he does come through."

"We're at one-eighty-K. By tomorrow evening, we should be out of the woods. I can't wait to pay 'em his money, too. Fuh real. This is stressing me the hell out. We can't get any sleep. People steady calling, coming, got me all paranoid and shit. A bitch might need a lil' vacation or something."

"Hell yeah, I feel you. I'm paranoid as hell, too. I find it too hard to believe that Zoo can pop up, walked down the street into them crazy nigga's yard and put his foot down."

"Correction. Let an eleven-year-old put their foot down."

"That's even worse, bitch. I know damn well they're not gonna let no shit like that slide," Cresha voiced.

Zi-Zi felt the same but couldn't find the time to entertain thoughts since they were overwhelmed with a rush of customers every minute.

"They'll have to this time. It's our time to eat."

"That's my type of lingo right there. Let's go ahead and get organized. The four a.m. rush about to come around."

As she began sorting through bundles and packages, something out the corner of her caught Zi-Zi's attention.

"Bitch. Look." She got Cresha's attention, with a finger pressed to her lips, signaling to stay quiet.

Together they went to the window after cutting the bedroom light off. On the side of the house between the neighbors, a tall light pole stood, illuminating the area. It was also how Zi-Zi was able to make out a face.

It was this Tookie Williams look-alike, Cloud.

"There's another one. I think the house is surrounded," Cresha whispered.

Panic set in. They knew what the play was already. As she peeked out the blinds discreetly, she noticed a blue masked figure heading up the walkway towards another door with a large gun at his side.

Knock! Knock! Knock!

Three loud hard knocks got all their attention. Before they could contest, Dae-Dae was at the front door putting his eye to the peephole.

"No. Don't!" Zi-Zi yelled.

Bloom!

The gunshot obliterated the peephole, painting the living room wall with Dae-Dae's memories. Both women erupted in a rage of frightened wails. It wasn't until the second explosion when Zi-Zi realized not only were they under attack, they too would be robbed and killed.

"We gotta go!" She jerked Cresha out of traumatization.

176

"There's nowhere to go."

"They've come through the front; we'll jump out the back window," she cried in fear of dying.

In a hurry, Cresha grabbed her phone, then one of the two duffle bags while Zi-Zi did the same. As the front door came splintering off the hinges after a third explosion, together they eluded danger by jumping out of the window in the nick of time and into the trees.

***

That morning Queenie was excited to get her day started early since her nightmares seem to occur frequently, as she found herself avoiding sleep, afraid her father would catch up to her, and she needed to at least be awake to see him coming. She knew his capabilities. To what extreme he'd go to have her back home.

Gary laid across the bed asleep. It had been a long night for them both. He had been patient in teaching her how to sell crack until she had it figured out.

"I think it's time for you to wake up, too," she told him after squeezing his pinky toe.

"What time is it?" He stretched.

"Morning time."

"Any plays come, that shit should be gone by now, right?"

"It is. That's why I need you to get up so we can get more," she replied anxiously. "It's still people coming by."

He made a call. "My folks will be here in half an hour."

"Can I take a shower?"

"Can I get in with you?" he teased.

"Uh—no. No. What I look like?"

"I'm just playing. Go 'head. Don't take all day either."

She quickly shouldered her book sack and headed to shower. After fifteen minutes, she was dressed in some form-fitting jean pants that hugged her tender curves along with a blouse that left her shoulders exposed. Taking another five minutes, she did her hygiene and finished, smelling sweet.

"Umm, you smell good as hell, let me hug on you, "Gary said once she entered the room. "Ain't no way in hell you're gonna be around me all day and night and not gon' let me scrap them walls a few times."

Queenie blushed, loving the attention but couldn't let it make her weak. "Are you ready? I needa' get my hustle on."

"Wait, you're tryna go boost?" he asked, confused.

"Uhh. Yeah, I do need to try to find myself a place to stay for a while, too. I can't live here with you when I don't have to, and I'm all in your way."

"You trippin'. You can be in my way all you want, girl. But if you got somewhere to go, that's cool. Just sit tight." He left out of the room, then the apartment. Ten minutes later, he returned, handing her a Ziplock bag of a rocky substance.

"What is this?"

"Three ounces of crack. I call it Buck Troy. Friends love it."

"What's it worth?"

"At least six stacks. Hold onto it." He went and took a shower.

Thirty minutes later, they were sitting in a crack rental. They were yet to pull out parking space, and she was already overwhelmed with paranoia. He stuffed the pistol between the seat and middle console while sitting the huge bag of rocks in the cupholder. As she watched him, she couldn't deny that his thuggish demeanor was appealing. The longer she stayed, the more she figured him as a boyfriend wouldn't be a bad idea. But shook away the attraction.

"Your phone was blowing up like crazy while you were in the shower. Figured it was your girlfriend."

"Haha, funny." He checked missed calls. "Ahh...Shit!"

"What?"

"Almost fucking forget the homie, my cousin Ta'maine's funeral today. Damn!"

"Might as well go there now and get it to the way, right?"

"Fuck it, might as well." He shifted into drive.

***

The hundred or so family and friends stood around as the pastor finished with his sermon before finally lowering Ta'maine's corpse into the ground for good. There was a cloud of sadness and grief hovering above. His four baby mothers, despite their differences and long history of fighting one another, sat at the front of the tint, consoling each other as best they could. It would be absolutely challenging to raise their young alone, but they vowed to do it together.

As the service came to an end, everyone said their final goodbyes. It was then Zoo decided to entertain a few questions and concerns. He stood to the far end, surrounded by several goons who were on high alert due to unfamiliar faces.

"Hey. How are you doing today? Zoo, I hate to bother you, but are you still going to help us out?" Tiffany, one of Ta'maine's baby mothers, spoke up for them all once they approached. Each of them was young and gorgeous. There was no doubt in his mind that by the end of the week, one of them, if not all, would have a new man.

"Know that Ta Maines' kids will be taken care of. School clothes, shoes, programs, whatever it is, I got y'all. Haven't I proven true to my word? Now here's my number. Get at me."

As they walked away feeling reassured, another woman approached with a one-year-old daughter on her hip. "Hey, Zoo. Are you busy?"

"What's good, Mona?" He checked the time on his Rollie.

"I wanted to thank you again for buying me a car to get back and forth to work. It really helps out a lot. But I need you again. You told me if my sons start acting up in school or around the house again, to call you. It's getting too hard on me, and they don't listen to anything I say."

"Which one is it?"

"All four of them."

"I'll come scoop them this weekend."

"Say no more. I really appreciate it," she replied with relief.

"No problem." He turned as she walked away. "What's good, Lil Homie?"

"Big Homie, I've been calling you all night long," Lil' Stew, a fourteen-year-old and loyal goon, reported. "We gotta problem."

"What's up?" His eyes surveyed the crowded cemetery. Something was throwing him off.

"Last night, I was holding a post, sitting in a tree, keeping an eye out on twelve and the dope spots like you asked me to. When the police left, some niggas pulled up in two black Jags, got out, walked up the street, and disappeared behind the apartments. I ain't heard the shots, but I saw the flashes against the windows. I saw the niggas running up the streets with a black bag over their shoulders. I tried to call you, but when you didn't answer, I said fuck it and let that fuck nigga have it when I let the choppa talk." His demeanor changed.

The news had his stomach aching. Now was not the time to be in any drama, especially with Ta'maine's death under investigation. He was afraid one false move could cause them to lose it all.

"Why am I just hearing about it, Lil Stew?"

"I told you." The kid swallowed hard." The police just broke the door down and went up there. Breka, PuPu, and Moni, all killed—shot the hell up. And I heard that whoever the nigga was that did it, tried to set the apartment on fire, but it went out."

"Fuck!" He gritted. "And you say he left with a bag?"

"A big one."

Zoo shook his head, distraught. "Motherfucker jacked my shit. I can't believe this bullshit, dawg."

"I tried to stop 'em, homie."

"Don't worry 'bout it youngin. You did good. I'll get to the bottom of it." He dapped him up, sending him on his way. Hearing the new revelation had his mood dark.

"Everything a hunnit, bruh?" G-50 asked.

Zoo gave him the news.

"I haven't even been to the 'hurst yet. Boy, I tell you, if it ain't one thing, it's another," G-50 replied. By then, a gathering of at least 50 to 60 Bloods stood around, turning the burial site into a meeting. "But brah, the homies wanna holla at you, and I don't think this shit can wait any longer."

"Who the fuck wanna talk 'bout what?" He glared, agitated.

"All due respect, Big Homie." Shooter stepped up, keeping his aggression in check. "We're all paying our dues on time and following your orders to stay low and fall back off the radar, but niggas ain't with all that shit, bruh. Homies getting slumped left and right, and we ain't doin' shit 'bout it," he said brazenly.

'Nigga, when I say go, you go!" Zoo spat. "When I say fall back, fall the fuck back."

"Ain't that what we been doing?"

"That's what the fuck y'all needa keep doin'."

"Bruh, niggas don't give no fucks 'bout the feds being in town running down on mufuckas. We tryna crush shit and mash the gas!"

"Fuck is you talking, too?"

Shooter flared his nose, furrowing his brow.

Zoo waved his hand. "Zero-three-one this nigga. All y'all!"

Though half the group sided with the shooter's opinion, the order was given, and on command, he was blitzed for 31 seconds. Not a second longer, none less.

When the ordeal was done, Shooter was lumped up badly and needed help standing on his own two feet. Zoo flexed his muscle, showing he was still in charge. "Any of y'all niggas tryna flip, on shine, ya ass gonna get flipped on your fucking head." He made sure to emphasize the severity of his murderous threat.

"Matter of fact, since y'all so eager to out some fucking work in, everybody who've wronged us, owe us, it don't matter if they looked at us the wrong way, red dot special on all of 'em. So now you're back on the front lines, and first mufucka complaining get their head blown the fuck off, playing with me. Now get the fuck outta my face!" He growled, pugnacious.

Zoo stormed off towards the Wraith livid, with his youngins close behind, jumping in their respective rides. Baby girl started the car, nervous to be alone with him and his temper. It wasn't normal to see him visibly seething.

"Take me to my downtown condo," he spoke into the walkie-talkie.

He took strong deep breaths and relaxed his nerves. Setting his head back on the rest, he turned on the massage system to loosen the tension in his back. As the soothing therapeutic effect took its course, his anger lessened though his mind was sorting through the sudden madness. One more issue may blow his mind, sending him back in full kill mode. As he began to organize his thoughts, his phone rang.

"Yeah, what's up. Who is this?"

This fear in her voice snapped her eyes open. "Speak."

"The niggas down the street rushed the spot and killed my fucking brother," her voice cracked with grief. "It was so—"

"What? What about Cresha?" he asked incredulously.

"She's right here with me? We barely got away."

"Fuck!" He gritted. "What's the status of my shit?"

"Gone. We didn't have a chance to get anything, either them niggas got it, or the police did. I'm sorry, bruh. I'll try to pay you back every dime." She cried.

"Forget it. I'ma get mine. Call me when y'all somewhere safe." He hung up. "Ain't this a bitch!" He punched the seat. "Motherfuckers think this shit's a game."

***

"How's everything going?" Queenie asked Gary once he returned to the car an hour later.

He cranked the car. "The funeral was nice, sad, crazy."

"There's something else on your mind I can tell."

"The Big homie, Zoo got us back on our bullshit. Red Dots on everything, everybody." He shook his head. "It's finna get crazy again."

"What's a red dot?"

"You ain't Blood, so I can't tell you."

"Where are we going now?" She laid back in the seat to avoid being seen.

"Walnut Street to pick up money this nigga owes me,"

She turned to him. Something was odd in his tone. Before she could pry, their drive came short-lived when they parked out front of a house.

"Get out, follow me." He took the keys, gun and crack, She followed reluctantly." Is everything okay?"

He chuckled with mischief. "We good. I need you to do me a favor. Put this in your purse." He handed over the dope and keys.

"Listen, Gary. We got too much going on to be –"

"I ain't gonna let my grandma handle me outta no money, so I damn sure ain't gon' let no crack head nigga handle me." He peeked around the corner.

"But-"

"Shut up. When you're in these streets like me, you're gonna learn to react the same way." He headed around with a pistol drawn.

She didn't know what to do, but strangely her heart led the way.

"Nigga, get your pussy ass up against the house. What you just thought I was gon' let you run off with my work and not do shit 'bout it?" he growled angrily.

"Aye, G. Don't kill me, man. It's only two hundred dollars I owe you. I got that for you, man, please. Don't hurt me, nephew." The fiend trembled with his hands held to the sky while staring down the barrel of the gun.

Queenie watched the scene unfold. Something urged her to run away, listen to Krissy's voice. She had enough going on mentally as is. Yet, another part of her felt obligated to have his back no matter what.

"Bitch ass nigga, you should've thought about what you knew I'd do if you ever took my shit and never paid for it. Now I got yo' ass slippin', and you wanna cop deuces. Nah, nigga." He smacked the fiend with the strap. "You know I ain't no pussy nigga."

The fiend stumbled sideways, crashing up against the house, both stunned and frightened. Blood trickled from the deep gash above his temple.

"Queenie, hold this." He thrust the pistol into her hands before launching a hail of heavy-handed blows to the man's face.

The fiend began fighting back for his life. Each blow given by Gary sounded off. "Next time you take my shit—" Gary rocked the man between words. "—I'm killing your ass."

Gary sat on his chest, raining blows. When he stood feeling the fight was over, the fiend hurried back to his feet in confusion, attacking him. Like a wild savaged beast, the fiend growled, swinging and hitting Gary in the chest, knocking the wind from him.

"Oh my God." Queenie grimaced.

Gary bent, clutching his stomach in a desperate struggle to catch his breath as the fiend returned the hard punches that threatened to make him crumble to his knees.

"Uh-huh. You thought you was tough lil' nigga?" The fiend punched him in the ribs." Look at chu'."

"Fuck you pussy!" Gary retorted,

"Get off him. Gary beat his ass!" she yelled.

The fiend glared at her. "Shut up, bitch."

"Nigga, you shut up!" she returned angrily.

Wham!

The punch landed with Gary's Jaw. The Junky was almost twice his size and double as strong. Queenie felt helpless and growing angrier by the second.

"Gary beat his ass!"

"He can't do shit with me. Look at 'em!"

"Gary."

He tried to swing wildly, hoping to catch the man with something vicious. However, he was winded and unable to land.

"I'll beat your young ass and take all your shit in front of your girlfriend," The fiend boasted.

However, before he could take advantage of Gary, she dug the pistol out, chambered a round, and aimed. The deafening explosion froze them all in place. It's round landing in the dirt beside the fiend.

"Get your hands off him, or I'll shoot you next time," she said, feeling a wave of courage and superiority with the gun in hand.

"Okay, young lady. Chill, you got that. Here." He dug into his pocket and tossed the money onto the dirt. "Don't shoot me."

"Nah, nigga, fuck you." Gary snatched the pistol from her grip before beating the fiend down to his knees. "Better be lucky I don't kill you." Gary snatched up the money, looking at her. "Let's get the fuck outta here."

Chapter Twenty-Four

"We gotta park somewhere."

"Why, what's wrong?"

"It's hot in the streets. You don't see all the police?"

"No, I haven't seen any." She looked around.

"That's 'cause you don't know what they look like but trust me, they're riding hard, and we got to get out on foot before we fuck 'round and get pulled over." The serious tone he spoke with made her worry.

"What if they stop us while we're walking?"

"That's a chance we gotta take. They won't be too alarmed if a man and chick walk to the store together." He slowed the car pulling into a neighborhood park, parking at the gym. "So, grab your purse, let's get out."

She hurried and got herself together. "I think you should let me hold everything."

"Hell nah, that's my pistol. Nigga ain't finna catch me slipping over this mufucka and leave me down bad." He looked at her like she was crazy.

"I'm gonna hold everything. If anything happens, you should know I have your back," she said, opening the door and climbing out.

Gary smiled, getting out as well, locking up the car. "You got that."

She noticed him wincing in pain. "Are you okay?"

"I'm good. Crack head ass mufucka 'bout beat my ass." He cracked up. "Crack pipe got dat nigga strong as hell."

Queenie burst out laughing. "Too funny. He was whooping your ass until I saved you."

The smile fell away.

"I'm joking." She chuckled. "Where are we going?" She realized they had been walking for a few minutes into the neighborhood.

"To the store."

She surveyed the community. There was no difference between it and Pinehurst. Soon into their short walk, she began to spot some of the same kind of people scurrying through the streets. Strangely, a part of her was beginning to feel comfortable and at home in the streets amongst fiends and drug dealers, with a role of her own somewhere in the mist to running things, she felt she belonged.

"I think we should put these on."

"The hell is this silly shit?" He studied it closely." A mask?"

"Put it on like this. It'll keep us from catching that virus and keep our faces concealed from the police."

Gary followed suit. "You want me to use hand sanitizer too?" he joked humorously.

Rolling her eyes, she smiled. "I sure do." Before he could counter, she was waving at a woman speed walking their way. "Hey Auntie, you good?"

The prostitute slowed. "Hell no, I ain't good. Y'all got something?"

"We got big twenty rocks. You can get two for thirty dollars," she spit the same game Gary had on numerous occasions before.

"Let me see."

She removed the sandwich bag from the front of her pants and quickly handed the woman two stones, watching her closely.

"Damn! These boulders compared to the crumbs they selling around here." The woman tasted the rocks. "And it's good.

Here, I got thirty dollars." She handed over the money. "Where will y'all be at? If it's good-good, I'm coming back."

"We'll be walking around," Gary said.

Queenie was all smiles as the woman walked away with haste. "That was some bold shit. Your ass is crazy."

"We gotta make this money, duh."

"True, but not over here. These Green street boys are on some grimy shit. I would hate to have to kill one of these clowns 'cause they hatin'?"

"Well, it looks to me that we're the only ones here. We might as well serve the addicts, right?" She waved to another prostitute and gave her a spill. In no time, they accumulated sales while managing to avoid detection from unmarked police cars circling the block.

"Everybody starting to come back," she grinned, noticing the first prostitute was back with a fiend and more money.

"Well, hurry up and make this play, we ain't got all day, twelve gonna be spinning the block in a minute or two," Gary said, watching her back.

Queenie hurried and made to serve for a hundred dollars before catching up to Gary, who was strolling to the top of the hill for the dozen times a police cruiser came to a stop in front of them. Rolling down the window, the black man looked them up and down. "How old are you two?"

"Umm—sixteen," she spoke up, sensing Gary was ready to run.

"I've been working in this area for a long time. You two are new, huh?" His demeanor was cool and charismatic.

"We're hanging out at the park, walking around, talking. Feels good to be out the house for a few hours," she spoke politely.

The cop gazed at them, sensing nothing suspicious about the couple. "Be careful out here. This is a tough area. I'd hate to see you two get caught up in the wrong place at the wrong time.

"Thanks, officer. We will." She waved him away.

"I'm ready to get the fuck on now," Gary said.

"Fine, but it's another customer coming down." She wanted to take one last play. "After this one, we can go, boo." She enjoyed making money.

"Y'all hustling?"

"Yeah, what do you need?" Gary asked.

"For y'all to get the fuck on. This my block and y'all done made a few dollars, so get the fuck on before shit gets ugly," the tall man spoke with animosity." I'm not gonna repeat myself twice."

"Nigga, you got me fucked up!" Gary spat.

Queenie turned to survey the street. Others involved with the man stood in the distance, waiting for something to happen. It was evident they were outnumbered and outgunned. Gary couldn't fight them and win.

"No. I don't, nigga. You got *me* fucked up."

"Brick fuck them, let's go!" someone yelled from a distance.

"Fuck that!" Brick glared. "This is my strip. Y'all mufuckas get the fuck on or the meat wagon finna pull up early out this bitch." His frame swelled with each second, and he grew angrier. He was intimidating, but from the look in Gary's eyes, he wasn't showing any signs of fear, not backing down.

"G, fuck this street, let's go." Queenie looked around nervously.

"Listen to your bitch, lil' nigga." Brick pointed his finger, walking up on Gary in a threatening manner. "What do you think I'm playin'?"

"Shit, what's happenin'?" As Brick went to lurch at Gary, Queenie allowed fear to consume her. In the wink of an eye, she was in front of the guy with the gun aimed at his chest, hand trembling violently. Her index finger was tempted to apply pressure to her sensitive trigger.

Brick halted in his tracks, changing directions at full speed, taking off or jumping the gate., It wasn't a secret he was going to get strapped.

"We need to go, Gary." She shoved the gun away. Holding his arm, they walked up the street as quickly as possible to avoid police harassment. Entering the Orange Party Shop, a local neighborhood store at the bottom of Milwood Drive, they peeked out the store to be sure no one was following.

"Anybody?" Gary asked.

"No, but we need to get out of your car, so we can go."

"Let me get some grape swishers." He told the Arab, turning to face her. "Well, catch an Uber to the whip. I'm not going back on foot., You pulled a gun on a nigga and didn't knock 'em down. That shit can come back to haunt you later." He paid.

"The next time, I will," she replied with conviction.

"Uh-uh—" A breeze blew in when the store door opened. A face Queenie doesn't want to see. "Look at what we have here." The chick mean-mugged.

"Strawberry, if you don't get the fuck on with that fuck shit." Gary glared, "Nigga, ain't got time to be in yo' drama."

"Good, stay out my drama then. This is between me and your little girlfriend." Strawberry grinned.

Before Gary could protest, she pushed past him, but Queenie was ready.

"Hold my purse for me, let me and Strawberry talk," she spoke calmly. "It'll only take a second."

"We gon' get it right here or what, bitch?" Strawberry scowled." Ain't nobody here to jump in while I beat your ass.

Strawberry, a thick, big-boned chick twice her size, squared off, but Queenie wasn't afraid to fight. She wanted to show Gary she could handle her own weight.

"Bitch let's go!" She swung and missed. Strawberry stepped back and looked at her, stunned. She punched Queenie in the chin, smiling.

"That's right, take this ass whooping."

Her eyes cut to Gary, who was standing by, ready to jump in. The Arab was yelling for them to stop. This time when she swung, Queenie connected with her left hand, dropping her head and rushing in with wild swings hoping to make a point. "Stupid bitch, don't ever--"

Whap!

Queenie slapped the shit outta Strawberry. Gary jumped in the middle before the girl could redeem herself with a volley of heavy hands.

"Move, Gary, I'ma show this chick!"

"Ma'am, you need to leave." The Arab shouted with the store phone in hand." I've called the police. They're on the way."

"Fuck you, Abdul! And you, bitch, you lucky I got warrants, don't worry I'll see your ass in the hood. Gary, you better bring that hoe back to the 'Hurst." Strawberry back peddled out the store.

"We gotta get the hell up outta here." Gary grabbed her by the hand and led her next door to a small bar.

"You think I won?" she asked once they were safe.

"Mannn. You whipped her stupid ass," he drawled excitedly. "Don't get a big head, though. You still ain't got no thump in you."

"Whatever. How I look?"

"You got a red mark on your chin, but you still look good." He gazed at her. "What about me?"

"I can tell the guy you fought really laid hands on you really good." She tried not to laugh.

"I'ma shoot that nigga when I see 'em again just cause. Mark my word."

She chuckled. "I'm playing. And you go 'head and call the Uber? It's been a long day, and I gotta lay down somewhere." She straightened her weave and face mask.

Gary got his phone, making a call. "We gotta stand outside."

Following him out, the fresh air was cool against her skin. Yet, the moment they stepped onto the concrete before they could turn and head back in, a white chubby male police officer was waking up after exiting his unmarked vehicle.

The man called out. "You two, over here."

"Chill, don't panic," Gary whispered.

"Okay, don't panic." She followed over to the police.

"Where are you two coming from?"

"Don't panic," she told herself. "From the laundry mat."

"The laundry mats?"

"Yes, sir," Gary answered.

"Mind if I pat you both down?"

Mouth dry as sandpaper, she replied, "Sir, we are both minors."

"Where do you both live?" The cop gazed at them both with suspicion.

Gary touched her. "No disrespect, officer, but we don't feel comfortable giving out our information. Besides, how do we know you're even a real—police?"

"You wanna take a ride down to headquarters with me to find out?"

"That'll be a first-time experience; I'm down." He turned on the charm. "Where are your headquarters at?"

The officer grinned. "Never met some kids willing to go to jail. But no, I have no reason to take you in. That'll be a violation, and right now, with this virus going around, we can't risk sending people to jail unless it's for a serious crime."

"So, can we go? We have to get some more laundry detergent." Queenie was anxious to get from around the cop.

"Don't I know you?" The officer took off his shades to get a better look. "You seem too awfully familiar. I know you from somewhere."

She swallowed hard. "Mmm. No sir. Not that I know of."

"Are you sure? Take your shades off."

"Is all that called for, Officer?" Gary asked.

Queenie removed the shades. "I'm pretty sure we don't know each other."

He took a long, good look, trying to place the face. Her heart pounded hard in her chest, hoping officer Jacobs wouldn't place her. She slid the shades on quickly to conceal her identity.

"See, told you."

"I know that face. I can't put a finger on it right now. It'll come to me later when I'm not thinking too hard about it." He said, raking his memory.

"Can we go?" Gary asked.

The officer's radio came alive with static from dispatch. "You two have a nice evening, get that laundry done, and get home." He said, heading to his car. They wasted no time slipping through the cut beside the building that led them through a small patch of field then a back street.

"What about the uber?" she asked, afraid to walk the street.

"Forget the Uber. I'm calling my brother to come get us."

Panting, she glanced over her shoulder. "Shit, don't panic. Act normal. The police are coming down the street towards us."

"Mannn—" she drawled with fear. "Do I have the gun in my purse, or do you have it?" she whispered.

"You got everything."

Her skin grew hot. Another cop car turned onto the block as the other cruiser eased past. She tensed with fear. "I'm scared, Gary."

"Chill, if anything, I'll take the purse and run. Everything is mine, little scary cat." He smiled.

She chuckled naturally, forgetting the police driving past. Discreetly, she leaned back to see the street was clear. "Come on. Let's get off the street." She pulled him by the arm into the yard of an abandoned house.

"I can't keep walking. My feet hurt, I'm scared, and I gotta pee." She winced, pulling her pants down once behind the house, relieving her bladder.

Gary burst into laughter. "Your ass is crazy. That's why I fuck with you."

She wiggled the last drops away, pulling up her clothes. "I'm not leaving from right here. So, either you go get the car or call an Uber. I do not fuck with the police, and if you know what I know, you shouldn't either."

"Sit tight." He walked off. Queenie stood against the house, peeing around every few mites. The moment the white on white M5 BMW pulled along the curb, her phone rang.

"Hello?"

"Hurry up, come on crazy."

At the sound of his voice, she scurried across the driveway to the waiting truck.

Chapter Twenty-Five

"Meet me in Ashley's," G-50 said, pulling to a stop beside Gary's crack rental outside the park. "Stop by the Hurst first and handle that business for me."

"Sayless, bruh. I'll meet you there. Queenie, ride with my brother."

"No! I'm going with you," she countered.

"Listen, I need you to slide within. You are good, a'ight."

She glanced over to G-50, who was giving her a no-nonsense look. "Nigga, you can't just push me off on nobody I don't know like that like I'm baggage or something. The hell I look like?"

G-50 grinned. "I needa holla at you for a moment. We can speak while Gary handles his business. You're in good hands."

"So, I still don't care."

"Chill, yo' ass out." Gary kissed her cheek. "It's a short drive." He got out and closed the door. Queenie felt around for her box cutter. Something about G-50 doesn't vibe right."

"Climb up front. Make it quick."

She opened the door and got in the front passenger. G-50 pulled away from the cub. They rode in silence until he finally spoke up.

"What you like about my little brother?"

She remained silent, keeping her sights forward.

He chuckled. "That's what's up. I see why he likes you."

"And what's that?" Curiosity got the best of her.

"That's for him to know and for you to know, but keep going on and doing you. If he tells you, you might slack up."

"Then why say something if you weren't gonna tell me?" She frowned.

"Because I had to get you talking." He chuckled.

She sat back in the seat, mad she said anything.

Pulling into Ashley Apartments, Queenie was suddenly filled with a wave of nervousness.

"This is another one of my spots. Come in. You're good." He cut the engine before climbing out of the truck.

"How long before Gary meets us here?"

"You really like him, huh?"

"He's cool. We're friends."

"True. He'll pull up in ten minutes."

"Okay, well, I'll just wait for 'em right here."

"No, the hell you won't," G-50 sated. "Yo' ass getting out and coming in so we can have a conversation."

"I ain't coming up in your house."

G-50 shot an icy glare that froze her blood with fear. She knew it wasn't something about him. He was the devil. "We need to have a conversation. Let's get it over with."

Queenie followed him inside.

"You can have a seat on the couch. Want something to drink?"

"I'm good."

"Cool, let's get straight to it then, Lil' mama." He took a seat on the couch opposite her. "What's up with you and that hoe, Krissy?"

She grimaced. "What do you mean?"

"She brought you to my hood. You were obviously fucking with her at some point, right?"

"I mean kinda. I guess."

"My brother was at the club that night. You and Krissy was in the building turning up, right?" His eyes narrowed, staring into hers.

"I saw him there. What does that 'pose to mean?" The temperature was rising and seemed to be getting smaller each time. "Are you trying to accuse me of something?"

198

"Nah, I ain't got to that part yet, but since you put me there, let's talk 'bout it. My cousin got killed out here, Ta'Maine. Now, I ain't saying you done it, but you may have been with a bitch that crushed him if you know something about it."

"I don't know anything."

Grinning, his gaze grew with intensity making her feel the pressure. "The best thing to do would be to throw that hoe under the bus and let her get ran over on a solo mission. Because if you don't and the dogs find out you're lying for her, the pups gonna eat yo' ass alive right along with her."

Thinking about the situation she was now in, she chose her words wisely. "Okay, this is what happened."

***

"Lord, Goodness Gracious!" Krissy exclaimed as the gut-wrenching orgasm surged through her body, causing her to quiver with intensity. "Mmm—shit!" Her head flopped back on the pillow, lazy and exhausted. Panting heavily, her chest rose and fell as her fingers clicked off the power button to the battery operating vibrator. "Damn, you're the best." She sighed deeply.

Needing a second to regain her senses, she laid still until she came down from her orgasmic high. The masturbation gave her temporary relief from stress. And lately, stress was heavy on her mind.

Taking her phone from the nightstand, she debated whether to call one of her homegirls for conversation or to aggravate Dirty. She needed to do something to keep her mind busy, but the moment she pulled up her social media, a picture of Ta'maine and his funeral was at the top of her news feed. "Tsk! Fuck they keep celebrating this niggas life for?" She spoke aloud in disgust. "Like this nigga ain't got what he deserved."

She turned the phone off. Tensions were thickening in the streets as assumptions rose and speculation took its course. No one had come for her head yet, so she felt no one knew. Queenie didn't open her mouth. The moment she spilled milk, there would be blood, so she couldn't risk the chance of letting the homeless girl reach the wrong hands.

Suddenly she felt the desire to get out of bed. "Why the hell do I feel like that?" She spoke freely, climbing out of bed touching her beating chest. "I need to see my doctor about this." She stepped into a thong. "Ain't no way I'm supposed to be this anxious about nothing." She looked at herself in the mirror. "I know what it is."

"Are you sure this is what you want?" Lexus, a tall athletic-built man in his late twenties, asked.

She gazed down at the print bulging in front of his pants, lost in a daze.

"Krissy?"

"Huh?"

"Is this what you want?" His silky voice had her pussy thickening with nectar.

"Hell yeah. Where your baby mama at?" She looked around.

'Not like dat, Girl. I'm talkin' bout this pistol. This bitch might be too big for you."

"It might be," she replied with seduction. "Only one way to find out."

Lexus chuckled. "You don't quit, huh?"

"You been ducking this pussy forever, nigga."

"Because I know what I'll do to it. But since dirty a real nigga I ain't gon' cut his throat. If you were anybody else, I'll have it my way. So, stop playing and cop this piece or bop your ass up the street."

She rolled her eyes. "Y'all niggas make me sick with this bro code bullshit. What kinda gun is this again? What you want for it?"

"Be sick, then. This is an XD-forty-five, twenty-round clip. Needs seven hundred fifty for 'em." He flipped it over on its side. "Blow big holes in a niggas ass, too, know you're gonna find a mufucka to use it on."

She made an ugly face. "For that much, does this hoe re-load and clean itself, nigga?' she sassed, digging inside her purse for money.

"I'on know, but once you pay me, you'll be able to find out."

"Funny," she paid him. "I need extra bullets."

"It's a box right there for you,"

Testing its weight in her palm, she had to admit. "It's heavy and scary."

"Any nigga in front that hoe gon' get his mind together."

"Really?" She examined, chambering a round.

Lexus counted his cash. "Hell yeah."

"Whoa, whoa, whoa. Hold the hell up. What the fuck you doing?" He held his hands up high in distress.

Krissy burst into laughter. As quickly as it came, it vanished, her face was wiped clean of any emotion, "Dead ass serious. Strip, show me that dick nigga." she commanded.

"Huh?"

"Boy, you heard me! Your fine ass runnin' round here fucking all these ugly bitches when I been trying to give you some ass for the longest. I wanna see if it's me or your dick. It's one or the other." She aimed at his chest. "Now strip, show me something."

"This some pussy ass shit." He unfastened the Fendi belt sliding down his pants and boxers exposed.

A smile spread across her lips. "So, it's really me, huh?"

He pulled his clothes up.

She aimed the strap at the sky, grateful they were in a secluded area.

Blahh!

They both flinched at the gun's ear-piercing explosion echoing, leaving their ears ringing and pulse quickening. He glared at her crazily,

"Had to make sure she works like I need 'em to," she said. "No hard feelings. My bad."

"Get from 'round my damn crib, and don't call me no more either."

"I still love you, too, you big dick ass nigga," she clowned, getting behind the wheel. "Call me when you get something new." She backed out of the yard. There was only one way to keep her mind at ease.

Now that she had a new pistol with her first love on ice, she drove through Sunset Blvd and onto the beltline. Since most of the city was still out of business temporarily due to Coronavirus, there weren't many places she could enjoy herself without running into someone who intended on avoiding something.

"Hmmm, who can I sell this last key to?," she spoke about, tapping her cheek deep in thought. "Ooh—I know." She took her phone out.

"Who's this?"

"RJ, this Krissy. Is Ike around?"

"Nah."

She looked at the phone angrily as the call disconnected. "This nigga hung up in my damn face," she said, making another call.

"Tonio, this is Krissy you—"

He hung up as well. Her stomach tightened. Something wasn't right; she could see it. Instead of playing on the phone, she decided to pull up.

"Girrlll," Levi drawled as she exited her car, walking into the backyard where he washed the four-door, Porsche. "You know better than to be popping up in a nigga crib like this." He set the water hose down.

"I know. I was afraid if I called, you wouldn't have answered."

"And why is that?"

"Don't know." She folded arms over her perky titties. "You tell me."

"You know you got your name crazin' in the streets, right?" His brows met hers. If there was one person she could talk to about anything, it was him.

"That's some bullshit, though. People are assuming I had something to do with somebody getting murdered when I didn't. That shit fucking up my money."

"If you ask me, I know you did it because I know you personally. I know what you will and won't do. And hearing from the streets what happened, you had to handle yourself. Is it my business to speak on it to anybody, no?"

"So, everyone assumes I killed that boy?"

Cooly, he nodded his head up and down.

Exasperated, "Fuck it. I ant never gave a fuck what people thought about me anyways. Fuck all of them."

"What about me and what I think?" Levi asked. He was an old-school, dope boy who she had sex with years ago before she was legal enough to spread her legs. He would always buy her gifts and listen to all her young problems. Recently he married, and to everyone, he was nothing but a father figure to her.

"I ain't gon' lie; it is what it is."

He chuckled lightly. "So, what is it you come for? You know we can't mess around with that anymore. I'm a married man."

"I got a brick of some pure white. I want thirty stacks."

"I can't do anything with it."

"Please. I know you got it. Thirty-K is petty change to you."

"Sorry, but shit has slowed all the way down. Niggas is telling, and I'm not gonna be in the streets like a light pole anymore." He shook his head. "The dope game is dead for the vultures," his words were honest. "And I don't have a beak or wings, so I'm damn sure no bird."

"So, you're going to leave me out to dry?"

"I already told you, Krissy. It ain't happening. If you'll excuse me, I gotta take care of a few errands. He touched her shoulder softly. "Stay solid."

"Fuck you," she wanted to say but kept it classy. Instead of unleashing an onslaught of verbal lashing, she went back to her car. "Pussy ass nigga." She spoke aloud once seated behind the wheel. She strolled through her call log, searching for someone she could rely on. Since Dirty was out of town for at least two days, she needed to cover some small hurdles. Instead of calling, she pulled up.

Boom! Boom! Boom!

The door rattled each time she pounded with force.

Boom! Boom! Boom!

"Nigga, come open the door!" she swallowed her fears, glancing up and down the long hallway of the apartment building in downtown Columbia. "Pull that sticky ass dick out that hoe."

Boom! Boom! Boom!

"Come open this—"

204

"Fuck is you doin' at my spot?" He iced grilled her, looking up and down the hall. She suddenly felt horrid. Before she could open her mouth to answer, he snatched her inside by the back of her neck in an overly aggressive manner, nearly lifting her air bound. He slammed the door shut then locked it up quickly.

"And how the fuck you know I was here?" Zoo glared down at her.

"I do know where you like to hide when the streets get hot, remember? This is where you used to sneak me when your girl was searching for you." She glanced around the condo, impressed with the new decor.

"Bitch, fuck your thoughts and your memories," he gritted. "What the fuck are you doing popping up at my shit?"

His spicey tone and red-rimmed eyes had her filled with mist. "First of all. I can go wherever the fuck I wanna go, nigga. You don't tell me what to do. And last time I checked, I don't belong to you." She swelled her chest up at him.

Using lightning speed, his grip latched around her neck, turning and showing her back up against a wall. "What the fuck is you doing at my shit," his growl sent chills through her soul. "I ain't gon' keep asking."

"I need to sell another brick." She managed to say.

"What the fuck I look like to you?"

She pried his grip away. "Get the hell off me! I wouldn't have come looking for you if I didn't need you to buy this shit from me. You think I wanna be coming around you? Fuck no!"

"I ain't buying shit from you."

"Zoo, for real. I have been riding around all day tryna sell. Nobody fucking with me right now, and I don't know why," she whined.

"Oh, you know why they're not rocking with you."

"I wish mufuckas would stop tryna blame me for that nig-gas death before the police lock me up for it."

Zoo's voice was threatening, "Bitch, if I learn it to be true, the police will be the last people you'll have to worry about. What, you think this shit sweet?"

"I didn't say that, but Zoo, you're in the same position I'm in."

"How the hell is that?"

"Because I heard you had your little ratchet hoodlums kill Big Ray in Pinehurst."

"What?"

"Did you?"

He snickered. The glint of evil in his eyes had her uneasy. "Playing with fire. I'on know what the fuck you tryna prove, but you gon' force me to prove my point."

"What you gon' do, kill me to hush me?"

"I'ma give you a chance to walk up outta here and go home to your bae, Dirty, 'fore-"

"Before what?"

Again, he snatched her up. This time he backed her up to the wall, ripping her shirt and bra like wet paper, exposing her hard thick nipples. She gasped at his behavior as he yanked her naked. She wanted to protest. His glare made her cave in.

"That mouth doesn't do shit but get you in trouble."

"Hold up, wait."

"Shut up," he growled, spinning her around and pressing her face into the cool wall, snapping her G-string away.

"What are you doing?" she shuddered. "Zoo—what—" He pressed firmly into her. She inhaled deeply as the situation began to register; his expensive cologne filled her nostrils. His presence made her walk to her knees as memories of theory past stormed the brain.

"Zoo, stop my-my period is on," she whispered.

He smothered her body. Pushing and fighting him off was a struggle. "Nah, bitch." His zipper went down. "You are popping up to a nigga's spot with that tough shit. I'ma show you something," his voice a low growl, his breath warm with his lips pressed to ear. "Take this dick."

"No—Zoo—stop."

She gasped for air feeling his massive bulge on top of her asshole. When trying to turn and face him, he bent her back up against the wall. He sneak-kicked and spread her legs open. "This is what you want, right?"

"No, I don't," she whimpered.

He spat in his hand. "Yes, you do hoe."

"Please, oohhh—shit!" she yelled, standing on her tippy toes. "Don't do it. Let me go, Zoo." She moaned. "Don't—"

He pulled his dick out of her shorts and pressed on her tender hole. She tensed as the violation came when he shoved his pipe up her ass.

"Zoo. Shit!"

"Hush up." He grinned, easing up her stomach.

His strong, well-endowed dick lifted her off her feet as he plunged deep and hard. By the time he was finished, her knees shook violently, making it a challenge to stand. She fought back the tears that became hard. "Run and tell Dirty to keep his bitch home," he said before going to wash up.

She stood, confused, shooting him was out the window since she left her purse in the car. She wanted to press charges but was too ashamed and embarrassed. When he returned, she was slowly getting dressed?

"You ain't gon' yet?"

"Why do you do that?"

"Get the fuck out my shit." He opened the door. "Hurry up."

"Fuck you, nigga," she stormed away, ass out. "I got something for your ass."

Chapter Twenty-Six

"And you're sure that's what happened?" G-50 asked, staring at Queenie with intensity.

"Ain't that what I said?"

G-50 chuckled. "That's all I need to know."

The front door sounded with soft knocks.

"That should be your superhero." He went to a door, checking the visitor. When he saw Gary, the door came open, and Queenie couldn't be any happier to see him. G-50 had her creeped out with his menacing demeanor.

"Where is my girl?"

She stood. "I'm ready to go."

"Y'all finish. How'd it go?"

"Here's a few hundred dollars for your precious time, Princess." G-50 handed her a wad of twenties.

"I ain't no princess." She took the money with a twisted face. "I'm Queenie."

"You're a little girl to me. Out here, tryna walk in some grown woman shoes. Baby girl, you have to slow it down."

"Thank you, but you're not my daddy. And if you were him, well, I'd probably tell you to go fuck yourself, right now. Gary, I'm ready to go." She headed for the door.

"I'll get at you later, bruh." Gary gave his brother a dap before following her out of the apartment. "Queenie, you good?"

"I'm fine. Tired, too much shit in one day. I need to lay down. Your brother was nice enough to give me some cash for my time. I guess I can call it a day." She eased into her passenger seat.

"But you look mad."

"I am. 'Cause I ain't get to handle what I really needed to handle today like I intended to."

"What was that?"

"Getting a hotel room somewhere."

"I got a few stops to make, so if I can, I'll see what I can do to make it happen." He started the car. "How does that sound?"

She flashed him a tired smile.

Pulling outside a boarding house, Gary parked. "I'ma run in here right fast and see if I can get somebody to get you the room. Sit tight."

"Don't have me sitting out here all day," she replied, exhausted.

"Talking like that, you're gonna be my ol' lady.' He grinned, squeezing the inside of her tender thigh before hurrying away.

Queenie watched him swagger away and into the house. The longer she spent in his presence, the more she grew attached. At a point, she looked forward to his slick remarks and down to ride attitude. Her young heart was beginning to depend on his thuggish presence. Lazily, she watched the door expecting to see him return with good news. Instead, her eyes blinked heavily until she dozed off.

***

When the front door slammed above them, both whimpered in fear of what was to come. Due to their mouths being taped shut, neither were able to say anything and would rely only on each other's movements or groans.

***

Queenie was unable to adjust to the darkness making it hard to see her mother, only a few feet away. It had been two

210

days since Matthew took them prisoner. His sick mind was turning on him, on the mall, making each of them enemies in his head and subject to being punished by his sinister thoughts.

Listening intently, everything around them stopped, placing them in a horror film, hearing a creaking floor above. Neither was breathing. They prayed he'd forget about them. The basement door snatched open, allowing light to spill in and cascade a glow on his silhouette across the wooden steps. His eyes cut to Destiny's battered face. Though there was fear, her mother seemed to accept her fate. It broke her heart. The steps began to creek louder. She could see his legs descending slowly until he was at the bottom step. He hit the light switch before strolling ever.

"Hey, honey. I'm home." He offered a sly smile. "How was my day at work?" he questioned himself. "Well—it was grueling. Locked up a few bad guys, blacks, of course. Had to throw a pregnant woman to the ground and kick her ass pretty good, too." He rolled up his sleeves.

Destiny mumbled behind the tape.

"Huh? Uh, no. I didn't file for divorce yet, but I'm going to after I get a few of these legal issues resolved. No worries, honey. Your ass will soon be somewhere back in the hood with your nigger family and ugly nigger friends that I hope all die from aids and this new Covid 19 bullshit!" he spat with disgust.

He shook his head in disappointment. "Can't believe I actually married a black whore. The stupidest, dumbest thing a white guy can do. Now my cousins in North Carolina think I'm a nigger lover. Do you know how that makes me feel?" He chuckled. Pained. "To have kids by a black bitch?" He gripped her face forcefully.

Destiny's mumbling echoed inaudibly.

"No. I should have never bothered to be served by a black, prostituting whore!" he shouted, then hawked a glob of spit in her face. "You stinking bitch!"

Tears ran down Queenie's face watching her father with agony and anguish, sniffling, causing him to glance her way. The moment their eyes met, she regretted making a sound.

"Hey, baby girl, sorry to wake you," his voice was soft. "Me and your mother are just speaking."

Her eyes peeled away from his.

"What were we talking about?" he asked. "Well, she's a sack chasing whore. And the only reason I married this black piece of shit was because my reputation was on the line. I hate blacks. But I thought if I followed up a bet to have sex with one, maybe my mind would change." He circled Destiny with malice in his gaze. "It did for a moment. I had to pretend to love my black wife, whom I paid fifty dollars for a blow job and another fifty for hot pussy. That I had mistakenly gotten pregnant and had you." He grinned, seething.

Facing Destiny, he punched her in the stomach. Her face went pale. "Fucking skank, if you would've had an abortion, we wouldn't be at this point." He landed another to the gut, then the ribs.

Queenie screamed behind the tape. Destiny's eyes rolled into her head. Her cries fell on deaf ears as he took out a violent assault on her mother. The strong stench of urine and feces invaded the air. Destiny lost control of her bowels.

"For that, you're not gonna get anything to eat for two more days," he ranted. "Shitting every-got-damn-where." He slapped her face to make sure she was still alive.

Satisfied, he crossed over the puddle of waste to Queenie. She glared at him through water-filled wells. "How was your day, sweetie?" He ran a finger down her face. "A little tied up all day? I can understand," he spoke comically. "I know *you're angry about what I've done to mommy, but believe me, she deserves to get her ass beat and tortured."*

More tears slid down Queenie's face as she watched Destiny dangle, cuffed at the wrists.

"But you, unlike your mother, are going to be given a little shower time. Since mommy's no good, you have to make daddy feel better. And right now, only you can make me feel a lot better. That is unless you want me to fetch Precious," his voice went dark.

"No!" She shook her head frantically.

"Good girl. As long as you do what daddy needs you to do, mommy and Precious will be fine, okay."

Head nod.

"And keep in mind, if you try to tell any of your friends or run away, I'll kill Precious, understood?"

Head nod.

"I'm going to uncuff you. You're going to do exactly as I say." He removed the bracelets from her wrist. "Now, head upstairs to the top shower. Lead the way. Slowly."

She had every urge to run, but with him so close, she knew she wouldn't get far before he caught her. So, she would withstand the conditions for now.

"Turn the shower on to a temperature you like."

She did so.

"Now, slowly strip down naked."

She shivered, looking into his empty grey eyes, where she found nothing but shame and hopelessness.

"Get in the shower. Soap up good."

As she went to close the curtain for a moment of privacy away from the prying gaze, his voice made her jump in terror, "Open it so I can see you. I know how sneaky you little growing, teenage, nigger bitches can be these days."

Dreadfully, she opened it completely, taking a shower in front of a man she considered her knight, protector, her father. Instead, he was now a monster that stripped away from her innocence, with the intent of crushing her soul. After a long ten-minute wash, she cut the water off as instructed and stepped out, wet and exposed. Her gaze hit the floor, settling on the box cutter in the shorts pocket. Her heart raced when she got the idea.

"Turn around, face the wall."

She did so, shivering cold.

"Get down on your knees, place your hands in the tub," his voice was low and bitter.

Slowly she complied with his orders, too frightened to disobey. She tensed, hearing his zipper come down, her eyes set on the cutter. Trembling violently when he positioned himself and grabbed ahold of her hips. She cried out in a muffled pain when he entered. Using one hand to balance herself in the slippery tub, she used the other to snatch the box cutter, exposing its blade, and in one daring motion, she swung the weapon wildly, hoping to slit his throat.

"Arrgghhh!" He jumped to his feet, and blood spurted from his chest. Fear etched across his face.

Queenie tried to dash past him in a rush to save her mother, only to have her face meet with his fists, knocking her out cold.

***

Queenie jumped from the nightmare at the sound of the driver's door opening, and her heart pounded uncontrollably as her mind left off a troubling moment in her life. The nightmares never seemed to end. She breathed out slowly to calm herself, sucked in the tears as Gary flopped behind the wheel.

214

"What's going on? Did I take too long?"

She sniffed. "No. Are they gonna get us the room or what?"

"Queenie, you woke up crying. I saw you asleep when I was getting in the car. What the fuck is going on in your head, bruh?"

Wiping her face dry, she sat up in the seat. "Nothing Gary. Do you have some weed left? I want to get high."

"I got a few blunts." He retrieved the bag of Kush while keeping his eyes gaze on the side of her face as he tried to avoid making eye contact. "I tried to get them to get the room for you, but none of them crackhead mufuckas had their damn IDs."

"So, you know anybody else?" she asked sadly.

"Yeah. But we'll be better off starting in the morning, first thang." He handed her the weed and searched for a lighter.

"Morning sounds good."

"Are you gonna tell me what you were crying about?"

"I don't feel like it."

"Was it something I did?"

"No."

There was a long pause as he went into concentrating on rolling the blunt. She hoped he'd drop the subject. As bad as it was in her head, she did not want to speak on it, reliving it over and over.

"For what it's worth," he began. "If it'll make you feel any better, whoever it was that hurt you so bad, point 'em out, and on five, I'ma kill 'em," his tone was deadly serious. His words rang true deep in her heart.

"You'd really do something like that for me?" she asked, misty-eyed.

Gary sparked up the blunt in his mouth, "Damn right. And once you become my woman, anybody that fucks wit' you got something hot coming their way." He flashed the pistol, taking another hard pull, then passing it to her.

She blushed with a sly smile. "I believe you, too."

"I ain't gonna play with these niggas. Bitches can get it, too."

Naturally, she leaned over and kissed him on the lips. He was shocked. It lasted a minute before she sat back in the seat, swiping moisture with a satisfied grin.

"Damn, what was that about?"

"Nothing. Just talk to me." She passed the blunt back, getting comfortable as he pulled away from the curb. "And stop smoking cigarettes. It doesn't fit you."

He cracked up. "Fuck you, girl."

***

Now with his shift over, Matthew desperately needed to get home to situate a few issues. Since his daughter had run away, he hadn't been able to sleep. In fear she may fall into the wrong hands, his job, career life, and freedom were all on the line.

"Hey, Matt," his supervisor, Castillo, spoke on his way out. "Again, I know you're tired of the reminder, but I'm sorry for the loss of your wife. My condolences to your family. It'll get better."

He shook the short, stubby hand. "Thanks, Boss. Appreciate it."

"Anytime, Matt, anytime." He patted his shoulder.

Leaving the building, he strolled over to his Tahoe parked in the far end of the lot with urgency. However, before he could make it to his vehicle, a voice called out his name in the distance.

"Hey, Matt. What up, buddy?"

He turned, suppressing anger and frustration, replacing it with a fake smile. "Oh. What's up, Jacobs?"

"What's going on, pal? I thought I missed you again. Say, how's your day been?"

"Great. Why should something be wrong?"

"Of course not." Jacobs chuckled. "With all the chaos that has been thrown your way. I'm praying you can have a little peace."

"Yeah, well, the only way I can achieve that is if I get going." He held his temper in check." See you tomorrow, Jac."

"Wait, one more thing."

He froze in his tracks, facing him once again. "What's that, buddy?"

"I don't know your family situation, but I wanted to ask you if everything at home was together—despite your tragic loss?"

"Jacobs, my home life is not your business. I'd suggest you back off and give me some elbow room, buddy."

In surrender, he said, "My apologies, bud. I'm just asking because I found it awfully strange today when I was over on Mildwood Drive that I encountered a young man and woman."

"What does that have to do with me?" he asked, impatiently.

"Depends."

"On?"

"Whether your oldest daughter Queenie moved outta the house already and across town. If not, she has one hell of a lookalike," Jacob said with humor.

Matthew's face flushed but recovered quickly. "That's a helluva look-alike, Jacobs. Know what they say; everyone has a twin."

"That is what they say. But I'm sure the twin was too—"

"Jacobs. My daughters are home. I just got off the phone with them both," he lied. "And I have to get home to them. See you tomorrow." He walked off, climbing into his truck driving away.

He hit the steering wheel forcefully." Shit! Shit! Shit!"

Chapter Twenty-Seven

His hands rubbed across the smooth, cool skin of her ass. The feeling was sensational. He was causing her to purr in her sleep. The juices between the sweet folds of her flower began to seep through her panties, waking her completely. Slowly, her eyes fluttered open, locking with his dark browns. A smile formed across his lips. The longer she stared, the faster her heart pounded in her chest, anticipating the next move. Gary squeezed a handful of her ass forcefully.

"I'm sick of your ass. Get the hell up, dawg," he snarled playfully.

Queenie giggled, tickled by his frustrations. She removed his hand resting on her mound of ass. "Get your paw off me, Animal."

He laughed. "I got your animal."

Sitting up, she stretched, pulling her shirt down. "What time is it?"

"Time for you to stop playing and give me some of that pussy. I know that shit is super juicy."

"You don't need to focus on my goodies."

"Damn, let me suck yo' pussy or somethin'. Fuck it, let me smell it."

"Boy, move, get away."

"You're sleeping in my bed with these little booty shorts on and little ass shirt, acting like a nigga ain't gon' try to get some ass."

She pecked him on the lips. "I'ma take a shower."

After a long thirty-minute shower, Queenie quickly did her hygiene and cosmetics, dressed and ready to hit the streets by the time she exited the bathroom. However, making her way down the hallway toward the bedroom, she bumped into Grandma Ester.

"I apologize, ma'am. Almost ran you over."

"You damn right you 'bout ran me over. You 'bout gave me a stroke too, if I hadn't seen you in time."

"My bad."

"And how are you? Gary got so many girlfriends I can't tell who from who."

"Ummm. I'm not his girlfriend, though."

Grandma Esther checked her up and down. "Never heard of any friends sleeping in the bed together, cuddled up."

Queenie blushed. "I promise it's nothing like that."

"I can't tell. His dirty dick ass got rid of a few chicks just to move you in his room. If you had any sense, I'd never give him any ass. Make 'em sweat."

She caught the laugh before I escaped her lips. "Oh my god. That's too crazy."

"I'm telling you," she lowered her voice." See—I've changed that boy's pampers all his life. I know he's packing, and if you don't know how to keep self-control, that boy gonna fuck our brains all over the place and have you running around like a headless chicken."

Giggling, "I 'preciate the heads up," she said. "And—here, take this. It's a couple of dollars toward the bills since I've been camping here."

Grandma looked at two twenty bills. "Chile—how come I ain't been met you?" she asked excitedly, stuffing the money away. "This fools been bringing them no good ass bitches around when he could've brought you," she said, "Where the nigga at?"

Queenie followed as the woman burst into Gary's bedroom.

"Why the hell is you busting up in my room, grandma?" he glared.

"Bitch! Why haven't you introduced me to this girl?"

Confused, he responded, "What is you talkin' 'bout.?"

"You've had all the other stank pussy bitches up in my house. When you were supposed to have let me meet this one. She's cute as can be, with a good attitude and home training. I don't know what the hell she sees in your dog ass, though. "She frowned, tooting her nose up at him. "You can do way better."

"Queenie," she gave her name.

"Yes, you can do way better, Queenie. I'm telling you I know some real dope boys that got plenty of money and would love to spend it."

"Grandma, make me knock your ass out playin' with me!"

"You ain't gon' do shit, little ass boy!" she retorted.

"Get the hell out of my room."

"This my damn house, and I ain't gotta go nowhere. At least not until you give me something. "Her voice softened.

"No more credit. He stepped into his shoes. "The first of the month is too fucking far away, and I'm not tryna wait until then to get paid, Hell nah."

"I got money, see." She pulled out the two twenties, avoiding Queenie's astonishment.

"I thought you spent all of your money."

"This the last of it. Give me a bubble up." She examined it closely. "Put another crumb on this."

"Get the fuck on."

"Fuck you." She rushed out of the room.

Queenie stood taken aback. Seeing him dressed, she was anxious to get out of the apartment. "Did you find anybody?"

"Fifty got somebody who'll get the room for us. That's where we are going. Pinehurst." He shoved the pistol into his waist. He handed her the bomb of crack. "You hold the work. I got the strap. Team effort."

"Aren't we taking the car? I'm hungry."

"Nah, we're walking there. Anthony is at the corner of Chestnut and Two Notch. They sell some good food. We'll stop there."

"I am not in the mood to be fighting," she sighed, straightening up her wig and shades.

He kissed her cheek. "Don't worry. I got you."

While leaving the fast-food joint, Gary checked his surroundings while knocking on door B4 in the Four Seasons Apartments.

"Who?"

"Nigga, you're looking out the peephole dead at me," Gary said sarcastically.

"Talking 'bout who. Nigga me! Open the damn door,"

G-50 opened the door with a goofy smile. "Scary ass nigga. What, you think them two police sitting in them cars gonna come fuck with you?" he asked in a playful tone. Them bitches know better than to fuck with me. Have some young niggas air that shit out?" He stepped aside, allowing them in. He stood carelessly in the door with the M-90 draped over his shoulder.

"Make sure no roaches come tryna share my food," she whispered.

Gary burst out laughing. "Funny ass. Let me find out you're traumatized."

"I am. Pinehurst has gangsta roaches; they're not afraid to run up on nobody." She held a serious face, then burst into laughter.

"What y'all laughing about?"

Gary countered, "Why are you being nosey?"

"Cause nigga, I wanna know. A mufucka told me they seen y'all asses over there on Green Street selling dope on them niggas turf. Obviously, y'all tryna secure the bag. Either y'all getting the bag or tryna start some shit.

"Which is it?" G-50 sparked up the blunt.

"You are asking too many questions."

G-50 grinned, casting his gaze on her.

"It's both," she spoke up. "That's all you need to know."

"I told you I like your girlfriend, right? She is official," he spoke. "You know only because your story matched that of Krissy 'bout my cousin Ta'maine, she's still breathing." He took another pill. "But in my gut, I know somewhere, and somehow, shawty knocked my homie down. And whether he was right or wrong, that's the fam, and I gotta save face. Krissy better thank you for giving her more time to live."

"I ain't saving her. I'm just telling the truth," she said. That's what you asked me for."

"Fuck all dat. You got somebody to get us this room or not?"

"Y'all got all day, sit tight." G-50 left out of the room. As Queenie was finishing off her meal, he returned, setting the large bag of Rocky Substances on the table," How much time did y'all spend off over on Green Street?"

"'Bout an hour and a half, why?"

"'Cause if them niggas let y'all eat that long and make that much money, them niggas sweet as fuck. With a little muscle and brains, we can manhandle and take that whole strip."

He had her attention.

Gary sat up straight. "Nigga what's the move?"

"I need y'all to go back out here with this work. It'll put that whole block out of commission overnight. It'll be ours." He held up the Ziplock bag of brown rocks.

"I ain't doing that. Almost got into some shit yesterday."

"We gonna go back, fuck that!" Gary was amped.

"And I'm nobody's soldier. I'd rather work for myself." She sipped her soda.

G-50 snickered. "Y'all make a good couple."

"We're friends," she spoke.

Taking out her cell phone, she dialed her friend's number only to reach the voicemail box. Having no luck, she sent a text and gave up. As the day became active, so did they.

"If y'all want to, y'all can sit out the front door to get some fresh air. Police ain't fucking with nobody right now," G-50 said.

"Sayless," Gary replied, pulling her up to stand, guiding her outside. "I love my hood." He inhaled deeply.

"I don't like it. She twisted up her face.

He chuckled." Why not?

"It looks—like—trouble."

"It's the jungle. What do you expect? All these lions, tigers, gorillas, anacondas, and everything that is living in the zoo." He took a seat on the stool, pulling her down on his lap.

She got up and sat on the edge of the sidewalk out of view. A lot was running through her mind, it was still a process coming from modest living to the struggle, but she planned to adjust.

"And who's in charge of this? Zoo?" She glanced over at him.

"The big homie, Zoo. He runs all this shit. He bought up a lot of the houses in Pinehurst. He owns the small apartments across the street. He got his hands in everything and around everybody's neck."

"What about your neck?"

"I work for my brother right now. Soon I'll be working by myself and doing my own thing."

"I hope so," she replied sweetly.

"You ain't got no clothes? My damn baby mama burnt all my shit up last night in Belvedere. Got me mad as fuck, bruh," one said, sitting on the crate beside Gary, placing his pistol on the sidewalk for easy access.

"She doesn't do any of that goofy shit anymore. And she's fucking with me now."

The group of older men looked at him sideways. "When did all this happen?" Star Chain grinned.

"Gary. You don't have to speak for me. I can handle myself. Thanks though, and to answer your question well, that's none of y'all business," she spoke up.

"Say no more."

Queenie smiled. Her demeanor changed when she gazed down at the bloodstained concrete where Fat Sweaty got gunned down. Just when everyone was beginning to settle down, the sleek black Sedan turned the corner into the Four Seasons Apartments.

"Fuck this bitch doin' out here?" Tony picked his gun off the concrete.

Queenie couldn't see Krissy until the car was parked, and her red bottoms were tapping on the concrete as she made her way over with two arms filled with merch. She had to admit, the bitch was bold.

"Good afternoon, fellas." Krissy forced a smile. "I got something good for y'all to fight over today." She set the clothes on the Mustang.

"Right on time, what you got?" Tony headed over.

"Men's clothes." She went about setting everything out quickly, keeping her eyes on the place as well. Krissy couldn't see Queenie, who sat between two cars on the sidewalk. "I hope y'all made some money today. I know these streets are hot."

"Show me something that'll make me spend," Star Chain said.

Gary glared at her from the side. Though she noticed him as she walked up, she hadn't given him a second glance and kept her sights on the police.

"Everything is an official designer brand. I got YSL, Fendi, Chanel, Gucci, Prada. Belts, jeans, scarves, and shirts," she spoke quickly.

Star Chain counted off some bills. "Dress me with this stack." He tossed the money on the car's hood.

"For a stack, that's easy." Krissy glanced at him, then to his freshly shape-up haircut, putting together a fit.

"What about you, Tony?" She ignored Gary's icy stare.

Reluctant, Tony answered, "Give me a belt and scarf."

Queenie picked up her uneasiness. Tony's vibe was throwing her mood. If the police had been parked, there was a possibility things could get hostile.

"One-seventy-five," Krissy told him.

Gritting his teeth, he tossed the money at her feet. Krissy picked it up then threw the merch at his feet.

"Bitch," he mumbled.

"Pussy," Krissy murmured. She spun around to face Gary. "You tryna get something too, little boy?"

He glared at her with anger. Queenie could only imagine what was going through his mind. He could easily kill Krissy and receive a *stain* on his resume. He was considering the opportunity.

"You need to get the fuck from 'round here. You know ya ass playing with fire and ice."

"And what I did to you?" Krissy retorted.

Queenie braced herself. Gary clutched his strap.

"Boy, you ain't gon do shit."

Queenie jumped from her seat. "Fuck her, Gary, don't do it. Let her go on about her business."

Krissy was surprised to see her. "I need to speak with you, Queenie."

"I'm good. You heard my man, though. You need to leave."

226

"Bitches fuck all that. I need to speak with you."

"Maannn—"

"Stop, Gary. This is between two women. I can handle myself. Krissy, we ain't got nothing to talk about. I don't fuck with you. What, you think I'ma be cool with you after what you did?" She grimaced.

"That's what I want to speak about." She tried to pull her aside.

She swatted her hand away. "I don't wanna talk to you, bye!"

Krissy went to smack her. Star Chain caught her wrist mid-swing.

Queenie mean mugged. "Pussy ass, bitch. You hit me, and my nigga will kill yo' ass."

***

Energized, Brick rose from his slumber, looking over to see his wife sprawled naked beneath the sheets. Stark naked, he made for the shower. Twenty minutes later, he was out, hygiene done, and dressed. It wasn't until he noticed the duffle bag on the floor bedside him when it all came back to him. He'd been knocked out for a day and a half catching up on rest and laying low. Taking up the bag, he tiptoed into the living room quietly.

Slowly he removed the contents of Heroin and at least one thousand cash and four pistols. His body began to sweat with excitement staring at the Jackpot. Thinking quickly, he slid out his shirt, retrieved the two kills for his own product from the kitchen pantry over to the table along with other materials. In a frenzy, he moved rapidly, busting the wrappers on each kilo, dumping the off-white and brownish powder/rock substance into a large mixing bowl, and began blending. He cared less what it came out to, as long as he had potent and marketable dope.

"What? Nigga thought he was gon' stop my grind?" he spoke out loud, sifting powder carefully. "I'm mufuckin' Brick, bitch!" he ranted. "These niggas can't fuck with me."

The sound of the bedroom television coming on caught his attention but wouldn't slow him down. He moved fast and in a hurry to take his new mix to the streets. The block had suffered enough, and he wasn't sure how much longer Greene Street would survive the drought.

Rucci's footsteps could be heard as she came stomping from the bedroom. "Brick, tell me—please tell me that shit I just saw on the fucking news ain't got nothing to do with your stupid ass?" She stood on the other end of the table, stark naked, hair in disarray with fear glistening in her doe brown eyes. "Please tell me I'm trippin' this morning?" she continued.

He lacked concern. "What are you talking about?"

"Nigga, I'm talking about the three people that were found dead in their home yesterday in Pinehurst. They say it was a robbery," Rucci's voice dripped with fear. "You need to tell me something?"

"Ain't nothing to tell you! I ain't had shit to do with nothing in Pinehurst. What you can do is, go brush your fucking teeth, take a shower, get dressed, and help me bag this shit up so we can get this fucking money you can't live without," he spat.

She gave him a nasty look that bothered him none. "Swear to God if you have me in some more bullshit, I'm leaving your dog-ass. You got people pulling guns out on you."

"Ru, how about this. Here, take half the money. Get the fuck out of my face. Go do what you do."

"Motherfucka, don't play with me. I'll flush all this shit and shoot the fuck outta you with one of these damn guns," she exclaimed. "I'm your wife!"

"And you're this close to pissing me off, Ru. Either you gon' take that money and get the hell on, or you can clean up so we can get Green Street moving. The choice is yours. I ain't got all fucking day."

She rolled her eyes, disgusted, before turning on the balls of her feet and storming away.

Two Hours Later

Brick and Rucci sat in the trap house dead centered on Green Street after busting down two kilos of smack and dividing it up into five houses. At the top of the street, the house with a picket fence opened for four hours, selling $10 bags. At the bottom of the block, the house with a private fence opened for four hours after the first house closed, distributing grams only. Once the four hours expired, Brick's shop opened up for 8 hours, distributing $150.00 bundles as the day turned into night. The last two sold $20 bags while the last sold $5 hits.

He ran the block so that each of the spots pulled in the currency as well as confused outsiders, charging each location the next day. Every twenty-four hours, spots changed. No one would use the same trap two days in a row except him.

"This shit got me 'noid, baby." Rucci peeked out the front window as the last customer hurried off the porch after the drug-money exchange. She fingered the nickel placate .25 nervously. "All this traffic is crazy."

"Don't get scared now." He chuckled. "You wanted the block back pumping. Enjoy." He snickered, focusing on rolling the blunt of Boont perfectly.

"I didn't say I was scared. Just 'noid." Her face contorted.

"Sounds to me like you're on some scary shit." He licked and finished the twist of the blunt, adding flame. "Ready to go home for the rest of the night?"

"Are you?"

"Hell no. Not until these eight hours up, its two hours away, three a.m." He took a hard pull of the dangerous mixture.

"Are you good? You need to put that stink ass shit out, fuh real." She waved away the smoke. "That cannot be good for you."

He coughed wildly. Instantly his mood darkened as his eyes turned into glass red. "Wanna hit it?"

She craned her neck. "Don't make me slap the shit outta you."

He laughed. "Answer your phone."

"Hello?"

"Are you around the way?" The dope fiend asked.

"Yes, same spot," she answered, pulling the phone from her ear, staring at it strangely. "I'll be there in half an hour. Have me two ready."

She quickly hung up then snapped the flip phone into pieces.

"What's wrong with you?"

"My damn phone was echoing, baby."

He cracked up laughing.

"What the fuck do you find so funny?"

"Baby, you trippin'. Come over here and play with this dick," his voice was saturated with lust.

She took another glance out the window. The pitch-black, dark streets were haunted with junkies carrying back and forth. A black Suburban slowed outside then sped away. Her heart thumped viciously with fear. Yes, the old days were back. But as the money came, so did the paranoia.

"Hubby, listen—after our shift is over, I'm not ever coming back here with you. Not unless you get us a new spot."

"What's wrong?"

She peeked out the window again. "I got a funny feeling. You may have taken the dope from the wrong nigga. It's also like I can feel him getting ready to make a move on us."

Brick jacked the slide on the. P89 Ruger. "Let 'em come then."

Black Migo

Chapter Twenty-Eight

"Little ass bitch running around here like shit ain't real in my damn life." Krissy rubbed her fingerprints off the bullets as she loaded the new XD.45 bought days ago. "I know she told them niggas something. She had to." She set everything down on the bed, taking a moment to think.

Folding her legs under, her mind was in a dozen different directions. "Okay, so what if she does tell my business? She didn't see me shoot his ass, but I did confess. My word against hers? Right now, my say doesn't even matter. If she would've told 'em I'd done it, they would've killed me right there on the spot." She wondered. "No, they wouldn't have. The police were out, too many witnesses. Ughh!" she shrieked, pulling her lace front off in frustration.

"This shit is driving me crazy," she whined, unable to untangle her thoughts. "I know what I'ma have to do. Kill that little bitch next time I see her. She's a runaway. Ain't nobody gonna look for me behind her." She sat up with a burst of energy. "I can't do that shit!" She quickly changed her mind. "Fuck, man!" she yelled, exasperated, finishing the reload of her pistol.

Once full, she chambered a round then inserted another into the clip. "Twenty-one headshots. Don't fuck with me." She aimed at the wall, holding the gun steady with both hands, squinting her sight. "'Cause I'm not playing with none of them pussy-ass-niggas."

Climbing out of bed, she dug out the panties cutting into her ass. In one hand, she held her pistol. The other groped the three thousand dollars made earlier while she began pacing the floor.

"Them niggas tryna put me in the trick bag. They're gonna come for me, I know it," she spoke out loud, feeling helpless and cornered. "But when they do come. I'ma—"

Diinngg! Doonngg!

The doorbell sounded off. Her heart dropped into the pit of her stomach as fear swept over her in a hot flash. Suddenly she ceased to breathe, knowing the worst had come to her front door.

Tossing the stack onto the dresser, she stepped lightly into the hallway listening for sounds of intrusion. She was hipped of the tactics men used to commit homicides. The front door rattled with her nerves as they were knocking shook the walls. Easing closer, she had the XD aimed and ready to scream as she peeked out the blinds.

"Open the damn door!" Dirty jumped into view.

She jumped back, startled. "Fucking stupid ass nigga!" she bellowed. "You play too fucking much, dawg. Straight up. You too grown to be doing little boy shit," she complained, opening the door and turning on her heels, leaving him at the door with a goofy expression plastered across his face.

"I wanted my bitch to greet me, your ass the one scary."

She could feel his eyes on her ass and back. "What the fuck ever." She set the gun on the counter, opening the refrigerator and a bag of cherries. "You could've just called, and said baby open the door for me."

Dirty sat the Louis Vuitton bag down on the counter before wrapping his arm around her waist, biting into her neck playfully, "Baby, open the back door for me. Let me punch these walls." He pressed his erection against her ass.

"I'ma shit on you."

He laughed. "Open the front door then."

"My period on."

"That ain't never stopped us before."

She craned her neck, giving him a dirty look. The mention of sex had her disgusted since only a day ago, Zoo had pushed his log up her valley and seemingly broke something. Her soreness had not subsided yet, nor was she in the mood for more pain.

"Not tonight, Dirty. Tomorrow maybe, okay?"

He touched the front of her panties. "I don't feel no pad."

"That's because I got a tampon on tonight, damn. Now get off me. What are you doing back so early? Thought you were coming back tomorrow night?" She wiggled out his embrace, facing him, doing a quick study of his face for glitter or hickies.

"I handled my business early."

"And what happened? How'd it go?"

"I met with Monte in Orangeburg. He gave me that cash from what he owed my nigga Kwami. So, I'll give it to his family first thing in the morning. Take the pressure off 'em."

"How much was it?"

"One-twenty-five-K."

Her eyes widened. "And you're gonna give 'em all of it?"

"What the fuck you think?" He opened the refrigerator taking a V8 splash to drink. "That money ain't mine. It's Kwami's, and he's dead. So, it goes to his family."

"It's hard times too, bruh. Kids gotta eat. I gotta make sure they fed."

"What about what other situations? With them Four-Eight boys? I saw Blac Zac. He said you owe one of them thangs."

"Damn!" He snapped his fingers. "I was supposed to swing through there on my way here. And I got rid of all my coke, fuck. Matter of fact, me and you going to Sumter to holla at Krock."

"What time? Because I got shit to do."

235

"Whatever you gotta handle, put it on the back burner. And where are the bricks at?" He finished the drink. "Next time you try me on some sucker shit like that again, I'ma knock yo head off."

She giggled, taking the threat lightly." I sold 'em already."

"Bitch to who?" His brow furrowed.

"That's my business, Dirty, damn!"

"I see you got a new toolie. Nigga run up you gon' make another point, huh?" he joked. "That's right, baby, kill they asses dead."

"Sounds like you believe what they say."

He took his bag off the counter heading into the bedroom.

"So, you just gon' walk off when I'm tryna talk to you?" She followed behind, fearing she was in a fight all on her own.

"I'm your man. I'm with you when you're right or wrong. But if you say you ain't do it, then what do you want me to do? Shit, it is what it is. If you did crush that nigga then I wish you would've told me before you let me ride through the city among these niggas," He kicked his shoe off.

"*I did it,* baby. I knocked his chest in because he was gonna rob and kill us," she wanted to blurt out. "Well, I didn't, so fuck 'em. They're gonna think what they wanna regardless."

"I already know, now get over here and top me off. He laid back. Krissy undid his belt, yanked his pants and boxers down before serving him until he was dead asleep beside her, leaving her awake and staring at the ceiling, lost in thought.

***

Tap! Tap! Tap!

Queenie opened her eyes at the sound of someone hitting the car window. The car had dark, illegal tinted windows so no one could see into the new crack rental Gary managed to come across later that evening. She glanced over at him, asleep in the driver's seat. Recognizing the face, she hit the button, rolling the window down some.

"What's up, Auntie?" she asked the fiend.

"Y'all still working, right?"

"What do you need?" She removed the lump of crack from her couch,

"Gimmie a sixty dollar rock and a forty dollar rock. But I gotta go around the building to get the other forty," the fiend spoke fast. "Here's the sixty, Sweety. Look out for me on that." The lady looked around. "I gotta go around the corner to get the forty."

Queenie hit the light above, checking to see that the money was good. Figuring it was real, she set it in the cupholder then fished three chunky twenty rocks, "Here you go. I'm not giving you anything for that forty until you give me the money."

The fiend rushed off.

She shut the light off and put the bag in safekeeping. Instead of getting a hotel room at the last minute, they decided it was best to rent the car for a few days and stack their money. She was looking forward to the extra coins knowing it was putting her one step closer to her goal.

When the previous fiend turned the corner apartment building of Four Seasons, she sat up. They'd been stationary since 7:00 p.m. with all the other Bloods going to a club party to celebrate Ta'maine's life, leaving them free to profit off the lucrative dope. And since Gary had gone to sleep, she wasn't going to wake him. Instead, she took the pistol for his lap, sat in on hers, and rolled the window down as the three fiends approached.

"What y'all need?"

When the women were served and sent on their way, she double-checked the cash and put it away. After a silent twenty more minutes or keeping an eye on the streets, Gary was waking as the clock struck 3:00 a.m. He stretched and yawned, diggin' in his pants to choke his chicken.

"How long did I sleep?"

"An hour or so."

"You've been watching my back the whole time?'

"What does it look like?" She held up the gun. "I ain't slippin'."

Her comment cracked him up. "That's what's up. You're learning quicker than I thought. Now I gotta get you to be soft with me and mean to everybody else." He gripped the inside of her thigh. Tingles shot up her spine, and for a second, she was holding her breath.

She quickly removed his touch, loving it but disgusted by it all at the same time.

"Why are you playing so many games?"

"I'm not playing any games. What're you talking about?"

"I know you're not a virgin, so why do you keep acting like you're scared to take dick? You act like I'ma judge you if you fuck me."

"Whether I'm a virgin or not, I don't wanna talk about my pussy or what it needs. You're starting to turn into a bug." she curled her lit up.

He rested his palm on her leg. "I'm bugging you 'cause you know how I feel about you."

"And how do you feel?"

"Stop acting dumb. You know."

"No, I don't, so tell me."

"I love me some you," He licked his lips.

Queenie blushed, turning her smile away. He had a way of picking the strings to her heart and making her feelings flutter. "Whatever, boy." She brushed the comment off.

"I'm dead ass serious, and I want you to open up to me and tell me stuff about your life because I know it wasn't peaches and cream. You know more about me and how I'm living than I know 'bout you."

"What you wanna know, Gary? There's nothing to tell you but my life. It's regular."

"No, it ain't. Start by telling me why you flinch every time I touch your thigh?"

She sighed. "There's nothing to talk about."

"Got damn, bruh. Every time we getting somewhere, you shut me the fuck down. This some bullshit!" He spat in frustration. "Fuck this shit!" He sat up in the seat, preparing to leave.

"No wait," She stopped him. "I'll tell you this. Don't judge me."

***

Bone-chilling terror had them both living in fear. Being that Precious was out of the house somewhere, they couldn't reach, and the threat to hurt her if they tried to escape his household was evident. They could only abide by his commands. The phone lines were cut, so the call for help was useless. Although they were no longer chained in the basement and given the privilege to sleep in the bedroom after three weeks of torment and beatings—comfort, at this point, was worthless.

"Mommy, please. Let's just leave and go to the police."
Queenie trembled uncontrollably from the excruciating pains

jolting through her battered and bruised body. "They have to be able to help us," she cried.

"No, they can't. They won't." Destiny rubbed her back for consoling. Her eyes had busted blood vessels. Some may assume she'd been in a heavyweight match where she had been crushed. Her beautiful face was damaged beyond recognition. "Your father will still be able to kill us before anyone else can come to help us," she whispered.

"But mom, it hurts so bad. I can't take it anymore," she pleaded.

"Yes, you can, Queenie. Baby, look at me. I'm taking it."

"Mommy, please. Don't make me take it anymore. We have to run while we still can. The police will hide us from him. They'll find Precious and lock daddy away, mommy, please." She struggled to breathe while curled in the fetal position, clutching her stomach." Pleeaasee," she groaned, shuddering violently.

"Be tough, baby. We can't leave. I know your father. He'll find us and hurt us worst, baby. I know this." Tears fell from her face. Her voice was strained and heavy with hopelessness. Spiritually, she had died. Mentally defeated. Physically, Destiny was too weak to fight, and her only escape would be to die.

"Arrgghh!" Queenie shrieked in agony, her body covered in tremendous sweat. "I feel like I'm going to die, mommy. Please, it hurts."

"I—"

Boom! Boom! Boom! Boom!

The front door rattled, followed by the doorbell ringing.

"Lord, let this be your help." Destiny struggled to her feet.

"Who is it, mommy?" She winced.

"Ugh!" Her body rocked.

"I-I don't know, baby, hang tight."

"Noooo. Don't leave me."

Boom! Boom! Boom!

"Baby, I have to go see who it is. They may be here to help us."

Queenie vomited what little she had left on her stomach. "Help me to the bathroom," she said weakly.

Red streams of tears continued down Destiny's swollen face as she used all her willpower and strength to carry her daughter the short distance, closing the door behind her before heading down the stairs against her husband's demand.

Boom! Boom! Boom!

She couldn't see through the peephole since her vision was blurred severely. She spoke using a raspy, dry voice and as loud as she could, fearing the worst. If it was her husband, she was in trouble.

"Who-who is it?"

"It's me. Open up."

"Who?"

"Destiny, it's me!"

Her legs nearly gave out.

"Are you gon' open this door? Damn!" The strong masculine voice boomed. She quickly opened the front door as fast as she could after hearing the familiar voice of her brother Drew. The moment she opened the door, his massive shadow filled the doorway. She crumbled to the floor, exhausted.

"Destiny?" His tone was heavy with anger and pain. "Who? What?" Drew rushed in, kneeling beside her. His big hands touched her face gently as he looked with disbelief. Baby sister, talk to me. Are you okay?"

She sobbed uncontrollably. "Help us. He beats us every day."

"Where is that motherfuckin' bitch?" Drew growled as the veins bulging in his neck and forehead made him twice as

intimidating. "Where is he?" He looked around, pulling this pistol.

"He's not here. He's at work."

Drew scooped his sister from the floor with ease, setting her down on the couch before rushing away to close and locking the front door. His 6'0" and 205 pounds of good southern eating towered over her. "Why hadn't you been called us back at home? We would've come." He was seething.

"I didn't want you getting into trouble, D."

"Fuck dat, ya heard," he snarled, displaying his mouth of gold teeth. She knew he was in kill mode. "I've been calling and calling."

"He cut the phone lines and took the cell phones," she cried. "He's lost his mind, Drew."

Drew had come from Baton Rouge, Louisiana, when he couldn't get in touch with his younger sister. They'd always kept in contact despite her husband's occupation as a police officer and his trade and livelihood in drugs. "We gotta get you to a hospital, Destiny. Where're my nieces?"

"Precious is somewhere with Matthew's family. Queenie is upstairs." Just as he was going to lurch up the flight of stairs, Queenie's ear-piercing shrill sliced through the air. Destiny managed to rush up the stairs behind him.

When they got to her, she was sitting on the floor beside the commode, crying and frightened, covering her mouth.

"Uncle Drew." She sobbed as he rushed to her side. "My dad. He rapes me." She shuddered.

"Oh, my goodness, Jesus." Destiny stared in the toilet.

Drew's eyes were bloodshot red with murderous rage. His shaking didn't go unnoticed. A light coat of perspiration covered his skin as his temper began to boil and blow. "Don't worry, baby. Uncle Drew is here." He looked away from the bloody mess in the commode.

She trembled in pain. Fear. She couldn't stand the sight of the miscarriage. "Give me a second, Uncle. I can't stand. It hurts."

"Destiny, get her together," his voice was strong and assertive. "I'll be right back, so hurry up, ya' heard." He stormed off.

"It hurts so bad, mommy."

"I know, baby, let's get you cleaned up so we can get out of here. This is our chance to get away, okay." Destiny flushed the dead fetus down the drain nodding her head. Drew helped them to stand. "Get some clothes out for the both of you. I've already purchased a hotel room for you both a few miles up. Take my car. I'll meet you both there in a few."

"What about you? We can't leave without you?"

"Sis, take the damn car. I'll meet you at the Country Yard Suites. All the room information is in the first text message. The room is under my name. Now go!" He hurried them. "Take my second cell phone and hurry."

"Mom, let's go," Queenie complained. They dashed as best they could jump into the pearly white 650, leaving...

***

"Fuck dat, I done heard enough!" Gary gripped the steering wheel, studying her face under the fluorescent moonlight.

Every minute she relieved those dark moments, she seemed to die. "I wish I hadn't said anything," she mumbled.

"I'm glad you did. I'm mad at your pop." He shook his head in disgust. "I' on even know what to say, honestly."

She patted her misty eyes dry. "I know how I feel."

"The only place he can hide from me is in hell. Where is he at now?"

"I don't know. I don't even wanna talk 'bout it anymore tonight, Gary. Telling you that little piece has my head throbbing."

"So, there's more?"

She nodded. "A whole lot more."

He sat back in the seat, looking at her for a long minute, sorting out his thoughts. She wished she could read his mind.

Softly she asked. "Why are you staring at me like that?"

"I would've never known you been through some shit like that. You hide it so good. Laughing and sometimes smiling, talking shit—" He paused, thinking. "You're a strong ass bitch, bruh. No cap. And pretty as a mufucka. This whole time I'm thinking you were bougie and stuck up when really you're just protecting yourself. Guarded," he said, taking another long pause. "My brother told me one time when I asked him to make me in charge of one of the blocks so I can make a bunch of money like him, that everybody wants to be the chief, nobody wants to be the Indian. I ain't no damn Indian. I'm a chief." He chuckled lightly. "Then he had me shoot a confidential informant. I was mad as fuck, but I felt better inflicting pain, especially when it meant protecting my hood, my family, the gang, and myself. My brother told me I'd never be a chief until I learned to be Indian. Then I realized one day, I don't wanna be the chief or the boss, I'd rather be the Indian or the soldier."

"And why is that?"

"Because the chief has more responsibility. He has to look over things in order to take care of all of us. While the Indian has one job, to protect the chief. So I'ma soldier. And word is bond. I'ma kill your pops or whoever fucks with you. Point 'em out, on the five, on Pinehurst Posse, they hit."

She blushed. "Calm down, Gary. I already know what you'll do. You don't have to do all that."

244

"You're right. I don't. But to make sure you know, I do."
He squeezed the inside of her thigh.

"Whatever, stop." she swatted his hand away.

"Sit back," He held her, sitting back in his seat as well.

"What's goin' on?"

"Police spinning the block with the lights on." Once they
were gone, he leaned up, starting the car. "We are taking it in
for the night. You can finish telling me the rest of that story
another time."

Black Migo

Chapter Twenty-Nine

"I want her." Zoo rubbed his chin, voice silky with lust. "She better be lucky she with the little homie." He caught a glimpse of his crush.

"Sir?" Baby Girl turned on the music as he steered the Porsche cayenne through the late-night streets.

"Nothing. Thinking out loud."

Baby Girl giggled, glancing over her shoulder at him. "What?"

"That girl that hangs with Gary. You really want her, huh?" She smirked.

"There you are paying me too much attention."

"I'm just saying. It's my job to keep eyes on you anyways, right? Queenie, that's her name?"

"You do it well."

"Obviously, you see something in her that gets you excited every time you see her, am I right?"

"You've been around me too long."

"Cause you can't let me go."

"Because you belong to me. Am I right?" he mocked.

She sighed, licking her lips while fingering the long silky weave as she steered the sports truck. She mumbled under her breath.

"Sorry I couldn't hear you. Come again?"

"I said, you're right. It belongs to you, but all you want me to do is to drive you everywhere."

He grinned. "It's been a long time since I've dropped this wood in ya, too, huh?"

Blushing, legs shaking, and short breaths were a dead giveaway. "About three whole months."

He gazed down at the time on his phone. "Pull over right quick. Somewhere. Anywhere," he instructed.

Baby Girl pulled over into the nearest parking space out-side a shopping center, looking back in astonishment as he ripped open the gold wrapping and slid his chunk of meat into it.

Pants down, dick brick hard, he sneered. "Climb back and sit on this big mufucka."

Reluctantly, she came but not before pushing up the pas-senger seat for space. Positioning himself properly, she lifted her skirt, glad she wore no panties, using the front passenger seat for stability as he spread her succulent ass cheeks, easing down on his pulsating member.

"Suu. Ahhhh. Shit!" she gasped, wincing in pain. Damn. Damn. Damn." She descended on his long ride until he was halfway in, then rose back to the top, moaning loudly and freely. "This dick-soooo-fuuuckking good." She bounced.

Zoo palmed her hips, coaching her rhythm while easing more and more into her tight doorways to heaven.

Abruptly he brought her down roughly, "Sit on this big ass dick."

"No wait! Zooo!" she exclaimed. "Ooohhh. Shiit!" she murmured and bucked.

Forcefully he brought her down on him until she was con-vulsing wildly, body jerking as thick cum oozed down his milk chocolate body. Smacking her ass crazy, he sent her into a frenzy on his pipe.

"You ain't showing' me nothin'," he gritted.

"I'm trying' baby. It's too much."

Tightening his grips, he put in the work. Making her box gush and splash everywhere and her yelling, begging for mercy. He would not give until his load was filling the rubber in abundance.

Baby girl plopped back in the driver's seat, exhausted.

Snatching the condom off, he tossed it out the window before cleaning himself with a wipe. His phone ringing interrupted them. He answered it, "Be there in ten minutes." He hung up, smirking as his discombobulated driver was breathing hard. Zoo just shook his head to dismiss the fantasy of her being Queenie.

***

Pushing the DE .45 into his waistband, he stepped out of the SUV and headed up the bright stairway to the Bentley Court Apartments, where two blood homies stood to assure, he got inside safely.

"Poppin' Foo?" Shooter greeted him once he entered. Though he was still a mess after being disciplined days before, there was no hard feeling between the two. At least that's what they assumed.

"Where everybody at?" Zoo finished the gang shake.

"Backroom."

The dry remark made him uneasy. Discreetly, he pulled his strap, preparing to walk into a trap. He was no bitch, so he was going to face whatever lay ahead of him, even if it was a foolish mistake. Heading down the hallway, he gritted his teeth and inhaled deeply as he turned the doorknob until it twisted open. Pushing the door open, he entered the bare master bedroom. At least ten blood homies were posted around the room in a scatter pressed up against the wall. All eyes were glaring at the two individuals taped and bound to the dining room chairs.

"What's this?" he spoke with no emotion.

"You put the red dot on them Crip niggas 'bout that situation the other day." Shooter would do all the talking. "We followed that nigga, Cloud, all day and night. When we rushed his spot, Cloud ran out the side door and left these two," he pointed.

"And who are they?"

"We thought it was his ol' lady or something but turned out to be his fifteen-year-old daughter and ten-year-old son. What you wanna do wit 'em?"

"Did you all search the crib?"

"Top to bottom. Found nothing except two .357."

"Remove the tape from the boy's mouth."

One of the Bloods against the wall snatched the tape away violently. Zoo stood in front of the trembling boy, with eyes black as night while the atrocious scowl paralyzed the youngin.

"Where your crab ass daddy at lil' nigga?"

"I don't know. Let us go. We didn't do anything."

"Gotta tell 'em where the blue Cloud is first."

"But I don't know where my dad is. What did he do?"

"If you don't know where he is, then I can't let you go, lil man." Zoo grinned, "See, your dad took a lot of money from me. I need all mine back because I got homies and a bunch of kids to feed. Understand?"

"Yes."

"Good. So, where is he hiding? Who would know?"

The boy looked over to his big sister for help. The menacing glare in her eyes told him to shush. He blinked away tears. The sister fiercely tried to shake out of the bounds to no avail.

Zoo watched, amused. Slowly, he removed the girl's muffle. "Homegirl, you got anything you wanna say?"

"My daddy is a big Crip, and he's gonna kill all you pussies, cuz!" she spat venomously.

They all chuckled.

"She's been goin' off since we went there," Shooter said.

"Since she is so tough on super Crip time, put shoes on her and drop her ass in Broad River immediately," he instructed, directing them to put cement blocks on her feet.

"Nooo, wait!" she protested, but he had sealed her mouth back shut. She screamed behind the tape as tears flowed down her face, and her muffled cries caused her little brother to watch in horror as three goons carried her away, chair and all out the room, out the apartment.

"Now lil' man, you wanna go with her?"

"No," he cried.

"Then tell me where your pop's hiding?"

"My grandma—"

Zoo's blaring phone got everyone's attention. He answered, "Speak!"

"We tracked that Cloud to his mama's crib in Greenview Community. It's about forty Crips out there, though. What do you want us to do?"

He scolded the little boy with evil in his eyes. "Greenlight," he said, hanging up. "Lil man, your daddy crossed the line. What a nigga takes from me, I'on want it back. He can keep it. It's 2020, and it's about the principle. So, he gotta die 'bout dat. You, on the other hand, I'm your new daddy."

***

"I'ma go 'head take a shower," Queenie told him as he made for the door.

"I got two plays to knock down. You want something from the store?"

"Mike's and Ike's is fine."

Gary let himself out. "I got you. See ya when I get back."

She locked the room door behind him, grateful for a little alone time. Gary had finally got him a motel two days later, and she wouldn't be the happier. Figuring he'd be gone for another hour or so, she dug out her stash of money hidden in a bag of maxi pads pushed to the bottom of her luggage. After a quick count and double count, she was glad to have $1,700.00 to her name through a drop in the bucket compared to the dream goal she fantasized about reaching. It was still decent, considering a few weeks ago she had not a cent to her name.

Taking another brief moment, she thought out loud. "Gary has to make a play for this-this-that, and it's only 7:30 pm," she taped on her lip. "We would be able to re-up with that." She stashed the money again.

Once the cash was put away, she proceeded into the bathroom, where she started a hot bath. After a full body shave, she cut on the shower and stood up under the pouring hot water for half an hour, enjoying the burning sensation. Her stresses ran down the drain, but her worries would never leave. So, she needed to reach Precious coming soon if she wanted any peace. As long as they were separated, her soul was incomplete.

Cutting off the water, she giggled, thinking about Gary's silly self. She smiled. Having him around throughout the day made her feel better. She needed distraction from the chaos in his life, and only he made it happen.

Stepping out of the tub, she dried and headed into a room wrapped in a towel. Sitting on the bed, she rubbed lotion.

"Soon as I get home. Girl." Gary burst into the room unannounced, singing a track by Trey Songz and YNF Lucci, *All Night Long*. She was caught by surprise.

Queenie jumped up, covering her breasts.

"My bad, baby." He licked his lip with lust, closing the door, all the while keeping his hungry gaze locked on her exposed curves. "You just now getting out the shower?"

"Duh, what it look like?"

"Like you tryna give me some," he said flirtatiously. She rolled her eyes, playfully being caught. "What up?"

"Cause you busted in here without knocking, doesn't mean I'm naked tryna give you any."

"I can't tell." He sat the bag on the table, crossing the room. Queenie couldn't slow her breathing. His lustful gaze had her extremely aroused.

"Well, that's not the case," she answered shyly. "Pass me my clothes right there."

He smirked. "How 'bout you get 'em."

"Pervert."

"Damn right I am." he squeezed her hip.

"Stop," she whispered.

"Gimme a kiss." He wrapped her up in his arms, kissing her face.

"You smelling all good."

She bit her lip.

"Let me stick the head in."

Suddenly her mood changed. "Get off me."

"What did I do?"

"Turned me off, duh. I already told you what's up." She thought about how much pain it would be.

"Let me eat that pussy then. I ain't gotta stick nothing in and only gotta lick it up. You can suck me up after I make you cum."

Giggling, she replied, "You just don't give up, huh?"

"I don't."

"What if I don't know how to suck dick?" She bit her lip seductively.

'Hell, I can't eat no pussy, but I'm gon' try."

"Hmm. You better not hurt me." She sat on the edge of the bed.

Astonished. "You gon' let me do it for real?"

"Boy, hurry before I change my mind."

Gary slipped down to his boxers in a heartbeat kneeling between her thighs. She held her breath and pounding heart anxiously. Slowly and gently, he rubbed the inside of her legs, teasingly.

"What're you doing?' she sighed as he kissed her.

"Shh, don't panic," he whispered, laying her back.

She managed to keep one arm over her breasts, the other she used to prop herself up on an elbow in order to keep eyes on him down below.

His kisses were hot, each deliberate and arousing, making a trail toward the comb. The closer his lips came, the more she trembled out of control. Juices oozed from her slit. His breathing gave her softness a chill that caused a moan to escape.

"Ahh, boy, damn, it feels good!" She placed a hand on his shoulder.

"Babbyyy!" Ecstasy filled her veins while she sighed, releasing all built-up tensions.

Gary licked hard, then soft., she shuddered behind her on a blissful ride. "I-I t-think I-m cumming—I—yes, I'm cummmming!" she cried. The orgasm sent a gush of sweet fluids across his face. "Lord!"

Gary lapped her juices up. Putting on a show, slurping, moaning, and licked clean, he stood with a devious smile. He laid beside her while she regained her senses.

Panting. "Oh my God, I'm dizzy," she whispered.

"My turn." He removed his joint. Queenie turned, getting a glance of his. She had no idea what to do with him but had to meet her end.

"Ummm—you like it?" she asked in between bobbing.

"Keeping going, it's good," he told her, and she did add a bit more speed and spit. She went all out and was glad that he

was loving it. His cum shot up out his pipe like a volcano erup-
tion before spilling down her hand.

"Are you finished?" She smiled.

"For right now."

When she came back after washing her hands, he rolled
over on top of her and between her legs. Holding his semi-
erection in hand, he went to push in the head.

"What I said, Gary?" she frowned.

"I tried." He sat beside her. "So, after all this, where do we
stand?"

"I only did what I did to you because I thought we were in
a relationship."

"I'm just making sure 'cause I ain't finna be eating no
pussy on the regular if you ain't mine. And—"

"And the same this way," she sassed, kissing his lips.
"What's understood shouldn't be explained, right?"

"Right, and right now, I need some pussy. Since you're
my woman, you gotta gimme dat."

Rolling her eyes with attitude, she snapped. "We already
got that understood."

"Yeah, we do." He matched her tone, got dressed and left
out.

She looked around the room, baffled. "What the fuck just
happened?"

The next morning, she woke from her peaceful slumber in
high spirits. Last night drove her crazy. She called Gary but
got no answer. Seeing he hadn't returned had her both worried
and agitated.

She hoped he was alright and that trouble hadn't found
him. Because she was going to give him a piece of her mind,
she sent a text.

//: Gary, where r u?

Five minutes later, she sent another text.

//: So, you're ignoring me?

Five more minutes

//: Not talking to me is crazy. SMH!

Ten more minutes later. Still no reply. Worry set in with an eerie feeling knotted in her stomach. She wanted to cry when she got the voicemail. "I am not gonna cry today fuck that!"

"G-50, where are you at, bruh?"

"What up, lil sis. I'm leaving the hospital. Why?"

Her heart was hurt. "What's wrong?"

G-50 chuckled. "Nothing, dropping my baby momma off at work. Why? You good?"

"Come get me, please."

"Come out front. I'll be there in two minutes."

Snatching up the bag of crack and box butter, she headed out.

"I 'preciate you for coming, bruh." She sat in the front passenger seat.

"Anytime. Where's Gary?"

"He left the room last night and never came back."

"Y'all beefin'?" He pulled the M5 out of the lot.

She folded her arms across her breasts. "No, we just had a little disagreement."

"About?"

"That's between me and him."

He chuckled lightly." Respect. So, where you need to go."

"So, you haven't seen him?"

"Not since I got y'all the room. He ain't call me either."

"Call 'em on speaker?"

"Mannn…" He drawled. "I ain't got nothing to do with y'all beef."

"There's no beef. Call 'em." She handed him his phone from the cup holder.

"Looking for shit, you'll find it."

"Call 'em."

G-50 dialed the number. Voicemail.

"Try again."

Voicemail.

"Drop me off."

"Where to?"

She pouted. "Your grandmother's house."

G-50 cast his gaze her way, noticing she was seriously upset. "Call me if you need something," he said before pulling away.

I will, she told herself. After knocking, there was a short pause before she could hear feet dragging across the carpet.

"Hey."

"How you doing, Miss?" Queenie smiled sweetly.

"Lord, either I'm tripping, or I'm tripping." Grandma Esther's brow wrinkled with confusion, looking back into the apartment.

"Is everything okay?"

"Well—see—I thought. Come in, Queenie." She pulled her in, closing the door. "Keep quiet, alright."

She stood listening to the living room A.C humming loudly and pushing out freezing cold air. "When's the last time you've seen Gary?"

"Last night, he left me in the room."

"Slick little bastard." She grinned. "You gotta keep an eye on his sneaky ass, chile. He thinks he has all the sense."

"Have you seen 'em?"

"Oh, I saw 'em alright. She was here all night, too. And this whole time, I thought it was you back there about to give me a grandbaby."

"Huh?"

The woman put a finger to her lip, gesturing for her to keep quiet while grabbing her and stopping lightly down the hall. As they neared Gary's bedroom, the louder the noise came.

"Shiiittt! Gary, baby," the female cried in pleasure, exhausted. "You better not leave me again, nigga."

"Bitch shut up. Turn around, bend the fuck over," he demanded.

"Baby, wait. I'm tryna catch my breath," she whined.

Queenie listened, blood boiling, feeling betrayed.

"Told you I ain't got all day, Tempest. Now turn around, arch that back."

"Don't go too deep. Your granny gonna hear me."

"Fuck all dat."

"Ouuii! Gary, wait!" Tempest protested.

She tried the doorknob, and it was locked. Seething, she started to kick down the door, but the woman touched her elbow. She turned, facing the woman with misty eyes.

"She gotta come out eventually, and you'll be waiting," she whispered. "Now let Grandma Esther borrow a couple of dollars, and I'll whoop his ass together. That stank bitch, too."

"I don't have any money," her voice cracked with raging emotion. "And I'm sorry, but I can't wait for them to finish," She stepped past granny, angrily leaving out the back door in search for Gary's back window, which didn't take long since the sounds of sex spilled into the day.

Kneeling, she got a glance inside, finding Gary balls deep in Tempest, who was fighting to run away from his vicious dick drilling. She wouldn't get far since he had two handfuls of hair crushing her doggy style.

"Arrrghhh!" Tempest hollered. 'You're too deep!"

"Shut up, bitch. Take it!

She had seen enough. Witnessing his dick glisten with another woman's juices made her snap. Like a cat burglar, she eased through the window. The moment the two spotted her, Gary jumped out of her twat, leaving Tempest on the bed.

"Bitch—"

Queenie hopped on the bed, kicking the words back down the woman's throat before sitting on her chest and hammering her face. Out the corner of her sight, Gary was getting dressed.

"Bitch! Bitch! Bitch!" She punched Tempest's face unleashing a built-up rage. "You think you're gonna be fucking my man?"

"Gary, get her off me." Tempest bellowed, unable to protect her face as Queenie aimed for teeth. She tried to shift and twist her way free, but Queenie managed to stay on top. "This bitch is fucking up my face!"

She tried to retrieve the box cutter from her back pocket but with Tempest bucking like a bull. She had to keep leverage and continue her rain of blows.

"Fuck you and Gary, bitch." She punched her harder. "Y'all tried me," she growled, continuing to release the bottled-up pains.

"Get 'er off me, Gary!"

"You get her off you." He stepped into his jeans. "I ain't got shit to do with it."

"Yeah, you heard 'em hoe!" She snatched out her hair, and Tempest started fighting back aggressively. "You on your own."

"Fight me head up."

Bam! Bam! Bam!

She dropped a mean three-piece. "Shut up." However, seeing Gary sneaking off to the door, she jumped off Tempest with lightning speed and rushed him head-on, shoving him into a pile of dirty clothes. "Fuck is funny?"

He bolted out his feet. "Bitch you—"

Smackkk!

Queenie slapped fire and spit from his lips, digging for her blade as he grabbed her by the arms and slung her aside forcefully."

"I'll kill this bitch!" Tempest snarled, aiming a pistol at Queenie's chest. Her nose and mouth tore up; she stood naked and enraged.

"This hoe fucked up my face." She touched her hand to her cheek and it came back red.

"Swear 'fore God. You do anything to 'er, I'ma murk yo pussy ass." He glared.

The fire in Queenie simmered as she stared at the fully loaded gun with fright. For a second, life flashed before her mistress's eyes as the gun exploded, discharging a flashing hot ball that traveled for her face in slow motion. Her heart stopped beating as he closed her eyes, commenced in darkness.

The room filled with thick, rancid smoke. It was over until she heard Gary's raging voice. Tempest dropped the gun in terror, Gary retrieved it. Slowly she opened her eyes, ears ringing loudly, bearing witness to the man losing his mind.

"Bitch, you almost killed her." He rocked Tempest's jaw then began pistol-whipping her.

The chick balled up into the fetal position, shielding her head and face, begging for mercy.

Bangin' on the bedroom door added more confusion to the chaos. As her senses came back, Queenie yelled, "Gary, stop!"

The moment he laid eyes on her, he softened, but only for a split second before he returned to a murderous black. "Fuck that. Bitch, get out!" He scooped Tempest from the floor and hurled her out the bedroom window, where she crashed onto the dirt.

"Your ass is going to jail, Gary!" Tempest screamed, lazily struggling to her legs, staggering. "Both of you are. Watch!"

Black Migo

Chapter Thirty

"Did you really have to pistol-whip her?" she panted as Gary drove the crack rental.

"Fuck, kinda question is that?'

"She was bleeding. What do you mean?" She nursed her sore fist.

"Because you bust her ass up first."

"You ain't had no fucking business fucking her!"

He kept his gaze on the road. "I wasn't fucking her."

Queenie glared at him with a disgusted attitude. "You really gon' say that, Gary? Me and your grandmother listened outside your door. She thought it was me, and if I hadn't come to find you, I wouldn't have found the fuck out."

"So, what the fuck you expect?"

"That's your ex, though. Ughh!" She shook the thought of him deep in another woman's trap. "I can't even believe I'm going through this right now."

There was a long pause before he broke the silence. "My bad, I was on some bullshit." He tried to touch her and she swatted his hand away.

"I don't want you touching me."

"If you say so."

She pulled out her flip phone and dialed Miranda's number needing to occupy her anger. She was surprised after the second ring, to be sent to voicemail. After a few failed attempts, she sent a text.

"You bought that dope with you?" Gary glanced over.

"Here, take it."

He smiled, taking a deep inhale of her scent. She rolled her eyes. When Queenie didn't receive any replies, she dialed Ms. Pat's number, wishing she had more friends. Precious was heavy on her mind. She missed her sister tremendously.

"What the fuck this hoe want?" Gary answered, placing the incoming call on speaker. "What are you calling me for?"

"You thought that shit was cool to pistol whip me?" Tempest cried.

"I'on know what you're talking about, bruh."

"Pussy ass nigga, you let your homegirl get off on me, and you just stood there watching. That bitch fucked up my face."

"Still don't know what you're talking about."

"Bitch stop lying stupid. When I see her ass, she's dead. As for you, pussy, you're dead to me."

He laughed. "Like I—"

Before he could finish, Tempest hung up the call. He set the phone in his lap, cracking up. Queenie glared with disgust.

"What's so funny, Gary?"

"This hoe talking all that tough shit. Know she ain't built like at."

"Still."

"I ain't tryna hear that shit you talking either." He placed the new incoming call on speaker. "What's up, grandma?"

"Boy, where the hell is you?"

"Riding. Why?"

"That damn girl, Tempest, got a million police outside my damn house. They're beating and banging on my damn door."

She sat up, nervous.

"Shit, my Draco in my room. Hide it for me."

"What?" she screamed.

"Granny, hurry the hell up. Hide it. It's under the mattress."

"I'ma call you back." She hung up.

"So, what does this mean?" she asked, paranoid. "Are they looking for us?"

"We'll know later. My grandma is gonna find out." He pulled into the driveway of a crack customer. "Sit tight. I'll be right back."

She sat in the seat, shaking with anxiety. Taking a few deep breaths to calm her nerves, she tried to focus on something other than the possibility that she would go to jail. Happiness changed her day when she cast her sights down to an incoming call.

"Oh, my God, Miranda. I've been calling you nearly every day, and you haven't been answering my calls or any of my texts, like—what's up with that girl?"

She heard sniffling on the other end.

Queenie's mood shifted, "Hello, Miranda? Are you crying?"

"Hey, sweety. This is Tiffany."

"Mrs. Tiffany, is everything alright?"

The woman sobbed into the phone. "They killed my baby!" she shrieked. Her words were like knives slamming into her soul. "They murdered her!"

"What! Oh, my God. No, this can't be." Tears gushed. "When? How? Why? Mrs. Tiffany, tell me something. Please." She was freaking out.

"The neighbors." She sniffled, struggling to speak. "They complained about a bad smell coming from our house," she cried. "We hadn't been home in two to three weeks, and normally we would've come by, but this pandemic has had me and my husband at work constantly. We haven't been home until now."

"I've been calling her and—"

"They cut my baby's throat and tongue out!" She screamed. "Why?"

The pain cut deep. Her dead friend crushed her heart, making it hard to breathe.

"Mrs. Tiffany, it's gonna be alright."

"No, it's not a baby. Not until I get a hold of the animal responsible for taking my baby's life!" She hung up.

She stared at the phone, weighed down with grief, saturated in tears, and stuck with an assumption. "Please, God, let this be a dream I'm stuck in. Please don't let all this be my fault." She clutched her chest. The more she thought about it, the deeper it set in, the angrier and livid she became.

"My granny says that bitch, Tempest put the police on us, even gave them our names shit, so they're--" His goofy smile fell away when he noticed her face drenched in tears and bloodshot red. "Baby, what's wrong?"

She was too shocked to respond.

"Queen, tell me, what's up?"

"My best friend. She's dead."

"No. What how?" He hurt for her.

He leaned back, crushed. "Damn, baby. I'm sorry for you and that you had to hear that. How they say she died?"

She told him.

"Seriously?" He asked, confused. "I never heard of shit going on out there around the summit. Whoever did that is trippin'."

"I know," she murmured. "It's crazy."

"You think that fuck nigga had something to do with it?" Gary was curious to know.

"I think so," she replied before zoning out…

***

"Mommy, I think we should drive to the hospital and tell them everything. They'll be able to help us."

"Queenie, we have to be careful. Your father had friends that helped him. We need time to figure everything out, okay, baby?" Destiny rubbed her knee for comfort.

"I'm scared, ma. What do you think Uncle Drew is gonna do?"

"He's going to protect us. He's a big man. He knows what he's doing."

She wasn't so sure of her mother's words. As Destiny pulled into the hotel parking lot, sadness filled her up, knowing in some form she was in the fight of her life.

"Suite one-twelve." Destiny retrieved the room key.

Once they were inside the room, both seemed to be weighed down with fear and anxiety.

"I need an ambulance, ma. I'm hurting." She stood near the bathroom.

"Let me call and see where your uncle is. We'll get him to take us." She picked up the room phone.

***

"If you let them live, they'll have your ass locked away forever," the evil of his conscience told him.

"No, they won't. They're too afraid." He countered, all day while working, the inner demons had been waging war against his sanity. He thought he was strong enough to silence the voices echoing in his head, but the harder she fought, the stronger it resisted. With the meds, he was fighting a losing battle.

You have to kill 'em. Today! Or they'll get brave enough to run away from us. They'll rat it out, so listen to me, jackass. Kill 'em, trust me. You think you know it all, but you don't.

"Shut the fuck up!" He glared at his reflection in the rear-view.

267

"You shut the fuck up!"

Matthew laughed wickedly, scratching the scar across his chest then wiped away the pouring sweat leaking down his face. "I am not going to let you win." Tears welled in his red-rimmed eyes.

"Fine. Don't listen to me then, and you'll learn sooner than later. Your ass is going to rot in prison forever if you don't kill your victims, you sick disgusting bastard."

Matthew turned away from the sight of himself. Panic was setting in. Paranoia had him trembling violently.

"What you gonna do, pussy?" The voice demanded. Luckily, your mutt daughter didn't slit your throat. I would have made you.

"No, shut up!"

"Weak!"

"Alright! I'll do it!" He finally gave in, turning onto the highway, en-route his home. I'll do it if it'll shut you up!"

Turning onto his block, he formulated a method of kill and disposal. Being a cop and ex-marine, he knew what he could get away with. However, the moment he pulled along the curb of his front lawn and noticed the familiar face of Destiny's older brother, standing on the porch, a terrible feeling stuck in his gut watching Drew speak into the phone.

"How can I help you, Drew?" He stepped out of the car.

"Aye, whoadie, let me holla at chu', ya heard?" His deep southern drawl was spooky. He pushed the phone into his front pocket, waving him over. "I'm trying to reach Destiny."

Matthew was quickly unholstering the service pistol.

"Nah, don't reach you fucking bitch!" Drew swung the gun into view, squeezing the trigger twice. The force of both slugs landed in his chest.

Lah! Lah!

Queen of the Zoo

The impact sent him stumbling backward off-balance. With a quick recovery, he rolled to the left, ignoring the excruciating pains while taking up the kneeling position, squeezing off rapid rounds of his .45.

Klak! Klak! Klak! Klak!

The first three slugs crashed into Drew's abdomen area.

Klak! Klak!

The second two smashed into the man's horrid face.

Matthew was sure his target was down. He then touched beneath the bulletproof vest to be certain the rounds hadn't penetrated before rushing up the front steps into the house while getting on his walkie-talkie.

"Shots fired!" He relayed to dispatch in a frenzy. He dashed through the house. "Shit. No. No. No!" He ran from room to room. "Fuck! Fuck! Fuck!" He panicked. Locking up the house, he stood on his lawn, waiting for his backup. Fear was overwhelming.

"Where could they have gone?" he murmured, frightened. Once the paramedic cleared him of no serious wounds, he was approached by his captain.

"Are you okay? Castillo asked, setting a hand in his shoulder, casting a gaze of worry and concern.

"I'm fine, thanks. Shaken a little."

"Where's the family?"

"Luckily, they're out of town at my mother's."

Castillo nodded his head. "The man's driver's license is from Louisiana. My guys ran a background check. He has outstanding warrants for drug trafficking and murder. Whatever reason he's here doesn't matter, as long as you're okay, is all that does, understand?"

"Yes, sir."

"This'll be written off as a justified homicide," Captain told him.

"*Take a few days off to let things simmer down, with all that's going on right now. We all could use a few, right?*'

"*Thanks, Captain.*"

Castillo patted his shoulder once again before walking away. After doing another debriefing down at headquarters, Matthew rushed out of the building to his truck. He didn't want to stick around and chat with any of the union at the moment, with other pressing issues weighing heavy on his mind. His blood was boiling with anger since he wasn't able to retrieve Drew's cell phone from evidence. Mashing the gas, he sliced through traffic, then hastily soaring onto the interstate,

"*Son-of-a-bitch!*" His grip tightened around the wheel. Then it dawned on him. Drew's vehicle wasn't anywhere to be seen, which only meant his wife and daughter had taken it.

"*Think motherfucker, think!*" he told himself. "*Where could they go?*"

***

"*Drew isn't answering,*" Destiny said gravely. "*Lord, don't do this to us. Please don't.*"

"*Mommy, my vagina is hurting badly. You have to get me to the hospital immediately.*" Queenie cries in anguish

"*Let me think, baby, let me think.*"

Tears gushed. "*Mom, call the police!*"

"*We can't, honey. It'll only make matters worse.*"

"*Stop being scared, mommy. I'm hurting.*"

"*I'm not, I'm— I'm, I have to pee.*" Destiny rushed to the toilet. She was fed up with fear and the pain. Laying eyes on the room phone, she limped over, dialing 9-1-1-. Her father had to pay. They needed medical attention.

"*9-1-1 operator speaking.*"

270

"Can you send an officer to the Country Yard Suites, room one-twelve?"

"Okay, ma'am. What's your emergency?"

"Me and my mother have been abused."

"I'm sending a unit."

Queenie hung up before Destiny finished up. She winced in agony, taking a seat on the couch.

"This is what we do. We're going to the local health center and get medical attention under an alias. That way, your father can't track us down." She nodded her head and listened to her mother formulate a plan. She wanted to inform her but knew Destiny would refuse. Strongly, she felt her father had to pay for his actions, and the longer he remained free, the longer they'd live in fear.

"Mom."

"If we're gonna do this, we have to go now."

A soft tap sounded forth.

Destiny cringed in fear. "Who could that be?" she whispered.

"I called the police, mommy." She shrugged and opened the room door blindly. Before Destiny could protest. "Dad!" She jumped in astonishment.

Matthew rushed into the room with his pistol drawn. "And where the fuck you two thought you were going?"

"We, dad. Uhh!" Queenie back-peddled. "Please!"

Destiny pleaded the small light of hope was snatched away. "Honey. Please, don't hurt us."

"Did you think Uncle Drew could save you? He's dead, and I killed 'em. So, if you don't want to be next, come the fuck on." He yanked them from the couch. "What, you thought I wouldn't hear you over the radio?" He glared. "Let's move!"

They headed out, too, afraid to run.

***

Gary was livid. "I want to kill your pops."

"Me too." She wiped away tears, leaving out major details to him. "I know he's probably looking for me."

"Where's your mother? Maybe we can—"

"I don't wanna talk about that right now."

"Fuck that! I say we go look for this nigga. As a matter of fact, take me to where he lives. I'll bury his ass in the front yard by the mailbox." He snarled.

"No, I'd rather not bother."

"You on some pussy shit."

"I'm not."

"Yes, the fuck you are, bruh. I told you I got your back. If this nigga is the problem, then he needs to be dealt with ASAP."

"We need to focus on our money first, Gary. Your ex just put the police on us, and I have someone to help me get outta jail if we both go, so I have to be prepared, at least right? And you do too."

Gary sat back in the seat, rubbing the peach fuzz on his chin. "First chance we get, I'ma smack that dad of yours, and you better not try to stop me."

She glanced over at him with misty eyes. "I won't. Now, where are we?" He parked the car around back out of view.

"It's a bando. Why, you scared?"

"No. I just want to know my surroundings." She took in a quick survey of the area filled with an unsettling feeling. "What are we doing here?"

"This is where I'm parking the car. Across the street in those apartments is where we'll be." He pushed the pistol in the waistband, climbing out. She grabbed up the box cutter and followed close behind. Gary pushed open the back door of the apartment as he'd done so on many other occasions.

"And how long are we going to be here?" She looked around the litter-filled, two-level apartment. Broken glass bottles were everywhere beneath their feet, given each step its own crunch.

"For a few nights. It's a good spot to trap out of. This is where I used to hustle all last year, especially when I was on the run for attempted murder. I ended up beating the charge."

Disgusted. "Do these used condoms belong to you?"

He chuckled. "Probably, but don't trip. It's actually cleaner upstairs." Entering the room upstairs, it was indeed clean. The second room was also clean, with two lawn chairs, a small table, and a gas heater.

"At least I haven't seen any roaches."

"It's decent. No lights, cold water. A good spot to trap. I broke all the bottles so I can hear customers coming in."

"That's smart. So, are we gonna make some money? If not, I'd like to go back to my room and lay down. Too much has happened today for me. I'm stressed the fuck out badly."

Gary smiled, squeezing her ass. "We finna get this money. I got the plays coming through right now as we speak and my plug on the way so we can re-up too."

She took a seat positioned by the window. "Sounds like a plan to me, but don't think that goofy shit you pulled is forgiven. Next time, I'ma show you what my box cutter does."

And in no time, the bando was jumping with friends rushing from all directions to purchase the good product. Gary figured since the day was still young that they'd hustle downstairs at the back door to keep the smokers from entering and lingering about. Hours passed swiftly as the bright sun began to descend the sky. Queenie stood beside him in the doorway, wondering if the feelings brewing were actually real.

She gazed at him strangely.

"What are you doing with my box cutter?"

"Take a look." He stepped back.

Gary and Queenie.

She stared at the chipped wood front door. "That's cute." she hugged him tightly, knowing that feeling in her stomach wouldn't be empty but filled with love for him.

***

"Hey, Matthew? This is Jacobs. I got an incident earlier about a domestic dispute with a guy named Gary."

"What does that have to do with me?" He gritted, clutching the phone.

"The young fella was accompanied by a young lady named Queenie. Now I'm not sure if this is your girl, Queenie, but the description matched.

"Where are you?" Matthew sat up in the driver's seat of his truck.

"Pinehurst, Waverly Street. Would you like to meet me? Maybe we could team up and get to the bottom of this together. I know the area pretty damn well."

Matthew shifted the gear and sped out of the lot. "Jacobs, I can assure you that's not my Queenie."

Chapter Thirty-One

"Cuz, we gotta do something about them slob ass niggas coming up in your crib, cloud." C-Lo rented heartedly while pacing the floor. "They took your kids, man!"

"We need to contact the authorities." Cloud's mother, Lou, wiped away the streaming tears down her weary face. "If you say that they've retaliated for something you all may have done, then there's a possibility those animals will slaughter my damn grandbabies."

"Ma, fuck the police!" Cloud spat. "Now I'm pretty sure we can keep this shit in the streets. I don't see that nigga, whatever his name is, killing no kids. Maybe he wants back what we took." He paced the floor.

"That's the point, cuz. I wasn't shit left in there. Whoever jumped out the back window took everything."

"He ain't give a fuck bout no money when he came to the cribs that day with them youngins. That shit was about respect, principles. We came, killed one of his for nothing, and he got the homie kids in exchange. We gotta go to war." EBO said angrily.

"Oh, Lord, Jesus." Mama Lou stood, with her head throbbing. She went to the kitchen sink, retrieved a glass from the dish rack, and poured water from the tap to down the few Tylenol caps. "This is a big mess." she quivered.

"Don't trip, ma. I'ma find my kids." He massaged his temples. There were at least twenty Crips homies standing around the living room where they had all been since the kidnapping. The sun was rising.

A wave of uncertainty washed over them all. Though most of them wanted to be positive about the situation at hand, there was a sense of hopelessness looming overhead, fear Cloud's children may already be dead. He rubbed his bald head in frustration, sighing deeply as his heart broke into pieces. Angel would force him to throw all reasoning in the fire to burn. Having not been home in a full ninety days for his babies, he'd go back in a heartbeat. "Aye, cuz, where them girls at?"

"We are packing, ready to get in crackin'," C-Lo answered, war-ready.

"Good looking, we're going down ionn Pinehurst."

"Damn right, cuz!"

Cloud turned to his mother with fire running in his brows. They exchanged a brief knowing look that words could not explain. She knew him all too well.

In an instant, the metal chatter of assault rifles being fired simultaneously overwhelmed the entire house with panic as bullets ripped through the structure by the dozens. Before Mama Lou could duck low, .762 rounds entered the back of her head, exploding violently out her face.

Kah! Kah! Kah! Kah!

Rounds crashed through the living room, atrociously setting them in a war zone. Each of them hugged the floor to avoid the violent onslaught raging overhead.

Cloud was low, crawling over to his mother. He was shocked and traumatized. No matter what, Zoo would have to face the devil

***

"Dirty, where are you, and why haven't you been answering any of my calls?" Krissy snapped with plenty of attitude.

"I'll be back to the house in two seconds" He struggled to keep from moaning out loud but found the task difficult to do.

"And why you driving my car when you got your own?"

"Mannnn," he drawled. "Chill out. I'm finna pull up."

"No, you chill out," she fussed. Dirty could barely keep the phone to his ear as his new side bitch, Shay, ate the dick up whole-heartedly. The firm grip at the base of his nuts as she sucked long and hard controlling the show. "You better bring me my motherfuckin' car back now!"

"O-o-okay, baby." He shivered. Shay slurped on his mic ferociously, making even breathing difficult for him. "I-I'm on d-da way."

"Nigga—I know that better not be what I think it is?"

Shay's mouth sucked harder, filling the car with wet noises.

Sweating profusely, Dirty struggled to keep his composure. It wasn't until she removed her powerful jaws from his package that he was able to speak clearly.

"What is you talking about?" He panted lightly, watching Shay lick up spit from his bone, eyeing him hungrily.

"Dirty, do not fucking play with me. Bring back my fucking car 'cause I swear to God if you got another hoe in my shit, on God, Jesus, and dat pussy ass hoe virgin Mary, I'ma fuck all yo homeboys. Now try me!" she yelled into the phone.

"Chill the fuck out. I'm not with anybody." He pretended to be upset, hanging up the phone.

"Ummm, you better hurry up and nut down my throat before she comes looking for you." Shay licked the tip of his dick teasingly. She slurped dramatically.

"Fuck it, keep going." He titled his heavy head back, fighting to keep his eyes open. "You said she fucked that nigga Zoo, so eat that dick up. This'll be our little secret."

Shay lifted her skirt, sliding her bald pussy down on his pipe. "Suu-ooh-boy, this dick is amazing." She winced.

He pulled her down on his dark slab of chocolate. The tight squeeze was breathtaking. "Don't run, ride that dick." He palmed her soft ass cheeks.

She began bucking wildly as the orgasm erupted unexpectedly. "When you get back home, let that bitch taste my pussy when you stuff this dick down her throat."

Grunting, he skeeted his thick wad of seed up her pussy as she grinded her hips and tightened the sugar walls around his meat. When she was finished, she climbed over into the passenger seat, panting heavily while straightening her clothes,

"When do you wanna see me again?" he asked lazily.

She cast a satisfied gaze. "And let her suck that dick, make sure she taste my pussy, too. Whenever you're ready for some more of this good ass pussy, you better call." She leaned over, kissed his lips then climbed out of the car before slipping into her own.

He grinned mischievously, looking down at his ringing phone. Ignoring the call from Krissy, he pulled out of the parking lot on Broad River Road. At a red light, he reached over into the glove compartment for a non-scented cleaning wipe, oblivious to the two trucks pulling along both sides of him until it was too late.

***

Krissy jolted out of her nap in a cold sweat. When she didn't see Dirty in the bed beside her, rage consumed her completely, making her nauseous. She had expected to see him an hour ago, and now that he wasn't home still, she was beyond angry. Grabbing the cell phone off the nightstand, she was reminded of the news she had for her man when she laid eyes on the pregnancy test before rushing to the toilet to vomit.

"I gotta find this little bitch." She wiped her mouth dry and rinsed. There was an eerie feeling every time she tried to figure out how to get a hold of Queenie without her new friends around. "I know she can have me killed or put in prison. She couldn't fathom the thought. As she went to reach Dirty, there was an incoming call from a restricted number.

She cleared her throat, "Hello, who is this?"

"What's up, bitch?" The masculine voice asked.

"Whoever the fuck you are, you're the bitch." She retorted, disconnecting the call.

As quickly as she hung up, the phone rang. "What the fuck?"

The voice chuckled, sending goosebumps up her spine.

"Man, who the fuck is this playing on my phone? Dirty, if this is you, I am not in the fucking mood, and bring me back my fucking car before I scratch your shit all the way up!" she yelled, becoming emotional.

"I hate to tell you this, but Dirty ain't coming home."

Her stomach tightened. "What the fuck is that 'pose to mean?"

Chuckling, "It means you're lucky we missed."

Krissy pulled the phone from her ear, glaring at it, confused. "You lucky? I'm confused. Matter of fact, quit playing on my phone."

"Next time. Your head's gonna roll. As far as Dirty, we'll see you at his funeral." The line went dead.

Her blood went cold. In a frenzy, she dialed the number only to get sent to voicemail. Panic in full swing, she called his grandmother.

"Mrs. Jenkins, have you heard from Dirty?" She asked the moment the like picked up.

"We're all down at the hospital, baby." The woman sniffled. Krissy felt her legs give out beneath her. "Are you still there?"

"How is he?"

"You should come over."

"Lord, I'm on the way."

Krissy burst into the Richland Memorial Emergency entrance, distraught, searching for the visitor station. The first person she noticed was Dirty's grandmother, Avery.

"Oh goodness, baby." Avery rushed him, leaving the crowd of family behind in a waiting area. "Glad you could make it."

"What's his status?"

"The doctors just told us he'll make it. They have to do a blood transfusion and undergo another surgery, but my grandbaby is okay," She hugged her tightly.

She wiped away tears, grateful at the good news. She needed a chance to see him in order to reach the bottom of the hit. However, at this point, she was well aware the assassination attempt was meant for her, which could only mean Queenie tossed her slam under the bus. She wiped away the tears. "When can he have visitors?"

"Maybe tomorrow, sometime. He was shot up pretty badly. The car was a total loss with over fifty bullet rounds. Luckily, he survived the three shots."

Krissy sighed. "Whoever did this is so messed up."

"Don't worry; Karma will punish them all."

"Yes, she will," she replied softly. "I need to use the restroom, I'll be right back, okay."

"I'll be in the waiting area when you're finished."

She rushed off, shivering from the brutal chill in the bones. Sitting on the toilet, she relieved her bladder while silently thanking God for sparing her man's life. With her pregnancy, she couldn't imagine raising a child on her own, or rather she was ready to be a mother at all. One thing for certain, the cat was out of the bag.

Wiping dry, she washed her hands thoroughly while reading the information on the mirror beside the faucet. To be sure to protect yourself from Covid-19, wear the mask, wash hands and *practice social distancing*. Mindful, she removed a few masks and placed them over her face before heading out into the visitor's area.

She halted in her tracks at the nurse station, listening intently to the couple of officers speaking to Ms. Avery.

"Yes, her name is Kristen Burress. You may know her as Krissy. We have reason to believe she may show up here to show support to her longtime boyfriend. She's wanted in connection to a homicide several weeks back. Have you seen her or have any way of contacting her?" the tallest of the two male officers asked.

Her soul was snatched away with the law speaking loudly, standing several feet away and oblivious to her presence. The only person who could alert them was the grandmother facing her.

They locked eyes.

"No, I haven't seen her, nor do I have the woman's number."

Keeping her stride unalarming, she rushed away, thanking God for making thorough old folks. She walked briskly out the electronic sliding doors and past the two police squad cars parked at the entrance to the truck Dirty owned, flopping into the driver seat. She used a brief moment to calm her frazzled nerves and unstable emotions.

"This shit cannot be happening to me." She began to crumble. Across the lot, she watched the two cops exit the hospital headed to their vehicles before heading out. She could not relax, knowing they were on the hunt for her

"Hello?" she answered.

"I don't think they noticed you." Mrs. Avery spoke low. "Be careful, darling. This is something serious you're facing. Take care of yourself."

"I know, and I really appreciate what you did."

"I'm old school baby and nothing new to the game. Get yourself situated. When your man wakes, I'll let 'em know to call you first."

"Thanks, Mrs. Avery." She ended the call, resting her head on the steering wheel. "I'm wanted for fucking murder." She cranked the truck, wiping away tears. "Fuck dat. I ain't going to jail easily."

***

"So, you're gonna markup this whole apartment with Gary and Queenie?"

"Why not?"

Amused, she rolled her eyes playfully. "Whatever, that doesn't erase the fact I caught you acting up in your ex's box as if me and you weren't intimate the night before."

"I know I fucked up. I was horny. I should've just beat my dick in the shower, but I needed some pussy and—"

"And you ain't care if it hurt me in the process. I know, it's all good."

"I wasn't thinking."

A soft tap sounded on the back door. Queenie held the pistol with both hands, ready to do damage if someone entered unannounced. Gary was tickled seeing her in commando mode. She stood along the wall in the shadows as he gave the green light.

"Come in."

"Hey, nephew." The male junky entered with another customer in tow. "Boy, it done got dark as hell in here. You still working?"

"What you want?"

"I need a dime. My friend wants two twenties. We wanna know if we can give you a dollar apiece to get high here on the steps. Won't take us long."

"Nah, we ain't having that."

"C'mon   nephew,   its—"

The finger pressed against the highly sensitive button that bought the green beam alive and bright to the junkies' groin area. Both friends jumped, startled. "Unk, you already heard what my man said."

"My bad, Queen. You got it, miss lady." The two copped and hurried out. Gary cracked up lightly. "Me and you can rob some shit together."

"I'm not tryna rob nobody," she told him, thinking of Precious, who she hoped and prayed was still safe,

"It's a quick way to get our bag up. We'll put something together later. He stepped over into the shadows to kiss her lips and squeeze her ass, something she noticed him doing often.

"No, we're not robbing."

He pushed the door closed and locked it. "Let's go upstairs. It has slowed down for a while, so we can take a quick power-up nap if you want to. It won't hurt nothing." He led the way.

"Do we have enough dope to last another rush house?"

"It's a half-zip left that should last us until morning."

"If you say so." She locked the bedroom door. Gary placed the lawn chair behind the door in case someone tried to rush the spot.

"Sit right here on daddy's lap." He parted with a silly grin.

"Shut up," she blushed, loving his personality. She sat perfectly across his lap, snuggling up close to him.

"Tell me the rest of that story with your pussy ass pops."

Queenie took a long gaze into his eyes, feeling accepted and wanted. "It's gonna make me cry but fuck it," she began.

***

"You bitches thought that you could run away from me and I wouldn't find you?" Matthew growled, spitting in both their faces. His fist landed in Destiny's rib cage, with so much force the crack could be heard before the muffled screams of agony.

Queen watched in horror as her mother hung from the overhead pipe, bound by handcuffs, nearly unconscious. So, badly she wanted to tell him everything was her own idea, but her own mouth was taped shut, now she regretted not listening to her mother in the beginning when she made it clear to call the police.

"Don't worry. I'm gonna show you, Queenie, that my word is the law. It's your mother's fault that you're in this mess. And over her stupidity, I'm gonna make an example out her ass." He removed the cuffs from Destiny's wrist, and she scrambled to the floor at his feet. He lifted her from the floor, slugged her over his shoulder. He hauled her away like trash—

Gary broke up the story. "What did he do with your mother?"

She wiped away tears, sniffling. "She was found in a run-down motel, two counties over with heroin in her system, overdosed. The police reports said she intentionally tried to kill herself." She trembled, fighting emotions. "My dad told me that he did it to make it look like she took her own life with drugs, and if I ever tried to go to the police for help, he'd kill me or my sister and make it look like an accident."

"This some fuckin' crazy ass shit shawty." He gritted his teeth.

"Calm down, baby." She rubbed his shoulder. "That's why I don't like to speak about it either. It angers me and makes me feel like I have no wins."

"I swear before God. I wish you hadn't lived that shit." His eyes became glossy with both anger and hurt. Seeing him this way touched her. "So, what happened with you and your sister?"

"He let me live as long as I promised to stay in my room. He put a leg monitor around my ankle and told me it would go off when I left the room. I found out my sister was at my aunt's. I packed my stuff, jumped out my window, and ran." A weight lifted off her shoulders, having told some of her past.

"We gon' murk dat nigga and bury him together. That way, you nor your sister won't have to ever worry 'bout dat chomo," he said, referring to her dad as a child molester.

She kissed his chin, snuggling in his chest, listening to his beating heart. Before dozing off, she whispered. "Love will make me strong. Killing my dad will make me stronger."

***

"Hello, ma'am, I'm officer Wilkes," Matthew spoke politely once the woman answered the front door. He flashed his badge. "May I come in?"

"S—sure." Nervously she stepped aside. "I told those other cops. I know nothing about what's going on with my grandbaby or why they were fighting in the first place."

"Understood. See, I'm not concerned about your knucklehead grandson, Gary. What I come to ask is where I can find them? The young lady he's harboring—she's my daughter." His menacing glare gave her goosebumps.

285

Ester touched her beating chest. "Oh, sir, I didn't know that. I wouldn't have allowed her into my house."

Matthew took a look around the living room. His eyes landed on a photo mounted on the wall. It was of two boys, one older than the other. He figured it was Gary and an uncle or other brother.

Aggressively, he asked, "Where are they hiding out? Either you tell me, or I'll have to detain you for seventy-two hours. This situation could be troubling for you, ma'am."

"I knew I shouldn't have let that boy bring Queenie in here. I just knew something was off about her. Officer, I can't go to jail. I'm on section eight. I'll lose my place and—I don't want any trouble. You know kids these days think they're grown."

Clenching his jaw tightly, he envisioned himself removing the weapon from his waist to blow a hole in her face. "I don't have all day. If you know where I can find them, you better tell me now."

She swallowed hard. If her grandson knew that she would crumble, she'd never hear the end of it. "I—I think I may know this one place—"

Chapter Thirty-Two

Earlier That Day

"Ooohhh! Ooohhh! Ooohhh! Baby, slow—slow down," Rucci whined as Brick fucked her brains out.

He had her luscious southern cornbread-fed ass tooted so high that her thick pussy lips were kissing the ceiling as he held back in a steep arch. The pipe had her gasping for air and slobbering all over the sheets. She gripped the edge of the bed for support with nowhere to run while her head banged against the headboard with each violent thrust.

"Shit, Brick, baby!"

"Cum on this muthafuckin' chocolate," he gritted, muscles flexing as he spread her ass cheeks, threatening to split her in two. "Cum! Cum! Cum!" He pumped harder.

"Aahhh! Ah! Ahhh!" she bellowed. "Bitch!"

Brick went on a rampage when his wife's juices spurted from her pussy all over his pelvis area.

She shuddered uncontrollably as he continued to smash into her G-spot wildly. Her body convulsed in a heated frenzy.

"Yeah, that's what I like to see. Bust all over this thick mufucka."

"Brick, b—baby, I—I can't take no more," she complained, glancing back at his scowl.

Whatever was on his mind, he was dead set on taking it out on her love box.

"Pull out, baby. Did you cum yet?"

"Take this pressure till I finish." He rocked his hips with no hands. His pole glistened, saturated in her sticky nectar. He continued to stroke her crazily. His phone rang but didn't interrupt his stride as he picked up the blaring phone from the nightstand. "Yeah, what's happening? Fuck y'all want," he

287

barked, holding the phone in one hand and using his other hand to stick his thumb in her ass.

"Where you at, whoa?"

"Why?"

"Cause nigga, wherever you're at, you need to stay for the rest of the day," Cory, one of his Green Street block runners, told him.

"Why you say that?" He bit his lip as his wife moaned louder, throwing it back, making her ass clap in his lap.

"Weird shit has been goin' on 'round this bitch all morning. One of the customers came through on some 'noid shit, saying the Feds got us under surveillance. He saw them riding through in a mail truck, taking pictures of the whole strip. My daughter told me yesterday she was using her WiFi service when she noticed the FBI WiFi link. I'm telling you, something ain't right."

Brick chuckled. "Nigga, fuck the Feds, they can suck my dick."

"Mine too. I'm giving you the heads up. Change your numbers."

"If they want me, they have to kill me," Brick said arrogantly, increasing the speed of his thrusts. The climax was building. "Whatever you do, make sure it's revolving around you all making my muthafuckin' money. I'll be out there in a few hours." He hung up and tossed the phone aside.

"Ohhh—who was that, baby?" Rucci cooed.

"Grrhhh—" He leaned his head back in ecstasy. "Dammmnnn!"

Rucci went limp on the bed, Brick rolled over beside her, exhausted. Together they panted, allowing the room to stop spinning.

"Are you gonna answer me, baby?" Rucci asked again.

"You ain't got nothin' to worry 'bout."

"I heard you say something about the feds, though." She propped up on an elbow. "Talk to me, baby. I don't wanna be left in the dark."

Brick sat up. "It's nothing. I need you to take my lawyer twenty stacks. He called earlier and told me for twenty-K he can get them two attempted murder charges gone."

"But I thought they were gonna throw 'em out anyway, due to lack of evidence."

"Just go pay 'em." He palmed her ass. "I got shit to do."

Rucci watched him leave for the shower. She laid in the bed for half an hour pondering. Once he was out and dressed, she got herself together. The last couple of days were a blur. It had gone from nothing in weeks to pulling in tens of thousands a day and growing.

Dressed, she took out 20K from the floor safe, locked it back, and headed out. The sight of Brick standing at the dining room table bagging up large quantities of smack while placing stacks of money into the counting machine made her nervous and paranoid all over again.

"Love you." She kissed his face on the way out.

He didn't respond.

***

"One second, and he'll be right with you," the paralegal, a pretty woman in her early twenties, spoke softly. "You can have a seat in the waiting area if you'd like."

"Okay, thank you." Rucci took a seat. There was so much going on in her head that she had a small migraine brewing.

Ten minutes later, the paralegal returned. "You can head into his office now. He's waiting."

"Hi, Victor Lii," Rucci greeted.

"Hey, Mrs. Lawson, here for Brick, right?"

"Yes, I am." She took a seat.

"I was hoping he would come so we could have a serious conversation," Victor said.

"Is it about the current case?" Rucci asked.

"Uhhh—kinda."

"Well, he told me to drop this off to you." She laid the money down in front of him. His eyes grew wide. "It's for you to get those charges thrown out."

"Wow! Yeah, no problem. I was hoping we could've done it over the wire, but this is fine too." He stashed the stacks in a file cabinet. "Let him know I'll get everything situated today."

Rucci smiled shyly. "Ummm—can I ask you a question?"

"Sure," he agreed.

"Can you find out if my husband is under investigation by the feds?" she blurted, hoping Brick wasn't.

"Ahhh—" Victor sat back in the seat. "That's why he and I need to have a very serious talk."

"So, he is?" Rucci confirmed.

"You have to warn him that he's in a lot of conversations. It may be too late for him to fall back, being that he's been running things for quite some time."

"Jesus!" She sighed deeply. Her heart was ripping into pieces. "That's crazy! Do you know if I'll go down with him?"

"I am not sure. It could be a conspiracy. The only thing I can honestly say to you is if they do come for you, at least try to be prepared for them. Get yourself an attorney now and meet this head-on if it's coming your way. If you aren't under investigation, you may have a chance to save yourself. Separate from your husband's illicit dealings until this thing blows over."

Rucci felt weak, vulnerable, and unable to think straight at this moment. Standing from her seat, she shook his hand and left.

***

"Where you at, hubby?" she called.

"The 'hood, why? What's up, you handled that?"

"Yeah, uh—we need to meet somewhere."

"Later, baby, I'm—"

She hung up abruptly, staring at the phone strangely. Checking her rearview mirror, she slowed down on Gervais Street Bridge and tossed the cell out of the window into the river.

"Now I know I wasn't trippin'." The echoes put fear deep in her heart.

Reaching home quickly, Rucci wanted to stay and explain the sudden dilemma they were faced with as a team, but she knew speaking to Brick at this point was worthless. Even the lawyer said it. So, with a thumping heart and pumping adrenaline, she rushed through their home in a frenzy collecting valuables. She then pressed the buttons to the safe and opened it.

Tears flowed heavily. At reach, she had half of a million in hard cash. She didn't want to take it, but knowing the feds would, she decided it was best. Having her bag loaded, she hopped into her black-on-black Hellcat and left for Atlanta, Georgia.

"Love you, but I ain't going to jail with you, baby," were her last words before exiting the city limits.

***

There were two loud thuds below.

Queenie stirred in her sleep, heart racing for no apparent reason. Too exhausted to open her eyes, she snuggled against Gary's chest, enjoying his warmth. She heard the muffled thud once again but was too comfortable to lift her head, wanting to stay asleep as long as she could.

Crrunncchhhh!

The crunching sounds of broken glass being stepped on echoed below.

Crunch! Cruncchhh!

Gary's breathing quickened, matching his thumping heart. Radio static burst through the eerie silence but was quickly muffled.

His eyes snapped open. "Queenie, baby," he whispered, tapping her thigh.

"Hmmm—what, Gary?" Queenie asked.

"Shuuu—don't be loud, wake up."

The urgency and aggression in his hushed tone got her attention. Her eyelids opened, taking in his worried expression. "What's wrong, baby?" she whispered, glancing over at the makeshift barricade.

"Be real quiet. I think someone's in here with us." He lifted the pistol from the carpeted floor.

Immediately she became fearful. Alert! Gary had a fire in his browns burning like embers with his trigger finger ready to wreak-havoc.

"What do you want me to do?" she mouthed silently.

There was deafening silence around them, and it was intense.

Crunnccchhh!

Her heart skipped beats. Quickly and quietly, she stood as anxiety and panic rattled her nerves to the bone. Gary stood as well with his index finger on his lip, signaling her to silence.

Together, they peeked out the back window. Noticing nothing, he turned to her.

"Somebody is trying to rob us," he whispered. "Lift the window slowly."

She did as instructed, lifting it completely. Gary stepped over to the chair they'd been sitting in, picking up the bag of crack and boxcutter. He froze in place, hearing the glass crunch louder. He knew that whoever was trying to get them had come through the front door.

"Where are we gonna go?" She felt cornered.

"If they come up the stairs. I'm gonna shoot through the door, baby. Don't be scared, okay."

She nodded, agreeing.

Radio static echoed again.

Queenie gazed at Gary in confusion. All too familiar with the sound, her blood chilled with terror. It took only a few seconds for reality to register in her brain. "That's—"

"The police," he finished. "I know, go step out of the window on the back roof. We have to jump." He pushed the boxcutter into her pocket and shoved the stack of crack into his briefs.

"Hold on, baby. Wait!"

"Queen, get the fuck out the window!" he gritted with hushed aggression.

There was no win. Cautiously, she slung one leg over the window sill as the crunching grew louder and louder as the intruder approached the bottom steps.

Radio static blared through the darkness again.

"If it's anyone in here, I suggest you come out with your hands up!"

"Baby, hurry, go!" Gary helped Queenie.

The bottom stair creaked loudly.

"You want me to jump?" She glanced down at the grass below, then to the urgency in his face.

"Yes, jump. Then run to the car, a'ight," Gary instructed.

She was going to respond when the sinister voice cracked through the empty apartment.

"Gary? Queenie! Come out with your hands up so I can see them."

There was no mistaking the voice. She had run from it nearly every night in her dreams and nightmares, and here it was catching up to her. Frightened, she kissed Gary's lips before plunging to the bushes below. She landed on her legs, then ass with a painful yet muffled yelp.

Gary aimed his gun at the door, hearing the creaking steps grow louder. Slinging a leg over the seal, he had no plans for jail anytime soon.

Bloom! Bloom! Bloom!

Gary squeezed off three rounds at the door, hoping to crush the cop.

Shots fired back with a vengeance.

Clah! Clah! Clah! Clah! Clahhh!

He jumped out the window as rounds whizzed over his head.

"Get up, baby." Queenie rushed to his side, helping him to stand.

Gritting, he rose to his feet. "Ahhh shit!" He grimaced. "Help me to the car."

Shuffling into the backyard, she sat him in the passenger seat and slid behind the wheel. Feverishly, she pushed the key into the ignition, cranked the car up, and fishtailed out of the graveled yard, disappearing into the night.

Apprehensive, she asked, "Did you kill that police?"

He cocked the slide to be sure one was in the chamber. "Obviously not, that mufucka shot back."

Desperately she wanted to tell him who the voice belonged to but was more afraid he'd snap on her. "So, what're we gonna do now, Gary? I don't like this. Shit is getting out of control, too quick."

"Queen, I know, I was cornered. That's why I shot first. Luckily, we both got away."

"But he called both of our names. I heard him." She cast an uncertain gaze his way.

He smirked, gripping her thigh. "Black Bonnie and Clyde shit, we're on the run, girl."

***

After following his directions in a vacant home driveway, she asked, "What's back here?"

He got out. "Follow me, this is the cut that leads through the back of my apartment. You don't recognize it because it's dark." He limped away.

She trailed close behind him, suddenly afraid of the dark and what may lurch from its shadows. Gary quickly found his backroom window knowing the area well. Easing his bedroom window up, he climbed in first then helped Queenie inside. Everything was in disarray.

"Did they find your big gun?" Queenie whispered.

"Nah, my granny put it up."

"What are we doing back here, Gary? We need, no—I need to be leaving. Let me drop you off somewhere, so I can go get my sister and—"

"Fuck nah, bruh. You ain't droppin' me off no damn where. You my woman, we in this bitch together. So, we gon stick together," his voice rose in the silence of the apartment.

I'm just saying—"

The bedroom door swung open. Granny Ester stood in the doorway with a heated, disgusted expression painted across her face. "Both of y'all gonna get the fuck up outta here with ya hot asses. Got the police coming up in my shit like they run sumthin'."

"Grandma, where's my Draco?"

"Your brother G-50 came and took it with him earlier."

"I'm sorry we had the police here," Queenie said. "I didn't intend—"

"Gary, you need to get this young lady up outta my shit right now!" Granny Ester yelled.

"Why you trippin'?" Gary flashed her a confused look.

"Cause! Her goddamn cracker ass daddy came up in my shit!" she spat with pure hatred.

The color fell from Queenie's face. Her heart pounded rapidly. Gary had a violent scowl that mirrored his thoughts. "Her dad came here?"

Unsympathetically, Ester glared at Queenie. "Motherfucker sho' did. And he's the damn police." She dropped the bomb, knowing how passionate Gary hated the law.

He turned his furrowed brows and looked at her with a perplexed gaze. "You mean to tell me your fuckin' pops is twelve?" He gritted with his jaw tight.

"I left it out cause I knew if I told you, you wouldn't have looked out for me the way you did."

"We don't fuck with the police around here, little girl!" Ester said, furious. "Nigga's got too much goin' on to be harboring a police baby. That's inviting the whole police into our hood, our house, our home—look around. All this 'cause your fast ass wanna run away from home."

Tears welled heavily in Queenie's eyes. "I swear, I apolo—"

"Fuck dat!" Gary interjected. "You ain't gotta cry, baby. Grandma, fall the fuck back fuh I fuck around and knock your old ass out." His threatening demeanor radiated hostility.

She glared as if he'd lost his rabid mind. "Boy, who the—"

"I ain't tryna hear that. What that cracker came and said?"

"Nothing, looking for his daughter."

"And what you told him? I know you gave him information."

"And no, the fuck I didn't either."

"Yes, the fuck you did! Queenie, let's go! She sold us out on my spot." He helped her out of the window, afraid the police could still be watching the apartment.

"Nigga, fuck you! Don't bring your ass back up in my house either!" Ester yelled out behind them as they fled the area.

Gary whipped the crack rental into the street. It was evident he was deep in his feelings about being left in the dark. "You could've told me something, my nigga."

"I was going to. I was, I swear. It was just taking me time to trust you and open up. I didn't want to risk telling you and end up losing you at the same time, especially now that I have these feelings for you." She swallowed hard, overwhelmed with guilt and mental fatigue. Since everything was going wrong at the moment, she was weighed down with defeat. "I didn't even expect him to find me so quickly. I should've known better, though."

"If I had known your cracker ass pops was twelve, my word, I wouldn't have jumped out that damn window. I would've stayed, waited, and killed that cop—your pops, whoever it was."

"But I'm glad you hadn't, cause what if it wasn't him?"

He smiled wickedly. "Then I would've caught a body."

"I need you to stop smiling, Gary. This is a serious matter. My dad has a lot of friends. They're going to lock us up, especially you. I don't want to go to jail. Wherever we go, they can find us."

"Not if we leave Killumbia." He sped through the streets.

"And go where?" Queenie asked. "The money we have won't last long."

"We're both hustlas. We'll make it anywhere we go."

"I think we should split. Meet up later when things calm down." She sniffled. "I don't want my father to hurt you if he happens to find us."

"I ain't worried about dat nigga. I already told you, I'ma kill him."

"And I believe you." She wasn't so sure. "Where are we going?"

"We can't waste too much time ripping and running through the streets with the police hunting for us. I'ma drop myself off, get the rest of my bread I got stashed at a few spots, while you go to the room and pack up all your stuff. Meet me back in Ashley's Apartments at G-50 spot." He pulled into a driveway. "You remember how to get there, right?"

"Yes!" Queenie answered.

Gary kissed her lips. "Alright, go, see you then."

She wasn't as ready to leave his presence like she was moments before, but there was no time to go back and forth. "Call me soon as you can." She climbed over into the passenger seat.

"Love me some you, girl."

As he pulled out of the driveway, she felt his words in her soul. "And I love me some you."

Chapter Thirty-Three

Using haste, Queenie moved throughout the room, snatching up her panties and bras, tossing them into the duffle bag.

"I have to hurry! I have to hurry!" Her hands shook tremendously.

Every few seconds, her gaze shifted to her phone, waiting on Gary's call to come through.

"Lord, save my sanity," she said in exasperation, sitting on the toilet, relieving her bladder. She swiped away tears, praying Gary could hold to his word. "God, don't let that animal catch up to us." She exhaled deeply.

Wiping herself dry, she flushed the commode and washed her hands before collecting the rest of her belongings. After making sure she had every item, she hurriedly loaded up the crack rental, then slid behind the wheel. Her only line of defense was the trusted boxcutter, so she pushed it into her front pants pocket, hoping she wouldn't have to use it.

Easing into Ashley's Apartments, she cruised the parking lot slowly. "Where is it? Where is it?" she whispered out loud.

Though she found the building, there was no sign of his truck. Still, she searched for a place to park. Finding a spot across the lot, she backed in so that she could be pointed in the direction of G-50's apartment and easily leave when ready. Cutting off the car, she leaned the seat back slightly to hide from view while taking the cell phone out to check the time. It was a quarter past 4:00 a.m.

Impatiently, she sent him a text.

//: Baby, where R U? I'm here!

A few minutes passed with no reply.

Her leg shook violently as her nerves took a beating. She needed one moment of peace to recollect herself and figure out the next best move but was unable to push the thought of such an insane animal hot on her trail out of her mind. Each passing second without her moving closer to her goal, she finally outgrew her patience and busted the move.

First, she had to call Gary to be sure he was safe and sound. He answered on the fourth ring, panting wildly. "What's up, baby? You already there?"

"Yes, I'm already here. I've been here for like twenty minutes. Where are you?" Queenie took a peek over the dashboard.

"I'm at the second spot getting the rest of my money. I should—"

"Nigga, now you got the fucking nerve to be callin' your bitch while you're in my house!"

"Tempest, get the fuck outta the way. I'm only here to get my shit and get the fuck on, though."

"You ain't getting shit. And tell that bitch to brang her ass the fuck over here and get you, so I can fuck her ass up!" Tempest, angry voice blared.

"Bitch, chill out wit' yo' police ass."

Queenie was furious and hurt that he was even in his ex's presence again. Since she was the one that caused the police to be after them. He was making it hard to believe he could leave the chick alone.

"No, bitch, fuck you! Get your fucking money and get the fuck out my house 'fore I call the police again on your ass."

"Queenie, come get me from—"

She hung up in his face. She was not in the right headspace for any more drama. Too much was going on. She needed to get her sister. Cranking the car, she reset the seat and checked the gas hand.

"Don't worry, Precious, I'm on the way to get you now, baby," she spoke aloud, shifting the car into drive.

She pulled into the flying J on Fairfield Road, parked at the gas pump, ignoring Gary's call for the dozen time, and hopped out to fill the tank before jumping on Interstate 20 West to Augusta, Georgia.

"Fifty on pump seven." She handed over the cash then went to the ladies' restroom to relieve her bladder before the trip.

"Hello?" She finally answered her phone.

"So, that's how we doin' it?" Gary asked with attitude.

"What are you talkin' 'bout?"

"Hanging up in my face! Matter of fact, fuck all dat. Where you at now? Come get me."

"I'm peeing at the gas station." She kept her voice low, wiping dry.

"I'm pulling up to my brother's crib right now. Hurry the hell up, bae."

"Okay, I'm on my way now." She hung up.

Flushing the toilet, she washed her hands again before rushing out to the pump. Her feet shuffled across the parking lot toward the dark blue Impala. Her heartbeat quickened when she noticed the familiar black truck across the lot.

"What the fuck?" she mumbled, struggling to keep her grip on the nozzle as the tank guzzled down fuel. Her fears climbed to its peak when she realized there was no one occupying the vehicle. "Fuck all dis." She hung up the device, snapped the tank shut, and dropped into the driver's seat, trying to get a good look at any familiar faces in the store. She cranked the car, shifting into drive, hoping to outrun the looming darkness when the fine hairs on the nape of her neck stood tall.

The cold steel kissed her perspiring skin as terror paralyzed her entire body causing her racing heart to stop beating.

Click! Clack!

The perpetrator jacked the slide, chambering a heavy round. "Bitch, you thought you could run forever?"

"Oh, my God!" She became nauseous. "How'd you find me?"

"Pull out of the parking lot into the Hardy's across the street."

Queenie did as she ordered.

"Park!"

When she parked the Impala, she cut the ignition off, too afraid to make any sudden moves. "What do you want?"

"I should kill you right here."

"Don't!"

Krissy glared at the side of her face as if she'd lost her mind. "Who the fuck is you yelling at, little ass girl? I will blow your fucking head off, playin' with me!"

"Go 'head, do it, fuck it!" She could care less at this point.

"And you're ready to die?"

"Bitch, do it!"

Timid, Krissy chuckled. "You don't give a fuck anymore, huh? That's what it's come down to?"

"If you're not gonna shoot me dead, let me go about my business. I got shit to worry about that's more serious." Queenie tremored.

"I'ma give you one chance to persuade me to let you live because as of now, I'm wanted for murder. The police are looking for me, poppin' up at my people's spots tryna hunt me down for some shit done in self-defense. The only way they can charge me is if they got evidence. So far, you're the only witness that can either help me or hurt me."

"Gary and his brother G-50 asked me, and I told them it wasn't you. I was mad you put me out of your house, but I'd never tell on you because I know what you did was do or die."

"I wanna believe you, lil mama. I do!" She giggled. "But it's hard to trust that when them same Blood niggas shot up my man and got him couped up in a hospital fucked up."

Her stomach tightened with sadness as her phone began to ring. "I'm so sorry for you! I really am, but Krissy, that's the truth. If you don't believe me, then kill me. If not, I have to go get my sister. You can ride if you want."

Krissy stared at the side of her face. "You really wanna get killed out here, huh?"

"My sister is in danger. My father is hunting me down. And I need to get to her to be sure she's safe," Queenie's voice cracked up. "I'm wasting time."

There was a long pause.

"Bitch, you better not be lying."

"I'm not. I'm dead ass."

Another long pause.

"Where you going?"

"Augusta, Georgia."

"When are you coming back?"

"I'm not sure."

"Give me your phone." She gestured. Queenie handed it over. Krissy dialed her own cell phone so that the number was saved in her phone. "Now we got each other's number. When I call, answer. You were there that night. That makes you my codefendant. We either go down together, or we help each other beat this together. The choice is yours. Take this with you."

Queenie took the pistol apprehensively.

"Take it, bitch. You gotta make sure you're protected as well, in case them punk ass niggas come for you, too."

"I don't need it."

"Yes, the fuck you do. Take it, keep it with you at all times." Krissy thrust it back into her palm when she tried to hand it back. "Nigga run-up, pop his ass."

Shaken, she replied. "Thanks."

"Now take me to my car. Call me when you handle your business. We still have a lot to talk about. I need you just as much as you need me."

"I got you." She cranked up, driving to the truck, parked at a gas pump.

Krissy opened the door. "Be safe, big girl. And don't forget, call me." She closed the door, vanishing.

She hit the side button to her phone, ignoring Gary's call. Eyes set on the pistol in her lap, she wasn't sure how to feel and hoped she wouldn't have to use it in the near future. Pulling out the gas station onto the Interstate 20 West Ramp.

She spoke in a hushed tone, "She was going to kill me."

Chapter Thirty-Four

"Bitch, keep it together," she told herself while fighting the urge to stomp the gas pedal to the floor completely and race up the highway. "You have to stay tough, or you're not gonna last long."

She hoped the advice was somewhat true. Glancing over at the gun, she couldn't ignore the eerie feeling looming over. Something about Krissy didn't sit well with her, and although she wanted to utilize the time to think about it deeper, she couldn't bear the weight of having that on her mind.

Still, she knew she couldn't ignore him any longer as the cell phone continued to light up with Gary's number.

"Baby."

"Girl, where the fuck is you at?" he snapped. "Got me stranded over this bitch waiting on your ass to pull up."

"Bae, I'm—on my—way—"

"Where? Better be here, bruh."

"Georgia. I have to get my sister," she replied softly. "I don't need you to get into any more trouble."

"It's too late for that," he spat. "Turn around and come get me."

"I'm already halfway there."

He chuckled in disbelief.

"Baby, don't be mad at me. You in all this because of me."

"And that's exactly why you shouldn't have left me, bruh."

"I'll be back as soon as I get her." She hated to lie.

"No, you're not. You tried to get your money up, so when the time comes to get her, you don't have to ever come back," he said angrily.

Silence.

Tears cascaded down her face. She couldn't take him being mad at her and only wanted to protect him from her father.

He sighed. "The police are looking for both of us. Wherever you go, stay there. Get your sister. Y'all go somewhere safe, even if it means going somewhere far. Your pops is the law, and he'll be able to find you. So, protect yourself. I can handle me, love you." He hung up before she could respond.

Her heart was crushed when she dialed his number and got no answer. She loved him deeply. After being sent to voicemail repeatedly, she finally gave up, saving energy for the task at hand because, regardless, she was never returning to Columbia.

***

The two-hour drive was long, considering how anxious she was to reach her sister. After pulling into a rest area, she used the break to stretch her legs and use the ladies' room. After relieving her bladder, she took a quick wash up in the sink to freshen up. Staring at herself in the mirror, she could not recognize the pain in her brown eyes.

"I miss you, mommy," she whispered, needing the strength to keep herself together. "And we're gonna get through this." She stuffed clothes and hygiene items back in the bag.

Just as she was going to leave out, she noticed her phone lighting up with a caller. Her heart fluttered as she answered softly, "Hello?"

"Hey, chile," the woman's voice warmed her skin.

"Ms. Pat, I've been calling and texting you. Trying to reach you for weeks. How have you been?"

"A lot has happened, sweety. I'm sorry for not answering your calls. Lord knows, I would've if I could, but I ended up contracting that evil virus some weeks ago, and it would have put me on my tail if I hadn't had the Lord fighting for me," she said in a low, raspy tone.

"Seriously, I'm sorry you had to go through that."

"Thanks, Hunny. Jesus is my savior. I can count on him every time. Nothing we go through is by accident."

Queenie hoped that was true.

"And that's why I'm calling." Ms. Pat cleared her throat. "I had my grandson go to my job every day since I been here so that he could pay for your motel room a little longer."

"Are you still in the hospital?"

"I am until I'm cleared to leave."

"I really appreciated you for helping me and still trying. So much has happened since, but I'm okay and—"

"Sweetheart, you're not okay," she said gravely.

"What do you mean by that?"

"God came to me while I was in a coma and told me to warn you before everything is too late."

"Huh—too late? Ms. Pat, you're scaring me," Queenie replied, exiting the ladies' room and pushing her bag into the backseat. She made sure to take a good view inside to avoid any more intrusions. The sun had risen, adding urgency to her day.

"I could feel your spirit the moment I met you. You were trouble and on the run. From what, I'm not sure. But nothing moves like the devil. I can sense your distance. Wherever you're going, keep going. Don't return. Evil doesn't stop. Save yourself."

Swallowing hard, she asked, "Why are you telling me this? It feels like you're trying to tell me something but not saying it."

"I don't want anything to happen to you. Or learn you've done something you cannot change."

Ms. Pat had her head hurting with the indirect warnings. "Okay, call later. I'd really appreciate it."

"I will."

"Later," she spoke softly, then hung up.

Queenie closed the phone shut, taking a moment to recollect her thoughts. Taking a deep breath, she exhaled slowly. Having memorized her aunt's address long ago, she reentered the information into the GPS. When it came to life, reading the navigation, her heart skipped beats.

Precious was twenty minutes away. A drive she was ready to make. Pulling out, she continued on her way. The ride came short-lived.

"Your designation is on the left," the GPS notified.

She cut the engine and took a good look at the house. It was the same as she remembered when she visited as a child during the summer. The fresh, white paint did it justice.

"Relax yourself." She spun the block.

The sun was high and bright. She was comfortable knowing the shadows couldn't get her. Building confidence, she needed to confront her father's sister. She eased into the driveway, behind the blue Lexus and white Audi truck.

"Fuck it, here we go. Let's do this!" She tucked the pistol on her slim waist and climbed out.

Approaching the front door, she pressed the doorbell nervously.

The door opened slowly. Her Aunt Joanna clasped her gown shut, eyeing the Impala. "Hi, Queenie."

"Is Precious here?"

"Come in."

Timid, Queenie stepped inside the foyer. "Where's my sister, Aunt Joanna?"

Confused, she stared at Queenie. "Is that why you're here, baby?"

"Yes, it is. And I need to see my sister immediately."

"Precious hasn't been here since three days ago," she replied disdainfully.

"What do you mean, three days?"

"Well, your father came and got her. I thought you were in the truck with him when he came," she admitted. "They're both in Columbia."

Her heart shattered to pieces. "This can't be happening!" She rushed through the house. "Precious! Precious!" she yelled, going from room to room, finding them all empty.

"She's not here, sweety. Now slow down and tell me what's going on?" her aunt's voice was soft, caring, and concerned. "Talk to me. I can help you."

"Get off me! Get away!" Tears welled in Queenie's eyes. "I have to go!" She rushed to the door. "And please don't tell my dad I came here either."

Black Migo

Chapter Thirty-Five

"I went up on that scene like you asked, bruh," Zipper, a twelve-year-old, reported. "Four of them crab ass niggas got hit up. The big homie Crip, Cloud? His baby mama got smacked to sleep, so he gon' want pressure 'bout that." He smiled, standing ready to carry out the next order. "What now?"

Zoo glared down at his soldier. "You did what I told you to do?"

"Yes, sir. I told a few people in the crowd that it was them Bedrock niggas who came through and done it. The rumor spread quickly. Everybody believes it, so there's no heat on us," Zipper spoke excitedly. "What else you got for us to do? Give us something. Anything!"

Zoo rubbed his freshly trimmed goatee deep in thought, casting his gaze on Cloud's son, Mason, who was sitting on the living room couch in his mansion. The boy was scared for his life. Shivering and unable to grasp the severity of the situation. There were plans for the young boy. All of them would come in due time.

"Have Baby Girl drop four of you off on Green Street. Find out everything you can on that clown Brick. You got three hours."

"If we find him, can we kill him?"

Zoo chuckled. "Do him dirty."

Zipper slapped hands with Zoo, cheesing brightly on his way out.

Zoo returned his attention to Mason. "You hungry, lil man?"

"Can I go home?" his voice cracked. "Where's my sister?"

"Your sister—she's out for a swim. You—this is sorta your new home now."

"But—"

Zoo held up a finger silencing the boy as he was interrupted by his phone ringing. "Talk to me," answered.

"Turning in the yard now, foo," Shooter said, then hung up.

Zoo went to the long, wide back window that gave him a full panoramic view of his backyard. He could see his youngins scattered and on point, keeping a close eye on the white Dodge Charger as it came to a stop beside the Wraith.

"What's this I hear y'all little mufuckas wanna act up around the house?" Zoo put his stern face on while talking to the four of Mona's boys, ages nine, ten, thirteen, and fifteen, once they entered the house.

The youngest said in defense, "We ain't been acting up."

"That ain't what she told me. So, who's lying?" he asked, giving the pet parrot and baby monkey treats before shooing them away.

The boys swallowed hard, standing side by side.

It was no mystery that Zoo had all the kids around the hood worshipping the ground he walked on. Though many were under his thumb, the majority of the kids shied away, too afraid of him. It was rumored that Zoo would get the worst of the adolescents from the projects who were on paths of destruction, illiterate, and one step away from being eaten by the blood-thirsty streets of the Concrete Jungle, the Zoo and take them away for days even weeks at a time. When returned, single mothers who had given up on their sons would see tremendous improvements. Sons would go from skipping school to A and B honor roll. From disruptive and disrespectful behaviors to well-mannered boys. No one knew how it was done. Or how he could take soft-hearted young boys and turn them into vicious, heartless individuals.

Staring at the five boys before him, he planned to do just that. "Shooter, have a seat in the living room."

"Let me join."

"Have a seat. This ain't for you. It's for them," Zoo said assertively.

Shooter wanted to protest but knew there was no win, so he took a seat.

"All you boys, follow me." Zoo led the way. "Any of you scared of spiders?"

"Yeah," they all answered.

"Good to know." Zoo grinned, leading them up the stairs to the third level and in front of a bolted door. He gave it a secret combination knock. "It's me."

"How many?" her sweet melodic voice asked.

"Five, they're stupid and some pussies." He looked back at them with a devious smirk.

***

"Matthew, what's going on?" His sister Joanna called with concern.

Furrowing his brow, he countered, "What do ya mean, what's goin' on?"

"What's goin' on as in, why was my niece just at my home going from room to room yelling for Precious not too long ago?" she asked heatedly.

His face grew flushed red. "Uhhh—I'm not sure why she'd come there. I'm actually here at the house now with Precious. I'll be heading out to work in a few."

"That doesn't answer my question, Matthew," Joanna pressed.

"Look, Queenie hasn't been acting like herself lately and—and I don't want her negative energy to affect P. They're both under a lot of stress right now, especially since their mother killed herself with drugs. I lost my wife, and it's hit them both pretty hard. As family, I would expect you to understand," his calm tone was persuasive.

"You've been acting pretty strange as well. Maybe it's the stress of your job. Maybe it's something else that you're not telling me. I don't know. What I do I know is, Queenie was not pleased to learn that her sister was not here, as she expected."

Matthew sighed deeply, rubbing his burning red neck. "Joanna, there's nothing to be concerned about. Just some miscommunication between my daughter and I. We'll talk about this later if you don't mind."

"I do mind!" Joanna yelled. "I want you to help me make sense of this," she challenged.

Matthew gritted his teeth in frustration. "It'll have to wait, Joanna. I'm going to be late for work."

Matthew disconnected the call. She was a second away from triggering him. Learning that Queenie was going after Precious was both a blessing and a curse. One, he'd have to figure out a way to work to his advantage. However, calming his anger, he knew he had to find Queenie fast. She was responsible for him nearly getting his face blown off. It tickled and enraged him.

Peeking his head in on Precious, he watched her face as she slept in bed. He closed the door silently, locking it from the outside before heading out.

"G-A-R-Y!" he spoke out loud to his computer system once inside the cruiser. "J-A-C-K-S-O-N!" He hit enter. "And Walla, there's that little son-of-a-trifling-crack-bitch right there," he snarled at the monitor. He clicked the red flag notifications. "Warrants for criminal domestic violence 3rd Degree. Shooting in a dwelling. And felony assault," he read out his charges. "Bitch is wanted for a probation violation as well," he whispered, soaking up the data before heading through the streets to track him down, which could possibly lead to his daughter. "Last known address—security threat group—"

Matthew chuckled lightly. "A baby gangster running with the gangster, killer Bloods. No wonder the fucker shot at me." He shifted his car into drive, headed down Two Notch Road. "Schoolhouse Road," he murmured nervously.

The Pinehurst park community always gave him a nauseous feeling knowing the gritty history of the bloody, wild-wild, East-like mentality that its adolescents maintained, no matter how many federal indictments came down as R.I.C.Os.

Unlatching the strap of his holster, he proceeded down the stretch also and cautious. After circling the block a few dozen times, he was going to cruise Waverly Street for any signs of them together when he noticed a Black male swaggering through the park toward Four Seasons Apartments on a cell phone. Busting a U-turn, his veins filled with adrenaline.

"Where you going, Gary? Where's my daughter?"

***

Queenie was reluctant to park in her same parking space as the night before outside G-50's building in the Ashley's. There were no words to describe how she felt about being back in the city. She'd even cried her eyes out as she made the painful and dreadful trip back. She wondered if God was punishing her for not staying home and enduring what her mother had for so long? However, the call earlier from Ms. Pat had her feeling funny, as if the woman had seen her future and was warning her.

"Gary, where are you?" she asked once he'd finally answered.

"Why?"

"I don't wanna argue with you. I know I messed up for taking off, but I'm back in Columbia, and we need to speak face-to-face."

"I got too much shit goin' on. Maybe some other time."

"Stop tryna be mean to me. I know you don't mean that. Where are you? I'm gonna come pick you up."

"Where are you?"

"At your brother's place."

"Inside?"

"In the parking lot, sitting in the car. Should I go in?"

"Nah, sit tight and don't fucking leave this time."

"Oookayyy," she whined. "Are you on your way now, at least?"

"I'm meeting a play in Four Seasons first. Did you pick up your sister?"

Queenie replied sadly, "She wasn't there, and that's why you need to hurry up and meet with me because I would really like for you to go with me to my father's house to confront him and get my sister."

"We ain't finna chat and have tea wit' dat nigga. We getting your sister and leaving his bitch ass on ice, simple as that."

"Fine!"

"I'll see you when I get there." He hung up.

She sat back in the seat anxiously.

***

Gary was well aware of his surroundings, so noticing the police car creeping up the street to his left, he kept his stride smooth and natural while speaking with Queenie on the phone. Something about her quieted the beast in him. He was glad she was back and ready to finish off her father. The feelings he had for her were unexpected. Since hearing all that shit she'd been through, a part of him felt obligated to protect her by any means.

She had a spirit of a warrior goddess, and he knew she of all the chicks he'd dealt with would be the one to be extremely successful. So, no matter what, he had her back and couldn't wait to get back in her presence.

He hung up the phone and gritted, spotting the squad car that turned into the Four Seasons Apartments as he too neared. If he sped, he'd make himself suspicious, and having an ounce of crack, ten thousand dollars with a pistol on his hip was a deadly combination for disaster.

Thinking of the pistol, he spat, "Shit!"

The police car came to a stop in front of him, cutting into his path, and Matthew climbed out.

Gary was ready to take flight, and sure no cop could catch him. He slipped the phone into his pocket, watching the officer closely. Gary's eyes met with his brown eyes.

The officer called out, "Gary Jackson!"

"Damn." He touched his waistband and pulled up his jeans. "Fuck it!"

***

After fifteen long minutes of waiting, Queenie was growing overly impatient and wanted to hurry and meet with him before her father got the heads up from Aunt Joanna. However, as she sat up completely and cranked the ignition, fear rocked her guts as she spotted G-50 and at least ten other male individuals spill from the apartment with guns drawn, rushing with hostility into vehicles the fishtailing out of the parking lot. She dialed Gary's number to sound the alarm that something was gravely wrong.

She got no answer.

"Why do you wanna play with me?" She twisted her face up and re-dialed his number.

Still no answer.

"See, I'm finna leave his ass again," she said, frustrated.

Waiting had her growing agitated as the clock seemed to be counting down in her ear. As she shifted the car into drive, headed to Pinehurst to get her man, the ringing of her phone got her attention.

She answered with haste, "Gary, don't nobody got the fucking time to be playing with your stupid ass. Now, where are you? I saw your brother rushing off somewhere like there's a problem."

"Um—I'm sorry this ain't Gary."

She looked at the phone.

"Oh, my bad. What's up, Krissy?"

"Where are you at? It's important."

"Ashley Apartments, outside G-50's crip." She got a bad vibe from her, even more now that she had the same pistol in her presence that Krissy used to murder Ta'maine with, sitting in the middle console. Something was echoing in her mind not to trust the woman.

"Is something wrong?"

"I'm afraid it is."

"Then what is it, tell me."

"It's Gary."

Her body was hot and bothered. "What about him?"

"I saw the whole thing in Pinehurst. The police got him."

"Did they take him to jail already?" Her heart shattered. "I got money. I can pay to get him out."

"Girl—Gary's—Gary's dead!"

"What!" she exclaimed, shocked. "What did you say?"

"He's dead! The police gunned him down for no reason. He didn't even have a gun on him, girl. It was so sad. He was trying to run."

Queenie ended the call as everything around started moving in slow motion. She sat back, wanting to scream her lungs out so that everyone in the world could feel the pain she was suddenly doused with. It hurt like knives slicing through her heart slowly, yet she was too numb to react.

She was shocked. Paralyzed!

Tears welled heavily, blurring her vision. The excruciating torment had her ears ringing loudly. Blood cold as ice, soul bleeding with silent fury. Her tongue was too heavy to force a sound. Her life was speeding into a head-on collision, and she was crashing.

"God," she whispered for strength.

Her cell rang. Too weak and vulnerable to speak, without checking the caller's I.D., she pressed the side button of the flip phone, assuming to silence the ringer only to accidentally place the call on speaker.

There was a long pause.

"Hello, Queenie?" she asked in a hushed, raspy tone. "Are you there, Queenie?" the familiar voice snapped her out of the trance.

Her heart pulse started pumping all over again. She held the phone to her mouth. "Precious?"

"Yes, it's me," she whimpered, sniffling. "Are you okay?"

"Of course, I'm okay. Are you?" The thick tears finally fell. "Where are you?"

Precious struggled as her voice cracked, "I—I'm—"

"I'm coming to you right now. Where are you?"

Precious started sobbing.

"Big Girl, don't cry. Where are you? Tell me, please!"

"You left me." She sobbed uncontrollably.

"No, I didn't, don't say that. I'm coming for you." Her body shook violently. "You have to tell me where you are and what's wrong, baby."

"I was home. Miranda's mom came yesterday and left your number when I told her that I hadn't spoken to you." She sniffled again. "I left home today when dad left for work." She sobbed more.

Queenie shifted into drive. "Okay, good. So, where exactly are you?"

"I broke into the neighbor's house and called you," she wailed. "Please come get me."

"I'm coming to you, Big Girl. Just stay there."

"Okay."

As she whipped out of the parking lot, she couldn't help but feel the guilt for not getting to her sister quicker, sooner. "Now, tell me what's wrong. Did that sick motherfucker touch you?"

Precious cried harder, unable to speak clearly. "Qu—Queenie?"

"I'm here, P!"

"Dad—"

"Dad? Dad, what?"

There was a short pause.

Precious sniffled. "Qu—Queenie, I'm pregnant by dad," her words sawed into Queenie's heart.

Before she could think and react, she lost control, crashing into a parked car. Her forehead smacked the steering wheel, sending specks of white light through her vision. However, that could do little to numb and stomp the rage. The phone fell from her hand.

In an uncontrollable rage, she exploded right there in the front seat, kicking, screaming, punching, and fighting the car's interior. She snapped mentally. The weight of the world broke her sanity. So, the moment her sights laid on the box-cutter, she snatched it up, exposing the sharp razor. The anguish, weakness, and being defeated motivated her actions.

She wailed at the top of her lungs until her chest dared to explode, and her throat was sore and raw. Thinking of the unbearable experience, her sister had to face due to her selfishness. Her absence made her connect the blade to her wrist.

"God, I can't," she admitted hopelessly. "I can't take it no more," she cried out, folding and collapsing under life's pressure.

She pulled back on the blade forcefully and quickly. Once! Then twice! Blood spurted everywhere, and finally, the worries vanished as the world around her faded to black.

To Be Continued...
Queen of the Zoo 2
Coming Soon

Lock Down Publications and Ca$h Presents assisted publishing packages.

BASIC PACKAGE $499
Editing
Cover Design
Formatting

UPGRADED PACKAGE $800
Typing
Editing
Cover Design
Formatting

ADVANCE PACKAGE $1,200
Typing
Editing
Cover Design
Formatting
Copyright registration
Proofreading
Upload book to Amazon

LDP SUPREME PACKAGE $1,500
Typing
Editing
Cover Design
Formatting
Copyright registration
Proofreading
Set up Amazon account
Upload book to Amazon

Advertise on LDP Amazon and Facebook page

***Other services available upon request. Additional charges may apply
Lock Down Publications
P.O. Box 944
Stockbridge, GA 30281-9998
Phone # 470 303-9761

Submission Guideline

Submit the first three chapters of your completed manuscript to ldpsubmissions@gmail.com, subject line: Your book's title. The manuscript must be in a .doc file and sent as an attachment. Document should be in Times New Roman, double spaced and in size 12 font. Also, provide your synopsis and full contact information. If sending multiple submissions, they must each be in a separate email.

Have a story but no way to send it electronically? You can still submit to LDP/Ca$h Presents. Send in the first three chapters, written or typed, of your completed manuscript to:

LDP: Submissions Dept
Po Box 944
Stockbridge, Ga 30281

DO NOT send original manuscript. Must be a duplicate.

Provide your synopsis and a cover letter containing your full contact information.

Thanks for considering LDP and Ca$h Presents.

<u>NEW RELEASES</u>

MOB TIES 3 by SAYNOMORE
CONFESSIONS OF A GANGSTA by NICH-
OLAS LOCK
MURDA WAS THE CASE by ELIJAH R.
FREEMAN
THE STREETS NEVER LET GO by ROB-
ERT BAPTISTE
MOBBED UP 4 by KING RIO
AN UNFORESEEN LOVE 2 by MEESHA
KING OF THE TRENCHES by GHOST &
TRANAY ADAMS
A DOPEBOY'S DREAM by ROMELL
TUKES
MONEY MAFIA by JIBRIL WILLIAMS
QUEEN OF THE ZOO by BLACK MIGO

Black Migo

3X KRAZY III

De'Kari

KINGPIN KILLAZ IV

STREET KINGS III

PAID IN BLOOD III

CARTEL KILLAZ IV

DOPE GODS III

Hood Rich

SINS OF A HUSTLA II

ASAD

RICH $AVAGE II

By Troublesome

YAYO V

Bred In The Game 2

S. Allen

CREAM III

By Yolanda Moore

SON OF A DOPE FIEND III

HEAVEN GOT A GHETTO II

By Renta

LOYALTY AIN'T PROMISED III

By Keith Williams

I'M NOTHING WITHOUT HIS LOVE II

SINS OF A THUG II

TO THE THUG I LOVED BEFORE II

By Monet Dragun

QUIET MONEY IV

EXTENDED CLIP III

THUG LIFE IV

By **Trai'Quan**

THE STREETS MADE ME IV

By **Larry D. Wright**

IF YOU CROSS ME ONCE II

By **Anthony Fields**

THE STREETS WILL NEVER CLOSE II

By **K'ajji**

HARD AND RUTHLESS III

THE BILLIONAIRE BENTLEYS II

Von Diesel

KILLA KOUNTY II

By **Khufu**

MONEY GAME II

By **Smoove Dolla**

A GANGSTA'S KARMA II

By **FLAME**

JACK BOYZ VERSUS DOPE BOYZ

A DOPEBOY'S DREAM III

By **Romell Tukes**

MOB TIES IV

By **SayNoMore**

MURDA WAS THE CASE II

Elijah R. Freeman

THE STREETS NEVER LET GO II

By **Robert Baptiste**

AN UNFORESEEN LOVE III

By **Meesha**

KING OF THE TRENCHES II

by **GHOST & TRANAY ADAMS**

MONEY MAFIA

By **Jibril Williams**

QUEEN OF THE ZOO II

By **Black Migo**

<u>Available Now</u>

RESTRAINING ORDER **I & II**

By **CA$H & Coffee**

LOVE KNOWS NO BOUNDARIES **I II & III**

By **Coffee**

RAISED AS A GOON I, II, III & IV

BRED BY THE SLUMS I, II, III

BLAST FOR ME I & II

ROTTEN TO THE CORE I II III

A BRONX TALE I, II, III

DUFFLE BAG CARTEL I II III IV V VI

HEARTLESS GOON I II III IV V

A SAVAGE DOPEBOY I II

DRUG LORDS I II III

CUTTHROAT MAFIA I II

KING OF THE TRENCHES

By **Ghost**

LAY IT DOWN **I & II**

Black Migo

LAST OF A DYING BREED I II

BLOOD STAINS OF A SHOTTA I & II III

By **Jamaica**

LOYAL TO THE GAME I II III

LIFE OF SIN I, II III

By **TJ & Jelissa**

BLOODY COMMAS I & II

SKI MASK CARTEL I II & III

KING OF NEW YORK I II,III IV V

RISE TO POWER I II III

COKE KINGS I II III IV

BORN HEARTLESS I II III IV

KING OF THE TRAP I II

By **T.J. Edwards**

IF LOVING HIM IS WRONG…I & II

LOVE ME EVEN WHEN IT HURTS I II III

By **Jelissa**

WHEN THE STREETS CLAP BACK I & II III

THE HEART OF A SAVAGE I II III

MONEY MAFIA

By **Jibril Williams**

A DISTINGUISHED THUG STOLE MY HEART I II & III

LOVE SHOULDN'T HURT I II III IV

RENEGADE BOYS I II III IV

PAID IN KARMA I II III

SAVAGE STORMS I II

AN UNFORESEEN LOVE I II

Queen of the Zoo

By **Meesha**

A GANGSTER'S CODE I &, II III

A GANGSTER'S SYN I II III

THE SAVAGE LIFE I II III

CHAINED TO THE STREETS I II III

BLOOD ON THE MONEY I II III

By **J-Blunt**

PUSH IT TO THE LIMIT

By **Bre' Hayes**

BLOOD OF A BOSS **I, II, III, IV, V**

SHADOWS OF THE GAME

TRAP BASTARD

By **Askari**

THE STREETS BLEED MURDER **I, II & III**

THE HEART OF A GANGSTA I II& III

By **Jerry Jackson**

CUM FOR ME I II III IV V VI VII

An **LDP Erotica Collaboration**

BRIDE OF A HUSTLA **I II & II**

THE FETTI GIRLS **I, II& III**

CORRUPTED BY A GANGSTA I, II III, IV

BLINDED BY HIS LOVE

THE PRICE YOU PAY FOR LOVE I, II ,III

DOPE GIRL MAGIC I II III

By **Destiny Skai**

WHEN A GOOD GIRL GOES BAD

By **Adrienne**

THE COST OF LOYALTY I II III

By Kweli

A GANGSTER'S REVENGE **I II III & IV**

THE BOSS MAN'S DAUGHTERS I II III IV V

A SAVAGE LOVE **I & II**

BAE BELONGS TO ME I II

A HUSTLER'S DECEIT I, II, III

WHAT BAD BITCHES DO I, II, III

SOUL OF A MONSTER I II III

KILL ZONE

A DOPE BOY'S QUEEN I II III

By **Aryanna**

A KINGPIN'S AMBITON

A KINGPIN'S AMBITION **II**

I MURDER FOR THE DOUGH

By **Ambitious**

TRUE SAVAGE I II III IV V VI VII

DOPE BOY MAGIC I, II, III

MIDNIGHT CARTEL I II III

CITY OF KINGZ I II

NIGHTMARE ON SILENT AVE

By **Chris Green**

A DOPEBOY'S PRAYER

By **Eddie "Wolf" Lee**

THE KING CARTEL **I, II & III**

By **Frank Gresham**

THESE NIGGAS AIN'T LOYAL **I, II & III**

Queen of the Zoo

By **Nikki Tee**

GANGSTA SHYT **I II &III**

By **CATO**

THE ULTIMATE BETRAYAL

By **Phoenix**

BOSS'N UP **I , II & III**

By **Royal Nicole**

I LOVE YOU TO DEATH

By **Destiny J**

I RIDE FOR MY HITTA

I STILL RIDE FOR MY HITTA

By **Misty Holt**

LOVE & CHASIN' PAPER

By **Qay Crockett**

TO DIE IN VAIN

SINS OF A HUSTLA

By **ASAD**

BROOKLYN HUSTLAZ

By **Boogsy Morina**

BROOKLYN ON LOCK I & II

By **Sonovia**

GANGSTA CITY

By **Teddy Duke**

A DRUG KING AND HIS DIAMOND I & II III

A DOPEMAN'S RICHES

HER MAN, MINE'S TOO I, II

CASH MONEY HO'S

333

THE WIFEY I USED TO BE I II

By Nicole Goosby

TRAPHOUSE KING **I II & III**

KINGPIN KILLAZ I II III

STREET KINGS I II

PAID IN BLOOD **I II**

CARTEL KILLAZ I II III

DOPE GODS I II

By **Hood Rich**

LIPSTICK KILLAH **I, II, III**

CRIME OF PASSION I II & III

FRIEND OR FOE I II III

By **Mimi**

STEADY MOBBN' **I, II, III**

THE STREETS STAINED MY SOUL I II

By **Marcellus Allen**

WHO SHOT YA **I, II, III**

SON OF A DOPE FIEND I II

HEAVEN GOT A GHETTO

Renta

GORILLAZ IN THE BAY **I II III IV**

TEARS OF A GANGSTA I II

3X KRAZY I II

DE'KARI

TRIGGADALE I II III

MURDAROBER WAS THE CASE

Elijah R. Freeman

Queen of the Zoo

GOD BLESS THE TRAPPERS I, II, III

THESE SCANDALOUS STREETS I, II, III

FEAR MY GANGSTA I, II, III IV, V

THESE STREETS DON'T LOVE NOBODY I, II

BURY ME A G I, II, III, IV, V

A GANGSTA'S EMPIRE I, II, III, IV

THE DOPEMAN'S BODYGAURD I II

THE REALEST KILLAZ I II III

THE LAST OF THE OGS I II III

Tranay Adams

THE STREETS ARE CALLING

Duquie Wilson

MARRIED TO A BOSS I II III

By Destiny Skai & Chris Green

KINGZ OF THE GAME I II III IV V

Playa Ray

SLAUGHTER GANG I II III

RUTHLESS HEART I II III

By Willie Slaughter

FUK SHYT

By Blakk Diamond

DON'T F#CK WITH MY HEART I II

By Linnea

ADDICTED TO THE DRAMA I II III

IN THE ARM OF HIS BOSS II

By Jamila

YAYO I II III IV

A SHOOTER'S AMBITION I II
BRED IN THE GAME
By S. Allen
TRAP GOD I II III
RICH $AVAGE
By Troublesome
FOREVER GANGSTA
GLOCKS ON SATIN SHEETS I II
By Adrian Dulan
TOE TAGZ I II III
LEVELS TO THIS SHYT I II
By Ah'Million
KINGPIN DREAMS I II III
By Paper Boi Rari
CONFESSIONS OF A GANGSTA I II III IV
By Nicholas Lock
I'M NOTHING WITHOUT HIS LOVE
SINS OF A THUG
TO THE THUG I LOVED BEFORE
By Monet Dragun
CAUGHT UP IN THE LIFE I II III
THE STREETS NEVER LET GO
By Robert Baptiste
NEW TO THE GAME I II III
MONEY, MURDER & MEMORIES I II III
By **Malik D. Rice**
LIFE OF A SAVAGE I II III

Queen of the Zoo

A GANGSTA'S QUR'AN I II III

MURDA SEASON I II III

GANGLAND CARTEL I II III

CHI'RAQ GANGSTAS I II III

KILLERS ON ELM STREET I II III

JACK BOYZ N DA BRONX I II III

A DOPEBOY'S DREAM I II

By **Romell Tukes**

LOYALTY AIN'T PROMISED I II

By Keith Williams

QUIET MONEY I II III

THUG LIFE I II III

EXTENDED CLIP I II

By **Trai'Quan**

THE STREETS MADE ME I II III

By **Larry D. Wright**

THE ULTIMATE SACRIFICE I, II, III, IV, V, VI

KHADIFI

IF YOU CROSS ME ONCE

ANGEL I II

IN THE BLINK OF AN EYE

By **Anthony Fields**

THE LIFE OF A HOOD STAR

By Ca$h & Rashia Wilson

THE STREETS WILL NEVER CLOSE

By K'ajji

CREAM I II

By Yolanda Moore

NIGHTMARES OF A HUSTLA I II III

By King Dream

CONCRETE KILLA I II

By Kingpen

HARD AND RUTHLESS I II

MOB TOWN 251

THE BILLIONAIRE BENTLEYS

By Von Diesel

GHOST MOB

Stilloan Robinson

MOB TIES I II III

By SayNoMore

BODYMORE MURDERLAND I II III

By Delmont Player

FOR THE LOVE OF A BOSS

By C. D. Blue

MOBBED UP I II III IV

By King Rio

KILLA KOUNTY

By Khufu

MONEY GAME

By Smoove Dolla

A GANGSTA'S KARMA

By FLAME

KING OF THE TRENCHES II

by **GHOST & TRANAY ADAMS**

QUEEN OF THE ZOO

By **Black Migo**

Black Migo

<u>BOOKS BY LDP'S CEO, CA$H</u>

<u>TRUST IN NO MAN</u>
<u>TRUST IN NO MAN 2</u>
<u>TRUST IN NO MAN 3</u>
<u>BONDED BY BLOOD</u>
<u>SHORTY GOT A THUG</u>
<u>THUGS CRY</u>
<u>THUGS CRY 2</u>
<u>THUGS CRY 3</u>
<u>TRUST NO BITCH</u>
<u>TRUST NO BITCH 2</u>
<u>TRUST NO BITCH 3</u>
<u>TIL MY CASKET DROPS</u>
<u>RESTRAINING ORDER</u>
<u>RESTRAINING ORDER 2</u>
<u>IN LOVE WITH A CONVICT</u>
<u>LIFE OF A HOOD STAR</u>

Queen of the Zoo

CPSIA information can be obtained
at www.ICGtesting.com
Printed in the USA
LVHW051506231121
704247LV00010B/1021